"I hate it when children are involved with murder," Susan commented almost absently, watching as Kathleen peered under the dead man's eyelid.

"It's a little early to think of murder, isn't it?"

"Either someone killed him, put him in that chair, and covered him up, or else he sat down, died, and then covered himself up."

"Rigor is beginning to pass," Kathleen said, nodding.

"He's been dead for a while, hasn't he?"

"Yes."

"And he's been sitting in that chair for a while, too."

"Probably."

"We spent the night in the house with a dead man."

Kathleen sighed. "It looks like it."

Also by Valerie Wolzien
Published by Fawcett Books:

MURDER AT THE PTA LUNCHEON
THE FORTIETH BIRTHDAY BODY
WE WISH YOU A MERRY MURDER
AN OLD FAITHFUL MURDER
ALL HALLOWS' EVIL

A
STAR-SPANGLED
MURDER

VALERIE WOLZIEN

FAWCETT GOLD MEDAL • NEW YORK

This book is dedicated to my three nephews,
Christopher Shelley
Matthew Shelley
and
Ted Wolzien
And to Trevor's dog, Karma, who has taught me all I know
about golden retrievers.

A Fawcett Gold Medal Book
Published by Ballantine Books
Copyright © 1993 by Valerie Wolzien

Library of Congress Catalog Card Number: 93-90093

ISBN 0-449-14834-3

Manufactured in the United States of America

First Edition: July 1993

ONE

At four p.m. on July first, Susan Henshaw drove across the bridge to the island.

The trip to Maine had been typical of a holiday weekend. It started with the gentle crawl of early morning traffic as the sun rose on Connecticut; resisted any impulse to speed in front of the watchful Massachusetts State Police; became impatient at long lines snaking through the New Hampshire toll booth; felt a slight relief as fellow travelers detoured at the outlets in Kittery; ignored the urge to check out L.L. Bean in Freeport; marveled at the beauty of the Maine Turnpike; and then followed gigantic trucks pulling even larger sailboats down the two-lane roads leading to the sea.

Susan and Kathleen had chatted throughout the drive. They had discussed their children. (Chad and Chrissy Henshaw, sixteen and eighteen respectively, were busy with their own projects—too busy, they had insisted, for a family trip. And Alexander Brandon Colin Gordon, who was two and a half years old and known as Bananas, was spending some quality time with his maternal grandmother.) They had discussed their husbands. (Jed Henshaw and Jerry Gordon worked at the same advertising agency and were currently involved in a project that was preventing them from vacationing with their wives.) They had talked about diets, childbirth, the possibility of future face-lifts, politics, careers versus children, careers and children, the PTA, going to law school (Kathleen), going to a fat farm (Susan), sex, sleeping late, redecorating, cooking with tofu, menopause, and two or three

1

dozen other topics for the eight hours they had been on the road. But much of the day had been peppered with Susan's memories of summers spent on an island off the coast of Maine.

From her first visit to her aunt's summer home when she was seven to her honeymoon with Jed, from Chrissy's premature birth in the living room of the island's then only doctor right up to Chad's accident last summer that required a doctor at the new island medical center to take ten stitches in his scalp, Kathleen had heard tales of Susan's summer vacations.

And Kathleen had been a wonderful audience for Susan's stories. But now she was tired, a little lonely for her son and her husband, and in need of a bathroom for more important things than washing off the day's accumulated filth.

"We're almost there. The road is just around the next curve," Susan announced, switching on the turn signal. She was tired and looked every one of her forty-three years. "Then just a mile and a half of dirt lane before we get to the house. I can't wait!"

"Me neither," Kathleen, a striking blonde about ten years younger than her friend, agreed honestly. "You said the water would be turned on, didn't you?"

"And the heat—in case we need it at night. The man who took care of Aunt Raney's house moved into a nursing home last winter, but he found and trained his own replacement before he left. So everything will be all right. The people on the island are very reliable."

"Watch . . ." Kathleen began as Susan swung her automobile around a large pile of rocks.

"It's fine," Susan said, glad that Kathleen's opportunities for backseat driving were soon to end. "I'm used to it. That pile has been there for years, just getting bigger and bigger. Jed plans on building a wall around the garden, and he keeps collecting boulders from the beach and the sandbar. Chad's collecting now, too, so the pile's really growing quickly. They draw up elaborate plans every summer, but no one seems too anxious to actually start building. . . . Damn!"

The car skidded a few feet and then stopped, its front

bumper smacking into the long metal chain draped between two tall white pines. "Are you okay?" Susan checked with her passenger.

"Fine." Kathleen peered out the windshield. "Why is that thing across the road?"

"I don't know," Susan answered slowly. "It isn't supposed to be there." She opened the door and got out of the car. Kathleen followed suit. "Our house is the only one on this road, so unless we're here, the barrier is up. My aunt rented out the house for half of every summer, but we haven't ever done that." She paused to examine the metal links dangling in front of the car. "It's probably just the new caretaker—I can't remember his name. Maybe he didn't know that we expect the chain to be removed before we get here. . . ."

"Where's the key?" Kathleen asked as Susan left her thought unfinished.

"Key?"

"There's a padlock on this end," Kathleen elaborated. "It seems to lock the chain to the metal eye embedded in the tree. There must be a key. There's no way we could pull this thing out of the wood." She examined the large, rusty eye more closely.

"Not a chance," Susan agreed. "Aunt Raney had that put in while workmen were still roofing the house. The tree's been growing around it for almost half a century. That's permanent!"

Kathleen glanced up at the spindly old tree and wondered about the durability of this particular Henshaw tradition, but she wasn't about to say anything. She had more urgent problems. "You have the key, don't you?"

"No," Susan answered slowly. "It's in the other car. You see, we usually come up as a family and—"

There was a time for family tales and a time for trips to the bathroom. "So how are we going to get through?" Kathleen asked impatiently.

"There's a key at the house. It's not far. We'll just walk down and get it. Then you can look around, and I'll head back here and retrieve the car."

Kathleen hurriedly followed Susan around the barrier and they set off. They couldn't see any buildings. The one-lane dirt road ran through thick forest. Spruce, balsam, birch, and poplar rose in the air around them, competing for sunlight. The ground was covered with moss and ferns, and here and there pink granite pushed through the lush growth.

"You're pretty isolated up here, aren't you?" Kathleen commented when they had hiked for a few minutes.

"Not really. It's just that no one else uses this road. We have neighbors on either side of us—and, of course, across the cove. The coast of Maine is pretty developed—in a nice way."

They had arrived at a large field filled with white blossoms and patches of tall purple lupine. "We're almost there. You can see the house down by the water. That's the boathouse." Susan had described the area more than once during the trip, and Kathleen wasn't surprised by the charm of the four-bedroom shingled cottage that Susan had inherited from her aunt.

"What's wrong?" Kathleen asked as Susan stopped suddenly.

"The shutters aren't off the windows."

"I don't see anything."

"It's not easy from here. Only the side of the building that faces the water is shuttered all winter, but they swing around that far corner." Susan pointed. "They're usually down before Memorial Day."

"Well, you usually get up here earlier in the year. And with a new caretaker and all . . ."

"Hmmm. The markers for the driveway haven't been pulled up either," Susan said. "But the grass has been mowed and the paths raked. You're probably right. The new man just doesn't know the routine yet. Why don't I run ahead and get the key? It's hanging right inside the door, and then I can go back and get the car while you look around. Maybe you could put on some water and we can have a cup of tea?" They walked between tall white lupine and up the porch to the back door of the cottage.

"Great."

Susan unlocked the door and grabbed for a bunch of keys

on a nearby hook. "I'll hurry back. Look around. The bedrooms are upstairs; the kitchen is down the hall."

"Susan, it's wonderful!" Kathleen stepped into the house and admired the bright rag rugs laid on the pegged pine floor. Checked cotton curtains hung at the many windows, and white walls and simple pine furniture completed the pleasant picture. "I'll be fine. I'll get that tea you mentioned." Right after I find the bathroom, she added to herself as the door closed behind her friend.

When Susan reentered the house fifteen minutes later, there was a pot of tea brewing on the large trunk that served as a coffee table in the middle of the old-fashioned living room. Kathleen had returned to the kitchen, searching for glasses to go with the bottle of wine she had unearthed in an antique pine chest.

"You didn't start to empty the car by yourself, did you? There's no reason. You must be exhausted after all that driving. Why don't we have a cup of tea or some wine before we start? This is a vacation, after all, and . . . Susan? Are you listening?"

"No." She absently sipped the mug of Earl Grey tea that Kathleen had handed her. "I couldn't drive the car here. Someone changed the lock. The key doesn't fit."

"Maybe the new caretaker?"

"Of course. Something must have happened to the old lock and he changed it—and probably no one told him where we hang the key."

"Too bad we can't find this man."

"But we can. I'll call Jed at his office and he'll have the phone number. Jed'll be waiting for me to call anyway. I told him that I would as soon as we arrived. Don't worry. We'll be settled in before you know it. The phone's in the kitchen."

She hurried off, and Kathleen picked up one of the heavy wool blankets that covered the furniture in the living room, revealing a comfortable Lawson chair underneath. She folded the blanket, tossing it onto another piece of furniture. Apparently the new caretaker hadn't done much inside the house either. She glanced at the windows that lined one side of the room; wide boards eliminated the view that she had seen earlier when . . .

Kathleen hopped up and headed back to the upstairs bathroom.

Five minutes later, the two women met again in the living room, puzzled expressions on both their faces. Susan spoke first.

"Jed says he talked with the new man last week and that Burt—Burt Jamison is his name, I should have remembered—assured Jed that the shutters had been taken down and the house was set up for the summer." She looked around the room, beginning to feel angry. After all, what did Burt Jamison think they were paying him to do? "Including taking the covers off the furniture and ha—"

"Hanging the pictures." Kathleen finished Susan's sentence.

"Yes." Susan was puzzled until, looking around, she realized that the walls were covered with unadorned hooks.

"I love that watercolor you have in the bathroom upstairs," Kathleen said.

Susan, a surprised expression on her face, reached out for the cooling tea. "It is pretty, isn't it? Jed bought it just last summer. The artist lives on the island and . . ." She put down her mug and stared at her friend.

Kathleen nodded. "Everything is set up on the second floor. The pictures are hanging on the walls, the shutters are down, and the sun is streaming in the windows. Even the beds are made up with fresh white cotton sheets."

Susan wasn't waiting to hear more. She was on her feet and running up the stairs. Kathleen joined her a few minutes later in the middle of the central hallway, where they could peer through open doorways into all four bedrooms, the bathroom, a large linen closet, and a door to stairs leading up to the attic.

"Come on," Susan urged, choosing the stairs.

Kathleen followed until she was standing upright in a large, rectangular room with windows looking out in all four directions. She started to examine the views, but Susan had other plans. "Look at this!" she insisted, waving her arms around the room.

Kathleen glanced about and saw nothing unusual. Old chests stood against one wall, drawers tightly closed. Boxes were piled against walls. Three steamer trunks stood upright, and unusual U-shaped clips hung from one wall, awaiting an unknown burden. A neat pile of army blankets sat under a window, and there was a large stack of painted plywood in one corner. "Everything looks fine to me," Kathleen said, shrugging. "In fact, it's the cleanest attic I've ever been in."

"It's all wrong. Like those blankets. They're used to wrap up the pictures. Then the wrapped pictures are placed in one of the trunks—in case mice find a way into the house during the winter."

"There are pictures on the walls on the second floor," Kathleen reminded her.

"Yes. But what about the first floor? And look at the shutters." She pointed to the lumber that Kathleen hadn't identified. "Why are the second-floor shutters down and put away up here, and the first-floor left up?"

"Maybe the new caretaker didn't understand what he was supposed to do."

"I don't think so. We hired him to set up, and Burt told Jed that everything was done. I can understand that he wouldn't know that we pull out the markers for the snow-plows in the summer, but no one would open half a house. Damn! Just what I need to do—find a new caretaker." She ran both hands through her long, light brown hair.

"So what next?" Kathleen asked.

"I don't know about you, but I could use a drink. Let's open that bottle of wine you found." Susan started down the stairs, Kathleen close behind. It had been a long day; she was tired and confused. And that was before they found the dead man.

TWO

KATHLEEN POURED PINOT NOIR INTO TWO GREEN-stemmed goblets while Susan dialed the phone number of the new caretaker. She passed Susan a glass, and they toasted each other and their vacation as the phone rang.

"Hi. This is Susan Henshaw and I'd like to speak to Mr. Jamison, please. Oh, I'm sorry to hear that. Not until after the Fourth? Well, is there any way I can reach him? . . . No, it's not an emergency. I just had some questions, but really, they can wait. . . . Of course, everything looks wonderful here, and I wanted to let your husband know how much I appreciate his work," she lied. "Thanks, I'll call after the holiday. Sorry to bother you. Have a nice weekend. Of course." She smiled at the receiver and hung up.

" 'Of course'?"

"I agreed that we would probably meet each other at the parade on July Fourth—or the dinner on the town pier," Susan explained.

"And will we?" Kathleen asked.

"Probably. The entire island goes both places. Summer people and the islanders."

"But I gather Burt Jamison won't be there."

"No. He left this morning to take some people rafting up in Canada. He apparently works part time as a wilderness guide. That was his wife. She said that he can't be reached even in an emergency. Apparently the group he goes with flies into remote areas of Canada and then immediately starts

8

downriver. They're picked up a couple of weeks later at the end of their journey."

"So we'll open the house ourselves."

"I guess so. Since the shutters are off the second floor, it won't be difficult to finish the job. But I vote we go out to dinner first and maybe stop and do some grocery shopping on the way home. There's not much in the house."

"I found two more bottles of wine and a box of tea bags, but not enough for a meal. And I'm starving."

"I'm hungry, too," Susan said. "But I'd like to wash my face and hands first. Why don't you go upstairs and pick out your bedroom? Jed and I share the room at the front of the house—the one with the green and white quilt on the bed. Take any of the others."

"I already know which room I want," Kathleen insisted, starting up the stairs. "What usually hangs on all these?" she asked, pointing toward the thirty or forty assorted picture hooks, nails, and tiny screws scattered on the walls lining the stairwell.

"Photographs. They're probably still up in the attic. They're interesting—it's sort of a history of the house. There's even a picture of it being built, and supposedly one of each person who ever slept in the house, but they're mostly family photos." She reached out and touched a brass nail. "And they're practically the only thing left in the house that belonged to my aunt."

"You've changed a lot?"

"Yes. The rest of the family inherited everything of worth—there were some wonderful old oil paintings and a few antiques. Aunt Raney thought it was only fair that my cousins should get them as the house and land were coming to me. What was left in the house was pretty ugly, and Jed and I replaced as much as we could as quickly as possible. The first year, we bought new mattresses and sprayed the furniture with white enamel. For the past ten years, we've been replacing everything else as we could afford to. We started out shopping at flea markets, auctions, and garage sales. Recently we've been buying things in antique shops and art galleries. There's a hodgepodge here, but almost everything comes from Maine.''

They were on the second floor, and Susan headed to the bathroom. A few minutes later, she returned to find Kathleen standing in the smallest of the three unclaimed rooms.

Susan beamed her approval. "My favorite! This is the room where I used to sleep when I was little. I helped my aunt piece that quilt,'' she added, pointing to the bed. Then her attention wandered to the window.

"What are you looking at?'' Kathleen asked.

"The boathouse. Look. Down by the edge of the cove.'' Susan pointed. "See that little barn-shaped building sitting by the water?''

Kathleen nodded. Like the house, the building had weathered cedar shake shingles with white trim. Black shutters bracketed the windows.

"Look at the roof,'' Susan ordered.

"The roof . . . You mean the skylights?''

"Exactly. They're open. Which they should be. The building gets musty over the winter and needs to air.''

"So?''

"So the windows are still shuttered. It's the same as the house. Half-open. Half-closed. It doesn't make any sense.''

"Maybe if we think about it while we eat,'' Kathleen suggested.

Susan grinned. "Very subtle. Lobster dinner, here we come.''

"I've been hoping you'd come in tonight. I wanted to ask you what you thought of your new neighbors out on the point. The whole island has been talking about them.''

"We haven't—'' Susan began, but she was cut off by the enthusiasm of the young woman standing beside their table, menus in hand.

"Everyone says they've been throwing around money as though they never heard of the recession. It's offending some people, but I say they're crazy. If people want to throw around money, they should just go ahead and do it on this island and not someplace else. We need it. I was just telling my brother that I don't think we should criticize them or talk about how strange they are as long as they're willing to pay cash. We can't afford to be anything but pragmatic. What do you think, Mrs. Henshaw?''

''Maybe the ladies would like to order before you interrogate them, Halsey,'' the young man behind the cash register called across the small dining room.

The girl threw her long, corn silk hair over one shoulder and glared in his direction. ''Listen to him.'' She pushed her wire-rimmed glasses farther up her nose and gave the woman a knowing look. ''Just because he's five years older than I am, he thinks he's boss.'' She didn't even bother to glance over her shoulder at the man she was speaking of; she merely fingered the large gold pin with the B.U. embossed on it.

''Halsey thinks she's a pretty big deal ever since she got into Boston University. She seems to forget that some of us have to work for a living,'' the young man continued.

If Halsey had pushed those glasses any harder, she'd have broken them, or, at the very least, shoved them right into her forehead, Susan thought, taking the menu offered and hoping to order dinner before a murder took place. ''I'll have—'' But she had begun too slowly.

''I slave nine hours a day, six days a week, for you, and I have posters up all over town trying to get some jobs doing housework, so don't you tell me that I don't work, Danny Downing!'' She spun around and stuck out her tongue at her employer, and then snapped into position, order book held high, pen in hand, attentive expression on her face, presumably ready to record Susan and Kathleen's every wish.

But Susan had heard opportunity knock. ''Do you have time to help me open the house?''

''I can be there first thing tomorrow,'' Halsey answered quickly. ''I have to be here at noon for the lunch crowd, but I can come Saturday morning, too, if we don't finish tomorrow. My scholarship only covers room, board, and tuition, so I have to buy my own books and things. I really need the money, Mrs. Henshaw. I'm going to work for Mrs. Taylor

on Tuesday and Thursday mornings, but otherwise I'm free."
She raised her voice, a smirk on her face. "My boss here is
a cheapskate who doesn't believe in paying his employees
very well. . . ."

"He pays them as well as they work. It isn't a waitress's
job to let the customers starve—but I guess that wasn't information that you needed for your SATs, was it, my dear sister?"

Kathleen leaned across the table. "They're related?" she
asked Susan.

Susan, who had been coming to The Blue Mussel for years
and had watched these two grow up, just nodded and ordered
dinner.

Halsey hurried off to the kitchen, leaving the women alone
at the table.

"What house? Who are they talking about?" Kathleen asked.

"The house out at the point at the end of the cove," Susan
explained. "It was just completed. The foundation was finished about this time last summer, and they were still building when we left. It looked like it was going to be a real
showplace when I last saw it. And it didn't even have a roof
at that point. The people who own it are the Taylors—and
that is absolutely all I know," Susan explained. She had been
hoping all winter for congenial neighbors—a hope that was
going to go unfulfilled? Before she could start to worry,
Danny Downing appeared at their table. "Back for the summer? Where's the rest of the family?"

"They're still down in Connecticut. It's just Kathleen and
myself for the holiday." Susan introduced Kathleen, asked
about winter on the island, and exchanged stories about re-
spective families before Halsey returned with their drinks to
get back to the original subject.

"I wasn't just gossiping about the Taylors for no reason at
all," the girl explained, setting their glasses on the table.
"It's just that everyone is confused about them. At one minute they seem just like everyone else from off island. They're
friendly and they stop and talk and ask questions about the
island and . . . and everything. And then there are all these

strange rumors going around about the family. It just doesn't make a lot of sense! And I really don't want to jeopardize my chances to work for them!''

''Have you spoken with them yourself?'' Susan asked, concerned about what she was hearing.

''Yes. A few times. Mrs. Taylor met me in the market downtown when I was putting up one of my posters on their bulletin board. And she asked me to clean for her twice a week: Tuesday and Thursday mornings. Then when I appeared there this morning, she sent me away. She said she didn't expect me to start until the sixth—after the holiday. And she acted like I had done something wrong. And all I did was misunderstand her directions. It was strange. You don't think she has a personality disorder of some kind, do you? Or maybe a substance abuse problem?''

''You'd never know that Halsey is planning to major in psychology, would you?'' her brother asked, grinning. ''She's always analyzing everybody. But it was worse when she was a little kid. In fifth grade she wanted to be a dental hygienist and she spent all her time bribing her friends to let her scratch at their teeth with lobster picks. Now she merely tries to convince everyone that they're neurotic, psychotic, or just plain crazy!''

Halsey's eyes opened wide and she leaned closer to the two women. ''I hope you don't think I'm being bitchy. I'm just trying to understand. I was wondering if it was something that I'd done. . . .''

''If other people are talking about the same thing, then it's probably her, not you,'' Susan suggested. ''They're our nearest neighbors, but I've never met them. Although Jed was up here early last spring and he met Mrs. Taylor. They had just bought the property. . . .''

''Her ex-husband bought the property,'' Halsey said. ''It was his money. At least that's what everyone is saying. And, you know, that might be very difficult for her new husband, and if their marriage is in trouble so soon, she'd be feeling tremendous stress, and maybe that's why she acts so terribly. So they—''

"They might walk through that door any minute and find you standing around here speculating about their private lives." Danny, for the first time in the conversation, sounded truly irritated. "This doesn't strike me as real nice behavior—or good business either," he reminded his sister with a stern look.

The door opened to reveal a dozen or so prospective diners, and Halsey smiled vaguely and hurried off to greet them. "I just hope she still wants me to work for her," she muttered. "I really need that job."

"I hope you understand; Halsey is just a little keyed up right now," her brother explained. "Getting that scholarship means a lot to her. She's worked her butt off for the last four years and she got what she wanted, but it's left her a little . . . uh, stressed out. She's excited about going to college, but she's worried that she'll get down to Boston and everyone will have more money and culture and she just won't fit in. You know?"

"Everyone is nervous about leaving for college," Susan agreed, thinking that the situation would be more stressful for Halsey since she was leaving the island and a small community where she had been protected and loved since birth. "And I do need someone to help me for the next few days—at least."

"I'll let her know you're serious." He turned his attention, as men usually do, Susan thought, to Kathleen. "Is this your first time on the island?" he asked politely.

"Yes. It's beautiful," Kathleen responded with a smile as the door opened again and another large party entered the tiny restaurant. "Are you always this busy?"

"July Fourth starts the summer up here. If we weren't busy now, we'd be in a lot of trouble. And, since Halsey isn't free, I'd better go clean off a table for the family that just came in the door. Enjoy your dinner," he added, hurrying away.

The restaurant was filled by the time Kathleen and Susan had finished eating their salads and were cracking the claws on the large lobsters they had ordered.

"Delicious," Kathleen muttered, placing a large chunk of white meat, dripping melted butter, into her mouth.

Susan, busy eating, nodded her agreement. "We don't eat lobster anyplace but Maine. Even the best places in New York City can't compare with this . . . . What the . . . ?" Someone smacked into the back of her chair, surprising Susan so that she dropped her nutcracker into the tiny custard cup of butter, sloshing the liquid over the blue and white tablecloth and the sleeve of Kathleen's cotton sweater. "I'm sorry!" She made a futile effort to mop up with her napkin.

"Don't worry, it's washable," Kathleen insisted. "Besides, you shouldn't be apologizing. That child should be." She watched as the perpetrator, a girl in her early teens with a cap of bright auburn hair, ran by the window, down the road, and out of sight.

Susan, who had turned around in time to see tears running down the girl's pale cheeks, glanced over her shoulder, wondering who still occupied the table the child had left. She didn't want to stare, but she had time to note two younger versions of the deserter, accompanied by an attractive couple whom she took to be the parents of this threesome. At least they certainly looked distressed enough to be the parents of the unhappy teen, she thought, returning her attention to Kathleen.

"We're very sorry. I'm sure Titania had no intention of upsetting your meal."

The voice from behind caused Susan to look back at the table. "It's all right. . . ." she began.

"No." A handsome man, blond with a startling dark reddish beard, sunburned cheeks, and dressed in the navy anorak, jeans, and deck shoes of a weekend sailor, disagreed with Susan. "It is certainly not all right for her to act like that. She is being rude and inconsiderate. But thirteen is a difficult age—intolerant and emotional at the same time."

Susan smiled. "I have two teenagers of my own," she admitted.

"Then you know all about it," the woman, as blond as the man, spoke up. "We're praying it's just a stage." She laughed as if to make light of the situation.

"Everything is a stage at that age. Please don't worry about it," Susan agreed, hoping to end the conversation and return to her lobster. She turned back to the meal in front of her, but not before she had noticed that the two youngsters remaining at the table were scowling at their adult companions. She guessed that they would follow their sister if only they had the courage.

"Hope it wasn't my mother's cooking that scared your daughter off," Danny Downing said, coming over to the table behind Susan.

"I think she's just in one of her moods," the woman answered, frowning at the oldest of the two daughters still present as the girl opened her mouth to speak. "The food here is wonderful," she continued loudly as if hoping to force things back to normal. "Everyone told us that this was the best place to eat on the island, and I guess they were right."

"There are a lot of good places to eat on the island," Danny said gently. "You'll probably want to try them all." Their conversation ended as Halsey arrived, order book in hand.

"It was very nice of him to say that," Kathleen commented as they got back to work on their lobsters. "Although they probably are all good restaurants. We haven't had any bad food since crossing the bridge into Maine."

"Hmmm." Susan paused long enough to chew an enormous bite of her shellfish before answering. "Some are fancier and some are cheaper, but I like this place best. But Danny's not just being nice. Remember this is a pretty small island. Less than a thousand people live here year-round. And about two-thirds of them were born here. The rest are retired people, artists, craftsmen, and writers—people who can choose where they live and work. There are also a few leftover hippie communes around. But the natives are a pretty small group. And close-knit. They support each other. Danny will recommend other places if you ask him, and the people who own the other places will recommend this restaurant in turn. It's the way of life on an island."

"You make it sound like utopia," Kathleen said, digging into her baked potato.

"It isn't. There's the same percentage of rotten apples as you get anywhere. The island is poor and there's some crime and a few serious family problems. Alcohol abuse is almost encouraged by the long winters, when people pretty much have to stay inside. Drugs are smuggled in all along the coast, and people are just as likely to make unfortunate choices in their lives here as anywhere else. But, you know, the natives keep most of that from the summer people. And most of the island people are like the Downings—hardworking, caring, supportive. And," she added, "they make great desserts."

"Desserts?"

"Rice pudding, Grape Nut pudding, raspberry pie . . ." Susan began.

"Toll house pie, apple pie, coconut cream pie, lemon meringue, blueberry pudding . . . And there are more up on the board," Halsey finished, rejoining them at their table. She nodded to the chalkboard hung on the wall by the cash register.

"So you'll be over early tomorrow?" Susan asked while Kathleen studied the list.

"About seven-thirty?"

"Great."

"Lemon slice pie?" Kathleen asked, sticking to essentials.

"It's made with whole lemon slices. If you love lemons, you'll love it," Halsey assured her.

"I'll give it a try. And a cup of decaf."

"I'll have the coconut cream and decaf," Susan said. "And I'll see you tomorrow morning." She had noticed that Halsey was looking over her shoulder at the table behind her.

But despite Halsey's apparent nervousness, the meal ended peacefully. The voices at the table behind them were self-consciously subdued, and Titania did not return. Susan offered the family a half smile as she walked to the register to pay for their dinner, but either it was unseen or they all chose to ignore it.

"So where's the grocery store?" Kathleen asked as they walked to Susan's Jeep in the cool night air.

"About a mile from here—in town," Susan answered with

a yawn. "We'll be there in a few minutes," she added, getting in the car.

"Maybe we should have made a list while we waited for our food," Kathleen suggested as they backed out of the lot and onto the curving road.

"We need everything. Eggs, milk, flour, bacon, dish detergent, snacks, coffee . . . everything. I usually just wander up and down the aisles slowly and fill a cart. Then we'll be back first thing tomorrow for all the things we've forgotten," Susan said, as they drove slowly down the road.

"It sure is peaceful," Kathleen commented, peering into the lit windows of the small white cottages they were passing.

"Hmm." Susan steered the car off to the side of the road. "Where's the store?"

Susan pointed to the line of cars she had just parked behind. "Up there. This is the beginning of the summer season, remember? Welcome to one of the most popular places in town. In a few days, everyone will be settled in and we'll be able to shop more normally. Until then, we're going to have to stand in line for our food."

"Then we better get going. This place isn't open twenty-four hours a day, is it?"

"No, but it's open until ten tonight and reopens tomorrow at six. Most of the island is up early." Susan stole a look at her companion to see if she had taken the hint. They had gotten a late start this morning because Kathleen had overslept.

But Kathleen was looking at her watch. "At least we have lots of time to shop and then get back home. But it's going to be a lot of work carrying groceries to the house in the dark if we really stock up, isn't it?"

"True. I guess we should just buy what we think we'll need for breakfast—and to get through the night. I'm not sure there's any shampoo in the house, although I know there's soap and toilet paper. But we might need paper towels. . . ." She entered the well-lit store, Kathleen following close behind, trying to remember what they were going to find necessary in the next twelve hours. Kathleen headed for the shopping carts waiting just inside the door. Susan hurried to the public phone hanging on a nearby wall. "I think I'll call Jed. Maybe he could put an extra key in overnight mail or something. . . ." She picked up the receiver.

"Why don't I start shopping then?" Kathleen suggested, and started off without waiting for an answer. She was standing in front of a large display of freshly baked bread when Susan found her a few minutes later.

"We're in luck. Jed says he can mail the key out tonight and we can pick it up at the post office here on the island anytime after ten tomorrow morning. He had some stuff from the office sent up that way last summer, so he's pretty sure of the time schedule. Why don't we pick up stuff for breakfast now, and then I can come back tomorrow and buy everything else." She looked at the various choices. "I like these tiny little orange muffins," she said, taking down a box of a dozen orange cakes. "And the potato bread makes wonderful toast." She picked up a large loaf. "We should remember butter, and there is a selection of homemade jellies and jams near the cash register. . . . Are you listening to me?"

"Yes, of course; I just overheard something interesting. . . . But it was probably nothing," Kathleen continued, less confidently. "What were you talking about?"

"Breakfast, groceries," Susan reminded her. "Did you pick up some orange juice?"

"I got frozen. I thought it would be easier to carry."

"Good idea." Susan selected a bag of coffee beans and continued down the aisle. "Maybe we should buy some granola or cereal in case one of us gets up earlier than the other. . . ." She would have looked at Kathleen with a sly smile except that Kathleen was still back with the breads. "Kath? Are you all right?"

Kathleen held her hand up and shook her head vigorously; Susan didn't have any idea how to interpret this. She swung around the cart and headed back to her friend.

"I'm fine. Listen," Kathleen ordered.

"Listen?" Susan was puzzled when Kathleen didn't continue.

"Listen. To the people standing over there," Kathleen

elaborated. "I think they were talking about your new neighbors. . . . Damn. They've stopped now. Now they're talking about cooking. Something about Eskimo rolls."

"Eskimo rolls are what kayakers do, they're not bakery products," Susan said. "So what were they saying about the people who moved into the house at the end of the cove?" she continued as they found themselves alone together.

"I'm not sure. I . . . ." She stopped before finishing.

Susan looked carefully at her friend. Either she was taking this whole thing pretty seriously or she was yawning again.

"I think," Kathleen continued, her yawn finished, "that they were saying that someone is planning to kill Mr. Taylor."

"I can't believe it. Who would talk about murder on a shopping trip?"

"You're probably right. I suppose I just misunderstood. The Taylors don't look like a family waiting for someone to be murdered."

"What?" Susan was perplexed. "When did you see them?"

"The Taylors were sitting behind us. The people whose daughter ran out," she added when Susan didn't respond.

"You're kidding. Are you sure?"

"I heard Halsey say something to Mrs. Taylor—about working for her. I thought you heard it, too," Kathleen explained. "Susan?"

But Susan didn't respond. She was wondering what sort of summer this was going to be when their nearest neighbors were a family comprised of a girl going through a turbulent adolescence and a father apparently hated so much that people spoke of killing him while they were selecting cornflakes. And one of the things she had treasured so about her island in Maine was how little it changed from year to year!

But, as Susan was to tell her husband on the phone late that night, it wasn't until she and Kathleen found that the barrier keeping them from driving down the road to the cottage had been unlocked that she realized this wasn't going to be an ordinary summer vacation.

"Probably Burt came back and unlocked it," Jed insisted rather sleepily.

"I know I woke you up, hon, but at least you could listen to me," Susan insisted, sipping a steaming cup of herb tea. "Mrs. Jamison said that there is no way to reach him in Canada. . . ."

"Maybe they got up there and the boats were missing or there was a snowstorm. . . . Okay," he added before she could interrupt him. "I know it's July, so snow is out, but maybe the trip had to be canceled for some reason and they returned and, when he got home, his wife told him that you needed to have the chain unlocked and so he came over and did it. You could call there, you know," he added more gently.

"It's awful late." Susan glanced at the clock; it was midnight. "And you know how early everyone goes to bed on the island."

"Yes, so . . ."

"But you're probably right and there is nothing to worry about. I suppose Mrs. Jamison found the key and came over and unlocked the chain. I shouldn't have awakened you."

Perversely, Jed seemed inclined to take the opposite side of any discussion. "Maybe you should call the police to check things out. I'm a little worried about you and Kathleen. You're all alone on that side of the cove and—"

"Oh, no, we're not," she protested. "That's the other thing I wanted to tell you. The Taylors are here. And they're really weird, Jed."

"In what way?"

"Well, their teenage daughter ran out of The Blue Mussel tonight crying. . . . All right," she interrupted herself before he could. "I know teenagers are unpredictable, but that isn't all," she continued, and explained about the mother's mood swings and the anticipated death of the father. "But it all sounds pretty insignificant when I tell you," she admitted. "I'm probably just tired. It was a long drive today, and moving in is always a lot of work—it might have been easier if we hadn't been able to get to the house and had had to leave everything in the car overnight. I'm sure glad Halsey is coming over tomorrow to help with the shutters and everything.''

"You really should go to sleep—don't stay awake worrying about the Taylors. We don't have to see very much of them, remember. And first impressions aren't always accurate.''

"I know," she admitted. "You're right; I'm being silly.''

"I didn't say that.''

"You thought it and you were just too polite to say anything—and I appreciate it. Are you packed for your trip tomorrow? What time does your flight leave?''

"No, and nine-thirty.''

"In the morning? And you're not packed? How are you going to get to Kennedy before nine? There'll be rush-hour traffic. . . .''

"La Guardia. And I have to pick up Jerry on the way. Don't worry, I have the alarm set for six. . . .''

"Then you shouldn't be up. You should get to bed right away," Susan insisted, forgetting that her call was the reason he was awake.

And he was nice enough not to mention it. "I'll be fine," was all Jed said. "Don't worry about me; I can nap on the plane.''

"Will you call tomorrow night?''

"Don't I always? I'm sorry I don't have the name of the hotel we're at. . . .''

"I'm sure Kathleen does. She's suffering acute withdrawal symptoms from her family. But you'd better get to sleep," Susan suggested to her husband, and after a few parting words, she followed her own suggestion.

The wind blew through the trees, a red fox climbed onto the porch and sniffed at the front door, and out on the point, a little thirteen-year-old girl in a big house cried herself to sleep.

THREE

KATHLEEN HEARD A SCREAM. IT WOKE HER UP AND SHE climbed from the warm bed, tightly wrapped a flannel robe around her to keep out the early morning chill, and walked barefoot downstairs to the living room. Morning wasn't exactly her favorite time of day, and certainly this particular morning wasn't improved by the sight of a dead man sitting in one of the armchairs that stood on either side of the stone fireplace. Susan and Halsey Downing waited nearby.

Susan was the first to speak. "Did you call the police?"

"You need a police officer?" Kathleen asked, apparently sleepy enough to forget the years she had been employed in that capacity in both New York City and Connecticut.

"Didn't you hear me yelling? I wanted you to call the police," Susan explained. "The number's hanging next to the phone in the kitchen."

Kathleen ignored her and walked over to the body and gently touched the man's forehead.

Susan watched intently, then glanced at Halsey. "Why don't you call the police?" she suggested. The girl looked as if she was going to faint—she was better off someplace else. Susan and Kathleen were, unfortunately, more accustomed to dead bodies.

"I'll . . . ." Halsey began, and then apparently felt an exit would be a good idea. Instead of the kitchen, she fled up the stairs. Susan recognized the sound of the bathroom door slamming.

"Poor kid," Kathleen commented.

23

"I hate it when children are involved with murder," Susan commented almost absently, watching as Kathleen peered under the dead man's eyelid.

"It's a little early to think of murder, isn't it?"

"Either someone killed him, put him in that chair, and covered him up, or else he sat down, died, and then covered himself up."

"Rigor is beginning to pass," Kathleen said, nodding.

"He's been dead for a while, hasn't he?"

"Yes."

"And he's been sitting in that chair for a while, too."

"Probably."

"We spent the night in the house with a dead man."

Kathleen sighed. "It looks like it."

"How can you be so calm?" Halsey whimpered from the top of the stairs.

Susan and Kathleen exchanged looks. What could they say, *Don't worry, you get used to it?* "It's easier to deal with these things when you're older," Kathleen suggested.

Susan didn't say anything.

"Did you call the police?" Kathleen asked.

"On the way," Halsey answered, returning to the room.

"Halsey's uncle is the sheriff," Susan explained.

"But he's off island right now. My grandfather had a stroke in Florida last week, and my uncle had to fly down and find someplace for him to stay when he gets out of the hospital. It looks like the only person who can help us is Aunt Janet."

"Halsey's aunt and uncle are the sheriff and deputy on the island," Susan explained.

"His wife is his deputy?" Kathleen asked.

"Every other year," Halsey said, sounding a little more like herself. "This year she's deputy and he's sheriff, and next year she'll be sheriff and he'll be her deputy. They have a liberated marriage," she explained needlessly.

"I guess so," Kathleen agreed. "But have you had a murder on the island before?"

"Two. The first was back when I was a kid. One of the lobstermen killed another—said he had been stealing from his traps for years. The murderer just sat down by the body and waited for the police to come. He said any Maine jury would understand what he did and why he did it. Of course, it turned out he was wrong: he's still in prison. And then last summer there was another killing. They weren't islanders, though, just tourists camping out down near the island nature center. A man shot his girlfriend and then stuck the gun in his mouth and killed himself.'' She shivered. ''They were found by a woman whose husband owns a nearby farm. She says she still has nightmares about it.''

''But in both those cases, the murderer was known, so no one on the island has had to find a murderer.''

''Nooo . . .'' Halsey strung out the vowel for a few extra seconds. ''But there's a big section of mystery novels in the library, and they're real popular. I'll bet there will be a lot of people that think solving our own murder is pretty interesting.''

''Then they'll be wrong. Murder sucks.''

The three women spun around and stared at the apparition standing in the open door to the house. A woman, probably in her late fifties or early sixties, Kathleen guessed from the gray hair and her windburned and wrinkled face, stood before them. Short and heavy, in fatigue pants, much-worn rubber boots, and a chamois shirt of international orange, she looked slightly like a pumpkin.

''Not that there's much I can do about this one,'' the woman continued, walking across the floor to the body. ''Looks pretty dead, doesn't he?'' she asked dispassionately. ''Wonder who smacked him with that bait bag. And what was in it when they did.''

''What?'' Susan had no idea what Janet Shapiro was talking about.

''See that imprint on his temple? Unless I'm crazy, that was made by a bait bag going about fifty miles an hour and weighed down with something pretty heavy. The crisscross pattern in the skin was made by the woven twine—it's a pretty distinctive design. Although I suppose it might have been made by a handwoven purse or something similar.'' She removed her glasses for a close look. "Damn bifocals," she explained. "Can't see with 'em. Can't see without 'em. Of course, without is considerably cheaper." She grinned at her own cleverness.

"Are bait bags rare on the island?" Kathleen was anxious to return to their more immediate problem.

"Not on this island. Each lobsterman has about a hundred or so. And this one was probably filled with a heavy rock. You've seen our boulder beaches—rocks is one of the things we have more of than we have bait bags. They might be hard to find on Maui or one of the Aleutians, but on this island, they'd be easy to find once you thought it all out. Makes a kind of ingenious murder weapon, doesn't it? Snatch a bait bag or just pick up one that floated to shore during the last storm, stuff a rock inside, spin it around your head like a sling back in Roman times . . ." She paused and shook her head. "Ingenious. And that takes brains. And in my experience, brains are just as rare on this island as in any other part of the world.

"Not that I think it's going to be easy to find the murderer of Humphrey Taylor," she continued. "From what I hear, there's lots of people who would of liked to see him dead." She looked away from the body to the two women. "From the looks on your faces, I can see that the sight isn't pleasing you two all that much."

"Who is Humphrey Taylor and why is he dead in my living room?" Susan asked, getting right down to what she considered essentials.

"Why, Humphrey Taylor is your new next-door neighbor. Don't tell me you didn't recognize him? I just assumed that you knew who he was. Why, Halsey should have known him right away. . . . Or maybe she wouldn't. . . ." Her voice trailed off.

"I just talked with Mrs. Taylor when she offered me the job," Halsey assured her aunt. "I did see Mr. Taylor, of course. . . . I mean he was around . . . but I didn't get a good look at him. And . . . and I didn't look too closely at him just now. . . . " She stopped and took a deep breath, and Susan, afraid the girl was going to throw up again, started toward her. "I'm all right. Really," Halsey insisted. "It's so shocking. So upsetting. I guess, when I saw the body sitting there, I just didn't think."

"Don't worry about it," her aunt insisted. "Mrs. Taylor is going to have to identify her husband's body, not you. Something wrong, Mrs. Henshaw?"

Susan had been staring intently at the dead man. The bait bag, the rock, or whatever had hit him had crushed his right temple, damaged the eye socket and part of his cheekbone, but most of his face was still visible, and something was puzzling her. "This is not the man we saw at The Blue Mussel last night."

"And it should be?" the policewoman asked.

"I didn't know who it was at the time, but I thought the Taylors were sitting at the table behind ours," Susan said slowly. "You know," she continued to Halsey, "the table where the girl was so upset that she ran away."

"Oh." Halsey nodded her head. "That was the Taylors. But that was the first Mr. Taylor, not the current Mr. Taylor. That was Mr. Ted Taylor; he's the girl's father. Mr. Humphrey Taylor is the . . . was the," she corrected herself with a shudder, "stepfather."

"Mrs. Taylor—" Kathleen began.

"Tricia Taylor," Aunt Janet said, nodding to show that she knew who was being talked about.

"Tricia Taylor married two men with the same last name?" Kathleen continued her question.

"Stands to reason that they did. They were brothers, after all."

"Wait a second here," Susan insisted. "You're telling me that Tricia Taylor divorced Ted Taylor and then married his brother, Humphrey Taylor?"

Aunt Janet nodded.

"So her daughters' stepfather is also their uncle?"

"Yup. People around here think it might be a little confusing for those girls—especially the youngest."

Susan considered that an understatement—a magnificent

understatement. No wonder the family appeared to be in such turmoil in the restaurant last night. And if that much emotion was apparent in a public place, what was going on behind closed doors? She looked down at Humphrey Taylor and wondered if his death was the answer to that question. His murder, she amended her thought. "And both the current husband and the ex-husband are on the island?" she asked.

"Well—" Susan wondered if she saw a sparkle in Aunt Janet's eye "—at least the current Mr. Taylor is on the island. I'm sure we're going to want to know exactly where the other Mr. Taylor is—and where he's been for the past day or so, of course."

"You think he killed him!" Halsey was too excited to explain, but everyone understood what—and who—she meant.

"I don't know who killed him." The girl's aunt stared at her sternly. "I do know that we're going to regret talk like that. Now, Halsey, I have to make a few phone calls, and I'm sure Mrs. Henshaw won't mind me using her phone. I want you to run next door and see if the Taylors—the rest of the family—are home. Don't go knocking on the door, and don't tell anyone about this. Just look around, make a mental note of what you see, and that's it. And then I want you to head out to the main road. Just wait on that rock down by the turn-in. There's going to be ambulances and police cars from off island, and who knows what else. They're going to have to know exactly where we are, and you can direct them. But—" she raised her already impressive voice "—you are not to tell anyone about this. Not if you see a car marked state police, not even if you see a car marked God. You are there to direct traffic—not to spread around news that's no-body's business right now. Do you understand exactly what I'm saying?"

"I . . ."

"It's important, Halsey. Maybe the most important thing you've ever done."

Halsey was obviously impressed with her aunt's statement,

and Susan was amused to note that she almost saluted as she raced from the room. Susan, too, thought Janet Shapiro was pretty impressive. "What do you want us to do?" she asked.

The deputy sheriff was looking closely at the body, and the words caused her to start. She stared at Kathleen and then Susan. "Can't say I have any idea. I was just trying to get her out of here. . . . Halsey's pretty smart. Just hope she's smart enough to shut up about this." She looked hard at what was left of Humphrey Taylor. "This was one of the stupidest men I'd ever met, but I never thought he was stupid enough to get himself killed." She looked up at Susan and Kathleen. "I don't like it! Not on my island," she announced loudly, and headed for the phone.

Kathleen picked up a slightly moth-eaten Hudson Bay blanket, draped it over the body, and then joined Susan by the window. "Something interesting?" she asked casually.

Susan glanced over her shoulder, making sure that they were alone. "Maybe," she answered briefly, and nodded her head at the glass.

Kathleen peered out the window, across the weathered gray porch, down the strip of lawn between tall white pines, and to the cove. The tide was almost out, and much of the estuary's bottom revealed. Mussels, clam flats, tiny immature crabs running between rocks and shells, were attracting flocks of gulls. A large blue heron picked its way across a bar of plants and boulders. Pieces of beach glass gleamed where the sun struck, and huge mounds of rugosa roses dropped pink and white petals at the water's edge. Kathleen seemed confused. "I don't . . ." she began.

"Over there. By that large pink boulder next to the stand of birch," Susan directed. "She's crouching down, but you can just make out the green anorak and her hair. Do you see her?"

"No, I . . . Yes!"

"Shhh." Susan dampened her enthusiasm. "We may not want Janet to know this just yet," she whispered.

"Why on earth not?" Kathleen answered.

"Shhh! Because we certainly don't want that child accused of anything, do we?"

"What are you talking about?"

"That's the Taylor girl—the one who ran from the restaurant last night."

"So?"

Kathleen seemed to be awfully dense today, but Susan persisted. "We don't want her to be accused of a murder that she didn't commit, do we?"

"Wait a second. We don't know that she's involved in this, we—"

"We can assume it," Susan insisted. "Why else would she be over there watching the house through binoculars?"

Kathleen opened her mouth to answer and then closed it again.

"Unless there's a rare bird nesting on our roof, that girl is watching us. And why would she be watching the house if she didn't know about him?" Susan nodded back over her shoulder.

"Okay, maybe. But how do you know that she isn't just interested in what's going on here for some reason of her own that has nothing to do with this? Teenagers aren't the most logical of people, you know. Remember when Chad became obsessed with that French exchange student and he started following her around? He must have been twelve or thirteen then."

"And this is just a coincidence?" Susan glanced back at the wool lump in the middle of her living room.

"Probably not, but possibly. And, if it's not, she might have killed him—or know the identity of the person who did," Kathleen added quickly. "And she could be in some sort of trouble, some sort of danger. I don't think we should just stand here and ignore her interest in all this. I really don't."

Susan thought it over. "Okay," she agreed. "I'll go talk to her." And, startling Kathleen, she opened the door and left the house, heading straight down to the water.

"Are you crazy?" Kathleen called out.

"Excuse me?" The deputy was standing in the doorway, phone still at her ear.

"Uh . . . Mrs. Henshaw got upset and just ran out of here," Kathleen explained lamely, hoping the woman had too much on her mind to worry about an erratic housewife.

"Murder is pretty upsetting, but that body shouldn't be left alone, and I've got to go to my car, and the ambulance is supposed to arrive. . . . Would it bother you to stay here with it . . . him?"

"Not at all. I was a policewoman before I got married," Kathleen explained.

Janet Shapiro chuckled grimly. "Then you probably know more about all this than me. A whole lot more.

"I'll leave you then," she continued, starting toward the door. "And when Mrs. Henshaw comes back, you might ask her to stay, too, but I don't think that girl should come in here. Yes, the Taylor girl," she continued, seeing Kathleen's surprised look. "I noticed her out in the cove as I drove up. Whatever she has to do with this can wait. She'll be around for a while."

"There's not necessarily any reason to think that she has anything to do with the murder," Kathleen said.

"Really?" Aunt Janet was skeptical. "Well, you may know more than I do, but from what I hear about that family, there's more than one reason to connect her with this murder. Which is good reason to keep her away for a while, seems to me."

And with this statement, Kathleen found herself alone with a dead man.

Susan walked across the cove, wishing she had taken the time to put on rubber boots. Glutinous black mud oozed into the new Keds that she had dared not take off for fear of cutting her feet on the shells. She slopped through water to her ankles, too intent on her mission to notice the brine shrimp fleeing. She was watching for the girl, who had ducked out of sight when Susan left her porch. The birch trees wouldn't afford much protection, but certainly the child could take off and run through them and vanish before Susan had squished across to the other shore. She slogged on, determined to accomplish her mission even if she had to run through the woods wearing a few pounds of mud on each foot. But that turned out to be unnecessary. As quickly as the girl had fled from the restaurant the night before, she popped out from behind the rock and then disappeared. But from the wave the girl gave her, Susan felt she could safely assume that her presence was desired.

"Hi!" she called out. "I'll be there in a minute." Surprisingly, the child's only response to this was to point back across the cove, wave wildly, and vanish behind the rock.

Susan, glancing over her shoulder, saw the only ambulance on the island (which had been used to haul wounded whales, dolphins, and a pet seal as well as the island's ill) skid to a stop in the crushed pine needles that lined her driveway. She dashed around the rock and dropped to the ground next to the child. "Hi," she said again, after a few minutes of hoping she wouldn't have to be the one to break the silence. Apparently her hopes were not to be fulfilled. "You're one of the Taylor girls, aren't you?" she added.

"Titania," came the one-word explanation.

"I'm Susan Henshaw. It's nice to meet you," Susan said, trying to remember exactly what the literary reference was.

Titania almost, but not quite, bent her pale pink lips into a smile. "It's nice to meet you, too." Her voice surprised Susan with its warmth. "When you have a name like mine, you can tell about people right away: those that are happy to meet you and those that want to prove that they're literary, that they've read *Midsummer Night's Dream*—they always say something stupid like 'Oh, are you queen of the fairies?' Do I look like the queen of any fairies?"

Susan smiled. She looked like a very healthy, athletic thirteen-year-old American girl. There was nothing nebulous or exotic about this Titania. Susan decided not to admit that she had had trouble identifying her name. "I thought you wanted to see me," was all she said.

"I guess . . ." Titania's assurance appeared to melt.

"There's a body in your living room," she said flatly as if it had nothing to do with her, as if there were no way she could be interested or involved.

"Your father's body . . ."

"My stepfather's body!" Titania surprised Susan with her vehemence. "Don't call that man my father! I hated him! We all hated him!" The announcement ended in hysterical tears.

Susan waited quietly, giving Titania a chance to express some of her grief and misery. The crying was such a combination of tears, moans, and angry sobs that Susan hurt just listening to it. "Maybe," she started gently when the crying had slowed down, "this isn't a very good time for you to say things like that."

There were still tears in Titania's eyes, but also a look of comprehension. "Because he's dead and we don't know who murdered him yet, right?"

"Right."

Titania grimaced. "I guess I just told you that I've been in your house, haven't I?"

"And that you saw your stepfather's body, but that's really all I know. You weren't at the house this morning, were you?"

"No. I was yesterday evening, though—I found him yesterday," she admitted.

"Did you touch him? Did he seem stiff or anything?" Susan asked as gently as she could.

"He . . . he didn't seem stiff, I guess. . . . But you're wondering how long he's been dead, aren't you? I know a little about that. I read a lot of Agatha Christie last winter."

"Yes, but we can find that out other ways. He might have been seen on the island recently or something." Or he might have been lying dead in my living room for over a week, Susan thought. But Titania's next words denied that possibility.

"He wasn't there the day before yesterday. I guess," she continued, seeing the look of surprise on Susan's face, "I should explain."

"You probably should," Susan agreed when the child paused.

Titania took a deep breath and began. "Things have been a little stressed out at my house this summer. Family problems and things . . . Oh, you're going to hear all about it. Everyone on this damn island seems to know about it," she continued more loudly. "My mother and my father got divorced last summer, which was lousy but livable. You know?"

Susan nodded. She did know. Lousy but livable was a good description of a lot of things.

"Well, we were kind of adjusting to it. Living with my mom but seeing Dad on weekends and all. And then we had this big party on New Year's Eve. My sisters and I even talked my mom into inviting Dad. Everyone was allowed to stay up till midnight as some big special treat, which it was for my little sisters, but I'm thirteen, for heaven's sake. There are kids in my class who've been to Times Square to watch the ball drop!"

Susan nodded again and took a moment to wonder why there were always parents who let their children do just about anything, and why her children were always holding those people up as sterling examples of parenthood. But she had to pay attention.

"So at the stroke of midnight my mother gets up and insists that everyone fill their glasses with champagne—even my littlest sister, and she was eight years old at the time— and that we congratulate her." She gulped, and Susan could see she was again near tears. "Well, my father was there, filling glasses with this fixed smile on his face, and my uncle was standing next to my mother—and she explains that she's getting married again—to Uncle Humphrey. I couldn't believe it. No one could believe it. I thought I was going to be sick. And Theresa was, but she doesn't have much self-control. . . ." Another gulp. "We . . . my sisters and I . . . we didn't know what to do. No one did. Some of the neighbors who had been invited even laughed—as though it was a joke, you know? I mean, they couldn't really believe it!

"But it wasn't a joke. They got married, and less than a week later, they were on their honeymoon in Antigua. They even had the nerve to invite us to go along!"

"You and your sisters?"

"Exactly. My little sister even wanted to go because of the sun and swimming and everything, but I thought it was a disgusting idea, and in the end, we stayed home with my father—my real father."

Susan wondered just how much of that decision had been mutual. And how welcome they had been in the home of their father.

It was almost as though Titania could read her thoughts. "My father loves having us," she insisted rather vehemently. "He always says that we are welcome there any time at all! And my father doesn't say things he doesn't mean!"

"Sometimes adults can't always live up to the things that they say," Susan answered. "You were explaining why you've been inside my house," she reminded her.

Titania scowled but apparently thought she might as well continue—which she did, slowly. "We've been up here for months, and it's been awful! My father had the house built for the family. He planned it for years and then he had a windfall last spring, and the first thing he did was hire an excavation company to start digging the foundation of the house. We were really looking forward to spending the summer up here. And then it went to my mother in the divorce settlement! My father's never even spent one single night in his dream home—he stays at an inn on the other side of the island! Think how sad that must make him feel! I'm sure it's been hell! Absolute hell!"

"And it's been difficult for you, too," Susan suggested.

"Yes!" Titania seemed to think the older woman was extraordinarily perceptive. "And that's why I've had to get away sometimes—to your house," she added a bit hesitantly.

"How did you get in?"

"Oh, that was easy!" Titania started out enthusiastically until she saw the look on Susan's face. "I was just walking around back over Memorial Day weekend when we were up here to . . . to christen the new house, as my mother called it—with champagne and lobsters—and I noticed then that there was a shutter off on one of the second-floor windows, so I climbed up that pine tree next to the porch roof on the back, and then I went around to the front—to put the shutter back up—when I realized that the window was unlocked and I could open it by just poking a stick under the sill and prying it up, and . . . and I got in," she finished, plainly embarrassed at her breaking-and-entering stunt.

"You must have been desperate for some privacy," was Susan's only comment.

"You understand." Titania's words were accompanied by a sigh of relief. "I . . ." Titania looked over Susan's shoulder and gasped. "They're coming. . . . My sisters," she explained. "They don't know about this. Please don't tell them. Please!"

The three girls could only be sisters. Three heads of auburn hair were cut into three identical little caps which topped a trio of turned-up noses, six widely spaced hazel eyes, and fair skin sprinkled with innumerable freckles. They all wore jeans and faded T-shirts, the uniform of the Maine coast.

"Titania, where have you been?" demanded the smallest of the group. "We've been waiting and waiting, and when you didn't show up, we wanted to come and get you, but you said we should wait, and I told Theresa that we should do what you said, but she said—"

"I can talk for myself, stupid!" These words were accompanied by a quick jab in the speaker's ribs. The middle-sized girl didn't bother to hide her anger.

"Hey! That hurt! Titania . . ." The young girl looked to her oldest sister for protection.

"Stop it, you two," Titania insisted. "You're here and Mrs. Henshaw is here, and that's all that matters right now." She stressed her words by widening her eyes and staring intently.

Susan was wondering just what unspoken message she was trying to communicate when Titania turned to her. "My sisters," she said slowly, "are looking forward to seeing the inside of your house. We've been admiring the outside for months now."

Susan opened her mouth and then shut it without speaking. So only Titania knew of their stepfather's death! "I . . . I'd be happy to have you all over in a few days—as soon as we've settled in," she stammered, agreeing with Titania that this wasn't the time or the place for them to hear the news. "We just arrived last night, you know," she added, making an effort to sound normal.

"Yes. We saw you in the restaurant," the smallest sister agreed, opening her eyes wide and grinning.

"And you probably noticed us—or at least Titania—when she decided to make a dash for it," the middle girl added, frowning at her older sister.

"Everyone saw Titania!" the youngest girl agreed, grinning at the memory.

"We have to get back to Mommy now," the middle sister continued. "No one else seems to be around," she added, gazing intently at Titania.

Susan thought the number of significant looks flying around was possibly a record for the island.

"And thank goodness," the middle girl added. "I thought I would go crazy if Uncle Humphrey found us. He would have made us go on another of those nature walks. Just the other day, he was talking about hunting sea urchins. Can you believe that?"

"I'd like to see some sea urchins," the smallest child admitted.

"Tierney! How can you say that?"

"I said I wanted to see sea urchins! I didn't say I wanted to see them with him, did I? Titania, where have you been? Theresa has been picking on me all day long!"

"All day? We haven't even had breakfast yet, and Mom is going to be really mad if we don't get home in time for it, Miss Stinky Pants!"

"Don't call me that! No one but Daddy can call me that!

No one!'' Tierney stuck her face a few inches from her sister's and screamed out the words.

Susan was a mother. She couldn't just sit there and do nothing. On the other hand, she wasn't their mother, and she might learn something that related to the murder. She resisted the urge to interfere. Except that . . .

"Stop this right now!" Titania's orders solved the problem. Both girls jumped back, and Theresa had the grace to look embarrassed.

Tierney wasn't so sophisticated. "I don't understand," she protested. "I thought we were going to go ahead with the plan." The statement earned her the wrath of both sisters, who glared identically. "Well," she continued with a tired whine, "that's what you two have been saying—that no matter what happens, we have to go on with the plan, that we can't stop till Daddy is back where he belongs. . . ."

"Tierney!"

"God, you are so stupid!" Theresa growled.

"It's what you keep saying!" Tierney was obviously distressed; apparently the rules had changed, and no one had mentioned it to her. "And why are you here, Titania? I thought we were all going to meet down by the old well and we were going to collect thorns from the raspberry bushes to . . ." She looked at Susan and gulped. "To collect them," she ended lamely.

"You girls collect thorns?" Susan asked, when no one else spoke up.

"Not usually. Of course not." Titania spoke up. "Theresa loves to collect things, and she has a science project that she's doing over the summer. She has to collect specimens of lots of plants and classify them. You know, for extra credit."

"You do extra credit work in the summer? Between the school years?" Susan, who had always suspected her own children of glossing over anything more difficult than *Mad* magazine during the summer months, was impressed. And more than a little skeptical. "Woody plants or just bushes?" she asked.

"Everything! All the plants around here!" was Theresa's

enthusiastic answer. She waved her arms at the woods and the cove as she spoke.

Susan didn't even bother trying to look like she believed that one. "Should be interesting," she said blandly. "I hope you have a large notebook."

"I like to collect things. I collect rocks, and beach glass, lobster buoys, and—" Theresa started to explain before her enthusiastic sister interrupted her.

"Do I hear Mother calling?" Titania jumped to her feet. "Yes, I do!" she insisted. "It must be breakfast. We'd better get going."

Susan, who had heard nothing, wasn't surprised when she found herself deserted. "There's something going on there," she said to herself, leaning back against the sun-warmed granite. "Something interesting."

The three children ran back across the cove. The sun shone down on their heads, turning their shiny hair the same color as the beard on their father's face.

FOUR

" . . . AND YOU DIDN'T GET ANYTHING ELSE FROM them."

"I didn't have a lot of time. . . ." Susan began to excuse herself.

"But there's a story there." Kathleen explained her interest. They were sitting at the scrubbed pine table in Susan's kitchen, sipping hot tea and waiting while the body was removed from the living room. "Everyone who has come to the house, even the woman driving the ambulance, has made strange comments about this."

"Strange? In what way?"

"Oh, I don't know." Kathleen put her cup down on the table and glanced out the window. "No one seems very surprised that he was murdered. . . ."

"Might be that no one on the island is surprised by some of the odd things you summer people do."

Kathleen and Susan both looked up as Janet Shapiro reentered the room. "And then again, it might be that they don't want to be involved, that they want this to be a summer-people problem, not something that involves islanders. . . . I sure would love a cup of that tea," she added, joining them at the table.

Susan hopped up to get another cup. "There's only milk and sugar. I still need to go to the store, I'm afraid. We had some problems getting down the road last night," Susan added, and explained their situation.

"Thanks," Janet said, accepting the tea and taking a large

gulp of the hot beverage before speaking again. "Tell me something. If you had been able to drive right to your door and unload everything into the house and then shop and do all the things that you normally do the night you arrive at the house, would you have taken that cover off Humphrey Taylor before this morning?"

Susan looked down into the deep turquoise cup, made by a potter on the island; she loved the rings that led from its top to its bottom. "I don't know," she answered slowly. "The first trip of the year can be difficult—fun but difficult. Normally the shutters would be off the house and all the covers put away before we arrived. This year something went wrong with the planning, and none of that happened. . . ." She would have continued, but Halsey had just run into the house, calling for her aunt.

"We're in here, Halsey. No need to wake up the dead."

"She's on her way. She's right out there. There was nothing I could do to stop her, but I thought you'd want to know."

They didn't have to ask who she was talking about. Humphrey Taylor's widow was knocking on the door before Halsey had stopped speaking. Halsey looked around wildly and, apparently unable to decide what to do, dashed for the stairs. Susan got up and hurried to open the back door.

"Come in. You're our new neighbor, aren't you?" She heard the inanity of the words as she spoke them, but what else could she say? *Come in. You're the new widow, aren't you?* She was glad the job of informing Mrs. Taylor of her new marital status was going to fall in someone else's lap. In this case, the wide one of Janet Shapiro.

But it appeared that the subject was going to have to wait a few minutes; there were social amenities that had to be gotten out of the way first. "Hi. I'm Tricia Taylor. We haven't met before, but my oldest daughter interrupted your meal last night. If I'd known then that we were neighbors, I'd have said something more. You must think we're pretty rude."

"Of course not. I didn't know who you were either. I'm Susan Henshaw, and this is my friend Kathleen Gordon. Kathleen's up here for the Fourth of July—the other members of our families can't get away, I'm afraid,'' Susan explained politely.

"Oh, that's too bad. I was hoping you and your husband could come to our brunch on the Fourth, but maybe Kathleen could come with you? We certainly aren't old-fashioned enough to worry about having extra women.''

"No, there's nothing wrong with extra women,'' Susan said. "And we'd be delighted to come.'' She wasn't going to worry about accepting without consulting Kathleen. The only party that was going to take place at that house was a wake.

"And we can meet your husbands when they come up—I know Humphrey's looking forward to it.''

Susan opened her mouth, and nothing came out.

"Humphrey is your husband?'' Kathleen asked to fill in the gap. Of course, they knew that, in fact, Humphrey was her husband—her dead husband, not her ex-husband. Although, when Susan stopped to think it through . . .

"Yes. My second husband. We were married just a few months ago.'' Susan wondered if Tricia was going to explain her unusual family situation.

"He's on the island?'' Kathleen asked.

"Not right now. He was here last week, but he had to go back down to Boston for a business meeting. He'll be back in a few days, though. The man you saw me with last night was Ted, my first husband. The girls' father. He's staying at a bed-and-breakfast on the other side of the island. He says it's very nice.''

As nice as the dream house that he had planned and built and now watched someone else move into? Susan wondered.

"I'm afraid we have some bad news for you, Mrs. Taylor,'' Janet said, insisting on returning to the tragedy.

Tricia Taylor put her hand up over her face as though warding off a blow. "I don't want to hear about it. I am sick to death of people coming to me about my family.'' She looked at the startled women and changed her tone. "There are problems. There are bound to be problems in a second marriage.'' She took a deep breath and continued more reasonably. "I have spoken to numerous psychiatrists and family therapists. There is nothing unusual here. We're just going to have to live through it. I was speaking to my husband last night—"

"You spoke with Humphrey last night? What time was that exactly?" Janet asked.

Susan was interested: Tricia Taylor's expression had changed from polite interest to annoyance to irritation to anger in a few moments. And why the changes since, apparently, she didn't know Humphrey was dead?

"I don't know what's wrong with you people! Do you have such boring lives that you get your kicks by invading the privacy of others? I cannot imagine what sort of person would ask questions like that. You sound like a policeman or something and—"

"I am a police person."

"And that gives you the right to ask anyone anything? I think not!"

Susan, astounded at how quickly Tricia Taylor changed moods, wondered if Halsey had been correct. Maybe there was some sort of psychological problem here.

"I happen to know something about the law, Mrs. . . . whatever your name is . . . and you are not allowed to hassle me or cause me any distress. Being a policewoman doesn't mean you can do anything you want, you know." She emphasized the word *woman*, ignoring Janet's preferred form of address.

Janet Shapiro poured out a cup of tea and pushed it across the table toward Tricia Taylor. "We got off on the wrong foot, and I'm sure it was all my fault. I'm just not used to this type of thing." She took a deep breath. "I'm sorry I have to tell you that your husband is dead."

"T . . . He's dead? How . . . ? Where is he? How do you know that?" Strangely enough, she picked up the tea and took a sip, peering into the cup. Susan wondered if she was trying to avoid their stares. "So how did it happen? A driving accident? These roads are so terrible, so many curves, no shoulders. . . . "

"It wasn't an automobile accident, Mrs. Taylor. Someone hit him."

"Hit him? Hit him with what? Is this some sort of sick joke?"

"Mrs. Taylor—"

"Now, look . . ." Tricia Taylor put down her cup with a bang. "My family is going through a difficult time, I admit it, but there is no reason to make things more difficult than they are. I don't know what my daughters told you, but they are really and truly settling down and accepting their new father, and all I can ask is that you ignore any wild stories they tell."

Susan put her hand on Tricia Taylor's shoulder. "It's true. Humphrey is dead. We found him this morning . . . here. In my house."

Tricia didn't say anything for a few minutes. When she did speak, it was to Janet Shapiro. "You were talking about Humphrey. You were telling me that Humphrey is dead."

The policewoman looked puzzled.

"You thought we were talking about your first husband, didn't you?" Susan asked, thinking that she understood the confusion.

"Yes." Tricia Taylor stood up. "I . . . I have to go home. The girls . . ." She seemed confused. "The girls have to know about this. They have to know right away."

Susan leapt to her feet. "You shouldn't be alone," she insisted. "I'll go with you."

"I don't know what you can do. . . ." the new widow began.

"I'd feel a lot better if Mrs. Henshaw went with you," Janet Shapiro insisted. "She can take phone calls and things like that while you deal with your daughters. There's going to be a lot of business to attend to, I'm afraid. But first things first. Someone has to officially identify the body."

"I don't think I could bear to do that." Tricia Taylor paled, displaying the first anguish Susan had seen.

"Well, you're going to have to see him sooner or later, but

if you want to wait until you're more in control, that's fine with me. What about your first husband?''

"Ted?" Tricia seemed confused by the deputy's suggestion.

"You said he was on the island," Janet explained, "and I did hear that he's your second husband's brother.''

Tricia's manner became slightly frosty. "I don't see what that has to do with anything.''

"He could identify the body.''

"Yes . . . yes, of course he could.'' No one in the room could miss the relief that Tricia felt. "He's staying at an inn over on the other side of the island. Near the bridge. I think it's called The Land's Inn or something like that.''

"It's The Landing Inn—that big cottage down by the old ferry landing. It's run by some friends of mine. If you don't mind if I use your phone, I'll call over there and set someone to work finding your ex-husband.'' Janet headed to the phone.

"She could be wrong, couldn't she?'' Tricia asked after Janet had left. "Maybe the man you found wasn't Humphrey. . . .''

Susan knew Janet Shapiro wouldn't have been sloppy in her identification, and she hated to raise Tricia's expectations. "Unless he has a twin brother, I think you can be pretty sure it was Humphrey that we found.''

"But we do have to have official identification, and Cathy over at the inn says your ex-husband is out,'' Janet said, returning to the room.

"Then I'll have to do it?'' Susan thought Tricia sounded horrified.

"No. He told Cathy that he was going to look around some art galleries on the pier in town, so I think I'll just mosey down that way and see if he can be found. Do you have any idea just what sort of art interests him?''

"Anything modern or abstract. I wouldn't bother going to places selling realistic watercolors of waves crashing against the granite coast or seals on the beach.''

"I know the kind of thing you mean—and the places to look. My husband is a sculptor.''

"I thought you said he was the sheriff." Tricia sounded as if she were accusing Susan of lying.

"You have to do more than one thing to make a living up here," Janet said, heading toward the door. "I'll call your house when I find him," she added, leaving the room with a quick wave of her hand.

"A sculptor? Isn't that kind of a strange hobby for a sheriff?"

"It's not a hobby. Her husband studied at the Rhode Island School of Design, and he teaches at an art school on the island. Being sheriff is a way of bringing in a steady salary. It's like Janet said, it's tough making it up here, and lots of people do more than one thing to make ends meet. Janet sells silver jewelry that she designs and creates—she graduated from RISD, too," Susan explained.

"I know I sound surprised, but she doesn't look like an artist," Tricia said, starting from the room.

"Not all artists fit the image," Kathleen said, standing at the door. "I'll stay here in case anyone needs me."

Susan and Tricia strolled down the path in the woods between the houses. For years and years, when the land had been unoccupied, this had been the Henshaws' trail to the tiny point of land that jutted out into the water of Penobscot Bay. Susan and Jed had often sat here in the evening, a bottle of wine and two glasses keeping them warm as they watched the sun set over far-off islands. Last summer they had walked the same trail many times as the gigantic home grew on the point.

The Taylors' new house (for *cottage* or *camp*, the names usually used for Maine island homes, certainly didn't apply here) stood on the foundation of an old summer cottage, one of the first on the island. Abandoned years ago, the original mansion had been built directly upon the pink granite slab that rose thirty feet or so above the water at high tide. The rocks had been matched so that it was difficult to determine where nature left off and artifice began. Sometime in the spring last year, before the Henshaws had opened their house, the Taylors' contractor had destroyed the original building except for the stone foundation and the base of a large fireplace. On that he had created a large, modern structure that soared into the sky.

And now, Susan thought, the inside would be finished and furnished. Even the tragedy at hand couldn't entirely destroy her curiosity.

"I hope the girls haven't heard about this from anyone else," Tricia Taylor said, closely following Susan.

"It would certainly be best if you were the one to tell them," Susan agreed, stepping over a large beige mushroom that had popped up in the middle of the path.

Tricia, apparently unaware of Susan's conservation, gave the fungus a kick that sent it flying into the woods. Oh well, Susan thought, the woman had more important things to worry about. "Jed and I have been admiring your house. We feel like we know it well—we watched the workmen all last summer," she explained.

"I hate that house," Tricia surprised her by answering. "If the economy weren't so bad, if I had a prayer of getting my money back, I'd sell it in a minute."

"I—" Susan began to offer a soothing word or two, but she was interrupted.

"It's worth a fortune. Ted, of course, had to have the best of everything. Solid copper and solid brass. The most expensive traditional workmanship and the most expensive new technology all rolled together into one gigantic castle on the Maine coast. I know the recession is supposed to be only a memory, but there's no way I'm going to make money on that thing. People get divorces for a lot of reasons, but I swear that house came between us just as much as another woman might have. It's his first love, his creation—his Frankenstein," she ended bitterly.

As they rounded a curve in the path, Tricia's monster came into view. It was spectacular—and beautiful. "You're impressed, aren't you?" Tricia Taylor asked. "Ted planned for you to be. He planned everything about his baby. It always made me think of those spots at Disney World where you're supposed to take pictures because that's the best view. Humphrey and I always laugh about it. Or we used to," she added quietly.

Susan didn't know what to say, so she said nothing.

"The girls like the house, of course," Tricia added. "Well, they should. Ted consulted them about every little detail."

"Really? How nice for them."

"I suppose, but," Tricia began as one conceding a point, "it didn't make life easier for Humphrey. Ted was a hard act to follow. As a father, that is. As a husband, almost anyone would have been an improvement."

"It sounds like building the house was a strain," Susan commented.

"Building the house was a piece of cake. Ted wrote a check. Dozens of men on the island leapt for joy over his stupidity and largess, and then they got busy and built it." Tricia shrugged. "Planning the house was the killer. In fact, it occupied Ted every spare second of our fifteen-year marriage."

"I—"

"There's Titania," Tricia interrupted. "She's my oldest daughter."

"We've met," Susan said. Apparently Titania's mother was too distracted to ask when and where—if she cared.

"Where are your sisters?" Tricia asked, putting her arm around her oldest child. "I hope they haven't wandered off. I need to speak with you all."

"Theresa and Tierney are waiting for you—in the kitchen," their older sister explained. "They're baking cookies. Chocolate chip."

Tricia hurried away.

"I thought it would be best if they were kept busy," Titania explained quietly to Susan. "They didn't like Humphrey—we all hated him—but this is still going to be upsetting. You know?"

"I know." Susan thought it was going to be more than upsetting if they didn't find the murderer fairly quickly—or if it turned out to be someone the girls knew, someone they cared about. "This is beautiful woodwork," Susan said, trying to keep the tone light and motioning to the soaring gull carved into the door.

"My father found a woodworker who carved all the doors for him. Daddy designed all three of them; there are seals and starfish and sea urchins on the other two. But the best thing is the mantel in the living room. It's fabulous—everyone says so. It has the family history carved right into it."

"I'd like to see that," Susan said absently. They were entering the house now, and she thought she heard voices other than those of Titania's sisters—women's voices that seemed to be coming toward them from down a spiraling stairway at the end of the large flagstone entryway where they stood.

"Oh Gawd." Titania looked horrified. "They're here. I thought they were going for a ride on the mail boat this morning." She gave Susan a desperate look. "We have to keep them occupied. They shouldn't be around when Mom tells my sisters about all this. Please help me, Mrs. Henshaw."

"What do you want me to do?" The voices were getting louder; there was little time for questions.

"Ahhh . . ." Titania looked around as though expecting to find the answer to that question emblazoned across the pristine white walls. "Get them out of here. Take them someplace. They were talking about going for a hike in the national park this afternoon. . . . Please," she added, "it's very, very important."

Susan didn't understand the urgency, but she decided to do what she could to help the girl. When the two women followed their voices into the room, she was ready to introduce herself. "Hi!" She sounded unusually perky even to her own ears. "I'm Susan Henshaw. I have the next cottage down the cove."

"Oh? The little gray one?" This was said by the shorter of the two women, a shapely redhead.

"This is Mrs. Briane. Judy Briane," Titania identified the woman. She was wearing turquoise silk capri pants, a creamy silk man-tailored shirt, silver metallic sandals, and a small fortune in Navaho jewelry. She didn't look at home on the

Maine coast, but she looked spectacular. And her tone of voice matched her first question about Susan's cottage. Judy Briane might be short, but that didn't prevent her from looking down on people.

"And this is Sally Harter," Titania continued. Unlike her companion, Sally's clothing was exactly what one would expect to find on the Maine coast. Except that everything she wore was brand-new, still bearing the imprint of the plastic bags in which it was sold. "Mrs. Henshaw knows all about Acadia National Park. She can probably answer all your questions," Titania continued, talking to Sally Harter while she and Susan shook hands. "I'll go get that trail map like I promised, and you can do it right now." And, without waiting for an adult response, Titania ran from the room.

"Did I leave those maps in the kitchen?" Sally Harter wondered aloud.

"They're on the desk in the living room. She's probably just going to see that animal she likes so much," Judy Briane suggested, not bothering to change her tone of voice. Or possibly she was only capable of sarcasm? Susan wondered.

Sally seemed to hesitate, perhaps unsure what to do. "I do know something about the trails in the park," Susan assured her. "I've been hiking there since I was a child. In fact, we were planning on heading up Precipice this afternoon," she lied, hoping Kathleen was up to the hike.

"Really? Who's we?" Sally asked, leading the way to the two-story living room.

While Sally Harter looked over the pile of pamphlets and maps on a tiny cherry desk in one corner of the room and Judy Briane collapsed onto a large red leather couch as though too tired to live, Susan looked around. The massive stone chimney with its carved wood mantel dominated the room, even drawing attention away from the view, which was spectacular. Birch logs were piled high on heavy iron andirons which Susan recognized as the work of an island blacksmith. The carved mantelpiece would have to wait for closer examination. A handwoven rug lay on the floor, and a mobile flew from a crossbeam near the ceiling. And, except for the couch, the desk in the corner, and a half dozen cheap wicker chairs, the room was completely empty. No pictures on the walls, no shelves, no books, nothing.

"Ted believes that each piece of furniture should be chosen carefully over time—so everything will be perfect," Judy Briane explained in a bored voice, apparently having noticed Susan's examination of the room.

"Found it!" Sally announced, not giving Susan time to respond to the other woman. "Now, let's see. You said Precipice trail. Right?"

"Yes. We climb it every year." Susan moved a little closer to the window while speaking.

"And you're all going up this afternoon?"

"Yes." Susan stopped for a moment. "Well, no. My family isn't up here yet. But a friend is with me, and we're going to hike together." Susan was so busy watching out the window that she didn't see what was coming, and before she knew it, she had agreed that Sally and Judy should join them for the long trek. She would have preferred to do something that required spending less time with these two women, but she had promised Titania. In fact, she had enthusiastically endorsed Sally's suggestion before she knew what she was doing. She would have been more careful of her time and more selective of her companions if she hadn't been wondering what Titania was heaving into the ocean.

Three hours later, Susan and Kathleen were in Acadia National Park gazing up at Champlain Mountain from the parking lot at its base. In the distance, they could barely make out hikers climbing to the mountain's summit.

"You do this every year?" Kathleen sounded doubtful.

"Every year when the peregrine falcons aren't nesting— the trail is closed then."

"I wonder where our fellow hikers are," Kathleen said, leaning back against the trunk of Susan's Jeep. "The last time I saw them, they were right behind us."

"They pulled off back at Jordan Pond House. I was watching in my rearview mirror. I assumed that they had to use the bathroom since we ate lunch less than an hour ago.''

"Only an hour? I thought it was more than that!" After two days together, Kathleen's answer didn't come as much of a surprise to Susan. She reached into the back of her car and pulled out a navy day pack bearing the logo of the Audubon Society. "I picked up some munchies at the grocery and made a thermos of hot coffee so we can have a snack at the top.''

Kathleen smiled. "Great! Hey, isn't that Sally's car?" she asked as a white BMW pulled into the lot.

"It's about time. I wonder where they've been," Susan said, slamming her car door and locking it.

"Hi! We didn't keep you waiting, did we?" Judy asked, getting out of the car. She had a bigger smile on her face than Susan had seen there before. "We found this wonderful gift shop and I just had to buy some pillows for my daybed in the study. They're hand-stenciled—not tacky tourist stuff.''

"We have been waiting," Kathleen said. Susan admired her lack of tact.

Her comment was ignored. Both women were staring up at the mountain. "Are you sure we can just walk up that thing? I saw some kids in hiking boots with ropes and stuff going down the road. . . ." Sally began.

"That was a group from Outward Bound. They're learning technical climbing. This is nothing like that," Susan assured them. "This is a hike, not a climb. The worst that might happen is slipping on a rock and twisting an ankle.'' (She glanced at everyone's choice of footwear. She had been very definite about the need for boots or sturdy hiking shoes, so she didn't feel guilty about the slipperlike things Judy wore.) "Come on," she urged. "Chrissy was going up and down this trail when she was three years old.'' She hoped to get the women past the large warning sign at the beginning of the ascent. She wasn't sure, but she thought that there was some mention of past fatalities on this, the steepest trail in the park.

"How long is the hike?" Kathleen asked.

Susan wondered if she was anxious to get to the snack. "It depends on how fast we walk. Chad once made it down to the bottom in thirty minutes. Of course, going up is longer." She didn't mention that Chad had run down the trail and that she and Jed, going their fastest to keep up, had taken over an hour. Information like that wouldn't encourage her companions—nor would the knowledge that there were dozens of metal ladders and rungs placed in outcroppings of rock to prevent climbers from falling into large boulder fields below.

"Well, the sooner we start, the sooner we'll be finished," Sally said logically, lifting a tan leather pack from the backseat of her car and slinging it over her shoulder. Susan could see that it was stuffed full. More lunch?

"So let's start." Judy was less well equipped, although a pair of very expensive German binoculars hung from a cord around her neck.

Susan hastily finished locking her car and trotted after the other women. Fortunately a large group of young people was huddled around the illustrated sign at the bottom of the trail, and apparently no one thought there was any reason to delay their start and wait to read it. They started up the trail, Susan in the lead following the red splashes of paint.

Half an hour later she was at the rear of the group, actively discussing various islands with Sally in an attempt to pretend that she didn't mind not being able to keep up with Kathleen and Judy (inappropriate shoes and all).

Another hour had passed before she was sitting on the top of the mountain. Unlike those less fortunate than herself, she had managed to reach the peak without breaking anything other than all the nails on her left hand and the skin of her knee. "At least I've got the food." She forced a smile to her face and started to pull the backpack off her shoulders.

"Oh, we've already eaten," Sally said.

"But we were so hungry that we ate up everything we brought. Kathleen said that you had your own snack," Judy added. "What did you bring? We've had fresh cream cheese on some zucchini bread that Sally made, gingersnaps, peaches, and white wine.''

"I brought coffee, apples, gorp, and lemon drops,'' Susan said. "It's what we always bring on Precipice.''

"Traditions are so nice,'' Kathleen offered, but she had the grace to look embarrassed. "And Susan's family has been climbing in the park for years.''

Susan thought that Kathleen was straining for enthusiasm just a bit. She bit into an apple rather defiantly. There was a worm trail through the white flesh. "Some view, isn't it?'' she asked.

"Sure is,'' Sally agreed enthusiastically. "Everything in Maine is beautiful. We've been having a great time ever since we arrived at the Taylors'. I just wish Trish had come with us. She really could have left those girls alone. Sometimes she's so overprotective!''

"Can you blame her?'' Judy asked. "Just think how terribly they've been acting since the divorce. I've never heard of anything like it. You'd think no one had ever had divorced parents—or that Humphrey is some sort of monster.''

"I think—'' Sally began, glancing at Susan and Kathleen.

"Every store we go into seems to have people standing around talking about Trish and Humphrey and the girls! I think there are a lot of silly rumors flying around the island, and it's time they were stopped,'' Judy insisted, not waiting to hear her friend's opinion.

"There might be good reason to keep everything quiet,'' Sally said.

"If you're talking about those death threats, you can just sit back and relax. No one is going to kill Humphrey Taylor.''

Susan was so startled by Judy's assertion that she could only stare. Kathleen was less intimidated. "Exactly who said anything about murdering Humphrey Taylor?'' she asked quickly.

"I don't think we should talk about this,'' Sally insisted loudly enough for a couple of young hikers to glance nervously in their direction.

"I think you should," Susan said, putting away her snack uneaten. "If you don't want to tell us, you could speak with Janet Shapiro—she's the official law enforcement on the island. You see, Humphrey Taylor has been murdered."

Neither woman said anything, although Sally opened her mouth, glanced at Judy, and shut it again.

"Mr. Taylor is being identified by his brother Ted—"

Susan's explanation was interrupted by Judy Briane. "Exactly how do you know this?" she asked.

"I was with Janet Shapiro when she left to find Ted Taylor. And there's no doubt that Humphrey was murdered," Susan continued.

"How did it happen?" Sally asked quietly.

"Apparently he was hit on the head with a heavy object," Susan answered, deciding not to tell more than necessary.

"How Agatha Christie," was Judy's only comment.

"When . . ." Sally began.

"Yesterday probably," Kathleen answered the unasked question.

"I don't understand why you two know about it—about the murder. You don't have anything to do with the Taylors, do you?" Sally asked.

"Mr. Taylor's body was found in Susan's living room," Kathleen explained.

"He was killed at your house? What was he doing there?" Judy asked.

"We don't kno—"

"He may not have been killed where he was found," Kathleen interrupted Susan.

Susan glanced at her gratefully. She was more interested in the reactions of the two women. Or, more honestly, Judy's cool response. Of course, she reminded herself, they could be only casual friends of the Taylors', the type of people you might invite for a visit to your summer home, hoping to become closer. But, naturally, where there was a murder, there were questions to be asked, relationships to be investigated.

Except, she reminded herself, this had nothing to do with

her. These people weren't friends or even acquaintances. They were only the people who had moved in next door, people who couldn't keep their dead bodies to themselves.

"We must get back to Tricia." Judy wasn't going to pussyfoot around. "I'd never have left her if I had known the pain she must be going through. How long will it take to get back down this damn mountain?" She glared at Susan. "And no more stories about your family—please!"

FIVE

Arriving home, Susan was surprised to find Titania perched on the steps leading to her front porch, a fluffy golden retriever by her side.

"Good," Kathleen said, spying a large box on the old wicker table standing in the middle of the porch. "There are the doughnuts we bought yesterday. I'm starving."

"That shouldn't be a problem," Susan said, greeting Titania. "You bought at least two of each kind the bakery makes."

"There were lots," Titania agreed cheerfully. "But I'm afraid Karma ate them. I hope she doesn't get sick. Sugar isn't good for her."

"Karma?" Kathleen repeated the word as a question. Susan, looking closely, saw that the dog had chocolate glaze on her whiskers.

"I'm sorry. She jumped up and grabbed them off the table before I was halfway up the stairs. This dog eats everything. She's always stealing food at home. Mom says she's a thief!" But Titania made the accusations in a loving voice as she caressed the animal's head, pulling the fur back from intelligent and satisfied brown eyes.

"The dog's name is Karma?" Susan guessed.

"Yes," Titania said. "She's only a baby—just six months old. My father gave her to me for my birthday. He named her. He said she would bring me good luck."

"She's beautiful," Kathleen said, reaching down to pet the animal.

"Isn't she rather large for a retriever?" Susan asked.

"She's a big golden." Titania was obviously ready to defend her precious pet against any slights. "Her grandfather was a champion."

"How nice," Susan commented, although she had noticed that owners were always saying that there was a champion somewhere in their pet's background. Either there were a lot of champions or a few dogs were awfully busy.

"My father says dogs are the aristocrats of the animal world," Titania insisted, hugging Karma.

"That's possible. I don't know much about dogs," Susan admitted.

"But you like Karma, don't you, Mrs. Henshaw?" the girl asked.

Sensing that the correct answer was important, Susan offered a polite lie. "She's a beautiful dog. It would be impossible not to like her."

"That's great!" Titania leapt up, startling the dog, who fled in circles around the porch. "We have to go home. I told my mother I'd take care of my little sisters this afternoon. She has to go to Blue Hill to make arrangements for the body or something. Oh, and my father is at the house. He wants to talk to you—he said it wouldn't take long. You'll come over, won't you?"

"Sure she will," Kathleen said. "I'm going to go into town and do some shopping. You were saying that you wanted to spend the afternoon just getting the house ready for the summer, remember?" Kathleen reminded Susan.

"Okay . . ."

"My dad will only take a few minutes. Please come. Please."

Susan, surprised by the desperation in Titania's voice, agreed to follow her to the point on the cove. She dumped her backpack on the porch, pulled Karma away from it, and headed out with the girl and her pet. They didn't talk much on the way, Susan preoccupied with questions about the murder but not wanting to interrogate Titania, who was kept busy pulling mushrooms, branches, moss, and broken seashells from her dog's mouth.

"She's teething," Titania explained as they entered the lawn behind her home. "She's going to get better about this type of thing as she gets older. . . . There's my father," she added as the bearded man Susan had seen in the restaurant last night crossed the lawn to meet them.

"Hi. I'm Ted Taylor," he introduced himself, and offered his hand. "I know that you're Susan Henshaw. My daughter has told me about you."

Susan was surprised, but didn't say anything. Karma was licking dirt off her knee.

"Why don't you and your dog go down by the water?" Ted Taylor suggested to his daughter. "Your sisters are there trying to find sea urchins—although I think they're going to have to wait for the tide to go out more."

"Great! Come on, Karma!"

But the dog seemed to have developed a compelling attraction for Susan's legs, and there was lots of pushing and shoving before the girl and her pet departed.

"Let's go in the house," the man suggested, leading the way. "I appreciate you coming over. I don't know what Titania told you. . . ."

"She just said that you wanted to speak with me," Susan explained, entering the house as he held the door for her. "But I would have come over tonight anyway. I wanted you to know how sorry I am about your brother. If there's anything I can do—"

"Actually, there is," Ted Taylor interrupted her polite offer. "I wanted to ask you a tremendous favor."

"Oh?" Susan, more than a little curious, followed him into the living room.

But it seemed that Ted Taylor was having trouble getting to the point. "How do you like the house? It's not decorated, of course, but . . ." He glanced around the room, apparently proud and definitely expecting a positive response.

Susan gushed praise, all the while wondering just what was to come. Ted sat down on the leather couch, patting the cushion at his side to indicate a space for her. Susan sat, prepared to hear an outrageous request for her precious vacation time. What she heard was the history of the house.

"Nice, isn't it?" he began, glancing up at the beamed ceiling and then out the windows and across Penobscot Bay.

"Very."

"Most people never get the chance to build and live in their dream houses. . . . Hell, for all I know, most people don't have a dream house stashed away in the back of their head. . . ."

"But you did."

"Yup. Even as a kid, I've wanted to build things. I wanted to be an architect before I knew what one was. I moved from blocks, to shop classes in junior high, to drafting classes in high school, and straight for a degree in architectural engineering in college. This house, with some variations, was my graduate thesis. But it's hard to get a job designing houses straight out of college. I've worked for rental car agencies, doughnut chains, and grocery stores. And finally, about six years ago, I got enough recognition for a chance with the best firm of architects in the country—if not the world. Recently I got together the money to buy this land and build this. . . ." He stopped and glanced around again, his gaze finally landing on the empty fireplace. "And here it is: my dream house. I sometimes thought I would kill to build this house. And I've never spent a night in it."

"It didn't take very long to build," Susan said, because she knew she should say something and she had no idea what was appropriate.

It appeared to be the right comment. Ted Taylor immediately launched into a very technical explanation of new building techniques, modular construction, and the like. Susan sat, tried to comprehend, and finally gave up; she couldn't relate all this talk of LED-controlled windows and computer-driven wells to the two old homes that she owned and loved.

Finally, after a complex explanation of radiant heat, he interrupted himself. ". . . but that's not what I wanted to talk to you about." He stroked his beard and gave Susan a long, serious look. "I wanted to ask you to help my daughters. I've been thinking everything over ever since I found out that Humphrey was murdered. You're the only person I could think of. You've met the girls and you know people up here. That deputy sheriff, what's her name . . . ?''

"Janet Shapiro."

"That's right, Janet Shapiro. Well, she said she'd known you for years. She said that you're one of the summer people everyone trusts, and you're involved because Humphrey was found in your living room, and she said you had been involved in solving murders before this. In fact, Janet Shapiro said you probably know more than she does . . . and I can't think of anyone else." He stopped with what Susan thought was a look of desperation on his face.

"To do what?" she asked quietly.

"Protect my girls," he said with finality.

"From what? I don't understand," Susan said slowly, knowing that with every question, she was getting in deeper and deeper.

"I'm afraid they're going to be accused of murdering their stepfather. . . ."

"Surely not! They're only children!" Susan was shocked.

"That may be. But you tell me—if someone has been threatening to kill someone and then that someone is killed . . ."

"Maybe you'd better tell me this story from the beginning."

"I . . . I can only tell you what I know. And I don't know that much. Tricia has worked very hard to keep me out of her new marriage."

"But you can tell me what you know. I really can't believe that childish threats against a new stepparent are going to be taken seriously. After all, lots of children tell their parents that they hate them at one time or another. . . ."

"It isn't quite that simple."

"Then why don't you explain?"

Ted sighed. "It's hard. I don't even know exactly when it started. . . ." He stared up at the ceiling, a frown on his face.

"When did you get divorced?" Susan asked, hoping to direct him.

"Last year. I moved out right after Labor Day. . . ." He paused and began again. "Oh, all this is my fault. And Tricia's. We should have let the girls know that we were having trouble, but we kept it from them. Even our short trial separation two years ago, we explained as a long design job that I had in San Francisco. We should have explained," he repeated sadly.

"So your moving out came as a shock to the girls?"

"Exactly. They had absolutely no time to adjust to the situation. One day I was living at home with them and their mother, and the next day I was gone and Tricia had filed the divorce papers."

"And your daughters?"

"Nothing at first. They were fine—we even took them to a family therapist, thinking that they would need some help to get through all this. But the woman talked with them and said they didn't need therapy—that they were handling everything with great maturity. And that's the way it seemed. They agreed to everything. Weekend visits to me. Weekdays with their mother. They helped me pick out an apartment with rooms for them, and they even helped furnish them. Tricia and I really thought everything was going well, that we had achieved the ideal divorce."

"But you hadn't."

He shook his head. "I don't know. Maybe it was the perfect divorce as long as one of us didn't remarry."

Susan remembered the New Year's Eve celebration that Titania had told her about. "And when your ex-wife remarried, all the trouble began?"

"Not until they got back from the honeymoon. Trish and Humphrey went to the Caribbean, and the girls stayed with me. And everything went well. Although they were planning what they were going to do while Trish was away. I didn't understand at the time, but later some of the things I'd overheard or didn't understand became pretty clear—very clear, in fact."

"So what happened?"

"Well, the first thing they did was booby-trap our house."

"What did they do exactly?"

"Actually they must have done that while the honeymoon was going on. My apartment is on the other side of town from Tricia's house—the elementary school is in the middle—and I guess the girls took a detour on the way home more than once that week."

"How did they booby-trap the house?"

"Let me think. They put tacks in Humphrey's shoes and jelly in the pockets of his sport coats. They put salt in the sugar bowl and sugar in the salt shaker. They poured all the Scotch down the drain (and Scotch is the only drink my brother ever touches) and filled the bottle with a similar-looking liquid that turned out to be food coloring and flat tonic water. They took out the top step of the stairway to the basement—"

"What?"

"That's right. They removed the top step so that whoever went down there would fall to the bottom."

"But that's serious! Someone could have been killed!"

"And that's what people are going to start to talk about now that Humphrey is dead, aren't they? You see what I'm saying here now, don't you?" he asked gently. "You see that I have to protect my girls."

"It does sound like you have a problem," Susan admitted. "And I gather that it didn't stop with that particular incident?"

"No. It got worse. At first Tricia thought that the girls were doing all this because I told them to—or at least that they had gotten the idea from me. Thinking that, she didn't even tell me about it at the time. She just sat the girls down and explained that she and Humphrey were married, that they were going to stay married, and that they were all going to have to learn to get along together. She grounded all three of them and took away Titania's phone privileges—because she assumed that Titania was the ringleader, and besides, she's the only one old enough to care whether or not she talks on the phone."

"And things settled down for a while?"

"No way. The three of them were stranded together, and

they spent most of their time planning to drive their new stepfather crazy. Motor oil from the shelf in the garage turned up in the imported olive oil that only my brother uses. Strange items appeared in the mail—COD in Humphrey's name. His name ended up on the lists of every insurance man in the state—poor Humphrey was seriously thinking of having the phone number changed, and Trish was so frantic that she called me and we set up another appointment with the therapist who had seen them earlier.''

"Sounds like a good idea.''

"Well, it was and it wasn't. Humphrey was pretty upset, as I said, and he went into the therapist's office and said that he didn't understand why all this was happening when this woman had said everything was going to be all right. Well, this didn't thrill the therapist, and she told him that it was all his fault. That he had been incredibly insensitive springing the remarriage on his own nieces the way that he had and that now he had to live with the results. She damn near spent the entire session lecturing him. The girls were in the waiting room, but the door was open. I remember glancing out at Titania, and she was thrilled to death, a huge smirk on her face.

"But things did calm down for a while then. I think maybe the girls realized how much their behavior was bothering their mother. And I made it very plain that they weren't doing me a great favor either.''

"How did you do that?''

"The next weekend they spent at my house—they spend each weekend with me when I'm in town—I took them all camping. We've been going since the girls were little. Well, I just waited until I thought the time was right and I laid it all out for them.''

"Do you mind telling me what you said?''

"I don't remember exactly.'' He looked out the window, watching a red and white lobster boat chugging around in circles, picking up lobster pots and then dumping them back into the water when empty. "I had thought about it a lot before starting. I knew it was very important to say the right thing, and sometimes I think that the more important it is to get something right, the more likely something is to go wrong. I remember that I started by explaining that I knew about the pranks they'd been pulling on my brother, and that I thought their behavior was inappropriate no matter how distressed they were. I told them that they really had no right to interfere in their parents' decisions about marriage. I told them that I understood they were hurt but that I had grown up in a family where my parents argued all the time and that they might find they were better off when Tricia and I were apart. I told them that they had a home with me always. And I told them to stop what they were doing. I think that's all.

"Then later the next day, I took Titania aside and explained to her that I thought she was the leader of the group and the other two girls would follow her, and that I would appreciate her cooperation in this matter. She said there wouldn't be any more pranks and . . . and we went fishing and came home."

"Did—" Susan tried to break into his monologue.

"Of course, I did it all wrong. I can see that now," he surprised her by saying. "I should have asked how they felt and listened to what they were going through instead of giving lectures. I was stupid." He shrugged, still watching the fishermen. "I just wasn't thinking at the time. Tricia was frantic and Humphrey was upset and they were both blaming me. And I saw how the girls were suffering. . . . I did the wrong thing." He looked at Susan. "Being a parent is awfully hard on the ego, isn't it?"

Susan smiled. "It is indeed," she agreed wholeheartedly.

"Would you like a beer?" he surprised her by offering. "It's been a long day and I'm thirsty."

Susan remembered that he had spent part of his day identifying the dead body of his brother and agreed that a drink would be nice.

"Then why don't we continue this in the kitchen? Now that I think about it, I missed lunch, too. Tricia always has a full refrigerator."

"Great," Susan agreed, getting up and following him. An

enthusiastic cook, she was anxious to see the kitchen as well
as hear the rest of his story. As she expected, the room was
wonderful. A long rectangle with windows across one wall
looked out into the woods, and a line of skylights looked up
to the clouds. There was a large green Garland stove at one
end of the room, and a Sub-Zero refrigerator at the other. In
between, mahogany cabinets lined the walls and displayed the
most up-to-date appliances from Japan and Germany. "Wow!"

"All the woodwork in the house was done by a man who
used to do the interiors of yachts—and he really outdid himself here. I was lucky to find him," Ted Taylor said, opening
the refrigerator and handing her a Coors. "Do you like Brie?
Or maybe some pâté? I don't know what these are. . . ." He
held out a ceramic bowl filled with ebony ovals.

"They're smoked mussels. And they're wonderful, but I
don't need anything to eat, thanks. Go ahead, though."

"I will." He peered at the mussels. "Do I eat them cold?"

"Yes. Usually on crackers or French bread," Susan suggested.

He had already popped two into his mouth. "Great." He
was filling the countertop near the refrigerator with food,
eating as he piled. "One of the worst things about being a
bachelor is that you have to plan everything—like if you want
a full refrigerator, you have to shop for food. When Trish
and I were married, I got used to living like this. And I miss
it," he finished wistfully.

Susan wasn't impressed. If she and Jed broke up (heaven
forbid!), she certainly hoped to be remembered for something other than her housekeeping. And how hard was it to
learn to shop for yourself? But she remained calm. "There
certainly is a lot of food here," she said casually, wondering
when they were going to get back to his story.

"There are a lot of hungry people here," he answered,
putting a dish of something on the turntable in the white
microwave.

"Your daughters and your ex-wife and Judy and Sally . . ."

"Don't forget Paul and Ryan," Ted said, pressing a few
buttons and leaning back against the counter.

"Who are they?"

"Paul is Judy's husband, and Ryan belongs to Sally. If you haven't met them, they're probably out fishing. They are born-again fishermen—can't get enough of it."

"You said you took your girls fishing."

"I like to fish. They live for it. But I'm glad they're here. It helps keep everyone busy." He turned to the microwave, which was now beeping urgently. "I hope this is done," he muttered, taking out the dish and opening it. Steam billowed out. "Looks like it. Why don't we sit at the table and I can finish the story."

But when they were seated, it seemed difficult to begin again.

"You were talking about the camping trip," Susan reminded him. "I gather things didn't get better when everyone returned home."

"It looked like it for a while. In fact, I was busy complimenting myself on what a good job I had done when we discovered that the girls had gone underground." He took a few bites of the casserole he had heated before continuing. "The story gets a little more complicated here—and a lot more serious."

"What happened?"

"They started acting alone. Tierney repeated some pranks—she put enough pushpins in Humphrey's jacket pockets to keep every bulletin board in her elementary school filled forever." He chuckled. "And she tried to put whipped cream in his shaving cream can, but of course, that was impossible and she just made a terrible mess in the bathroom and got in trouble. Titania and Theresa were the problems."

"Both of them?"

"One or both of them. We're really not at all sure. They've refused to tell on each other. They fight like cats and dogs, but they bond together against adults."

He leaned forward and continued. "The first thing that happened is that the brakes on Humphrey's car were oiled—and, of course, they didn't work very well after that. The attempt was amateur—fortunately—and Humphrey had a slight fender bender on his way to work one Monday morn-

ing. The mechanics at the local gas station made some not-
so-funny comments about someone trying to kill Humphrey,
and then Tricia called me and we lectured the girls, threat-
ened and punished. The next thing that happened is that
Humphrey discovered that someone had tampered with the
allergy medicine he takes—that someone had put talcum
powder in the capsules. Obviously this was all too serious to
ignore or treat as some sort of childish prank. . . .''

"So what did you do?"

"Well, the first thing we did was put a stop to Tricia running
to me for help. A friend of mine who is a psychiatrist suggested
therapy for the girls, and we insisted they go. He also pointed
out that the girls were getting us back together with their
pranks—even if temporarily—and that we shouldn't allow that
to happen. So we stopped letting the girls know we were talking
about them—and we told Theresa and Titania that unless the
pranks stopped immediately, they wouldn't be able to see me.''
He looked a little embarrassed. "It worked. Everything stopped
then and there. Until today, that is.''

Susan looked curiously at Ted Taylor. After the long, de-
tailed story he told, this ending seemed rather abrupt. Was
he lying? Or was he just hungry? she wondered, watching
him finish the casserole and reach for his drink. Was his
behavior at all unusual for a man whose brother had been
killed and who was worried that his children might be blamed
for the murder? What was usual in such an unusual situation?
"So nothing has happened for how long?" was all she asked.

"At least two weeks," he answered.

Susan wasn't terribly impressed with the length of time.
Anyone might say that they were just planning the ultimate
insult against their new stepfather. If anyone thought to ac-
cuse them at all, she reminded herself.

Ted Taylor seemed to be thinking the same thing. "Do
you think my daughters are going to be connected to Humphrey's death? They didn't want to hurt him. They did those
things hoping to get him out of the house. Everyone will see
that, won't they?''

Susan waited a few moments before answering. "I know

what you mean. When you talk about thumbtacks in clothing and mixing up concoctions that they hoped Humphrey would mistake for liquor, it all sounds like the kind of ineffectual shenanigans that kids resort to when they don't have any real power."

"Exactly," Ted Taylor enthused. "Don't you think we can get everyone to see that? It will protect the girls. I don't think they had anything to do with this—they couldn't have," he insisted, "but even being questioned would be a trial for them. They're too young to be involved in a murder investigation. You're a mother; certainly you understand. And . . ." He paused, looking for words. "And maybe you can make everyone else understand, too?" he ventured.

"The problem is that not everything sounds completely harmless," Susan began slowly. "They did tamper with Humphrey's car, and removing the top step to the basement really could have killed someone—and not only Humphrey."

"I'm sure they didn't want to kill anyone. . . ."

"I can believe that. But don't you see, that's exactly the problem. Someone could say that your brother's death was a prank gone wrong. That possibly one of your daughters caused his death even if they didn't mean for that to result from their actions."

"Manslaughter," the distraught father muttered. "It can't be. They didn't do it. They have to be protected. We have to keep this from happening—"

He was interrupted by the appearance of a ruddy man carrying enough fishing gear to equip Captain Ahab. "Ted! Hey, good to see you," he called out cheerfully. "I hear one of your girls finally got old Humphrey right where it counted!"

SIX

IT TOOK A FEW MOMENTS TO SORT IT ALL OUT. THE EN-
thusiastic fisherman with the large mouth was, Susan discovered, Judy Briane's husband. He had been out in a boat all
day and claimed not to understand the significance of his
words.

"I had no idea," he was assuring Ted and Susan for the
third or fourth time after they had explained about the murder. "How could I? Ryan and I left the house this morning
before daylight. The last time I saw Humphrey, he was . . ."

"He was where?" Susan asked, wondering why Paul
Briane had stopped speaking.

"I'm thinking. I saw him before breakfast yesterday. He
was heading into town to do an errand before he left for
Boston. Something about a sea kayak, I think . . . I didn't
really listen. You can't fish from a kayak. One quick move
and the damn things flip right over. Guess the last time I saw
him, he was standing in the driveway right out there—" he
nodded out the window "—getting into his Range Rover. I
waved and he waved . . . and that's all. You know, I feel
badly about that. There were some things I would have said
if I'd known that was the last time I was going to see him."
He looked away from the window and back into the room.
"We're all going to miss your brother, Ted," he said. "We
were just finding out what a fun person he had grown up to
be." He sighed. "This sure makes the things that have been
going on recently seem pretty insignificant."

So Paul Briane knew about the girls' activities! Susan

opened her mouth to ask a question or two, but Ted Taylor cut her off. Intentionally, she guessed.

"There are a lot of people who are going to think that the girls had something to do with Humphrey's death," Ted suggested, a stern look in his eyes.

"What?" Paul sounded sincerely shocked by the idea. "There's no way those sweet little girls could have had anything to do with something horrible like this. Who would say a thing like that?"

"It's one way to interpret what you were saying when you came into the house," Susan insisted. "And Ted and I were just talking about ways to make sure they're not involved in all this," she added, watching the two men exchange looks.

Paul was the first to speak. "I'm a professional therapist with almost two decades of experience, and I've spent a full week with those girls. It's my professional opinion that there's no way they could kill someone. I don't know what you've heard, but no one should think a thing like that for even one second. And I didn't," he insisted. "I had no idea Humphrey was dead when I walked through that door. If I had, I would have been more careful about what I said. I explained already that I was just talking about that Monopoly game the day before yesterday."

Susan didn't believe it for a minute, but she knew she was going to have to be patient if she was to learn the real story about the girls "finally getting old Humphrey right where it counted."

"It was bad timing. I was just telling Mrs. Henshaw that I was worried about people misunderstanding the situation between the girls and Humphrey when you came in." Ted tried to clarify the situation. Susan wondered exactly what—if anything—the serious expression on his face was meant to convey. "Mrs. Henshaw has some experience investigating crimes, and I was hoping she'd help make sure the girls aren't wrongly involved in this one."

"Good for you." Paul was immediately transformed from the sincere mourner into the hearty good friend. Susan thought for a moment that he was going to pat her on the head. "If I had daughters of my own, I'd hope they were just like Titania, Theresa, and that little one—Tierney. I always forget her name. Anyway, they're sweet girls, and I'm sure glad you're going to help keep them from being wrongfully considered suspects."

"Brilliant."

They all turned to find that Judy Briane had joined them— trailing silk and sarcasm, Susan thought, watching to see what reaction the men would have to her appearance.

"Catch anything?" she continued, walking over to her husband, removing the bottle of beer from his hand, and taking a long swig. "I'm thirsty. We climbed a mountain while you and Ryan were out in that damn boat," she continued. "Sally is in the living room telling Ryan all about it."

"Then why don't we join them?" Paul Briane suggested. Susan got the impression that he was picking up a cue.

"That's a good idea," Ted said, heading for the refrigerator. "Take a couple of bottles with you and maybe some of this cheese. I have no idea what anyone is going to do about dinner around here."

"We're going into Blue Hill to that place everyone recommends," Judy said. "Don't worry about us. We can take care of ourselves."

Ted Taylor looked relieved. "I'd appreciate that. I have no idea what time Trish is going to get back. I should probably find her—or that policewoman."

"Good idea," Paul agreed. "She really shouldn't be alone right now."

Susan glanced at her watch and waited, but no one seemed to remember that there were three children needing care and attention.

"We could drive you to Blue Hill," Judy suggested. "It will take Sally and me a few minutes to get our clothes changed, and the men probably need showers, but we could be ready in half an hour."

"Great! Why don't we all meet outside," Ted said. "I'll show Mrs. Henshaw out. . . ."

"Nice meeting you," Susan said, taking the not so subtle hint and heading toward the door. But once she got outside, her assumption that Ted was seeking an opportunity to speak to her alone evaporated.

"Judy and Paul are right. Trish needs me. I should have thought of that half an hour ago. I . . ." He looked around as though he couldn't remember why she was here.

Susan decided to help him out. "Why don't I find your daughters and feed them dinner?" she offered, deciding that if she waited until someone remembered the girls to make her offer, it would probably go unmade. "Then you won't have to worry about getting back early," she added, not that he appeared to be a man rushing to meet his children's needs. In fact, since Judy Briane's entrance, Ted Taylor had apparently forgotten he had children. Susan realized she was getting interested in the mystery in spite of herself. "I can even put them to bed. There's plenty of room at my house."

"That would be wonderful. And it's exactly what I was talking with you about. The further away from all this the girls are kept, the better. I know it's imposing, but—"

Susan interrupted with the standard polite reassurances.

"But I don't know what Trish would want. . . ." Ted apparently had a new thought.

"Why don't you just tell her that they'll all be at my house and she can come over and get them whenever she's free? It might make things easier for her, too. She already has a lot to worry about."

"You're right. Thanks." He looked around as though having no idea what to do next.

"You'd better get back to your guests," Susan reminded him. "I'll head to the water and find the girls."

"Thanks," he repeated, and disappeared into his dream house.

Susan followed the path to the granite stairs that led down to the surf. She heard a dog barking and assumed it was Titania's retriever; she just hoped the animal didn't expect to sleep with the girls. She started down to the water's edge, where more than one red head was shining in the sunlight.

The stone stairway had been built for the original house, and the steps were well worn and slightly slippery. Susan walked carefully, thinking over what she had been told of the Taylor family's problems. She was less than impressed with Ted Taylor's fatherly virtues after the way he had forgotten all about his precious girls in just a few minutes of his guests' company. Or had he? she asked herself, stepping around a small stream of water that was dripping from the rock. Was it possible that he was trying to keep his houseguests occupied and away from his daughters? She decided to think about it all later. The two youngest sisters had seen her and were waving their arms in the air and calling out. Susan hurried toward them, thinking as she went that no matter what else was happening, Tierney and Theresa, at least, were not mourning the death of their uncle and stepfather.

"Look what we found! A whole bucket full!" The youngest girl held out a tin pail full of miniature crabs, most less than an inch long. "Theresa lifts up the rocks, see, and I grab them before they run away."

"Nice teamwork," Susan said. "What are you going to do with them?"

"We're going to put them back," Theresa answered. "Then they can grow up to be full-sized crabs."

"Yes, we promised Titania that we would," Tierney announced. "She says that it would disrupt the environment if we took them away. She's very smart. She's in the gifted classes at home. . . ."

"She's not all that smart," Theresa said, jerking the pail away from her little sister. "I learned all about that in fifth grade. You don't have to be in the gifted classes to know things."

"I think you're all pretty smart to be caring so much about the environment," Susan suggested, hoping to avoid an argument. "Where is Titania?" she added. "I thought I heard her dog. . . ."

"You heard Karma, all right. Titania was making her go to your house, and she wanted to catch sea gulls instead. She was barking and barking and barking!'' Tierney shook her head to emphasize the commotion.

"My house? Why my house?"

"Who knows?" Theresa said. "Titania said she was going to take Karma to your house and that you would know what to do. Titania thinks she's so smart and then she does awfully dumb things, don't you think?"

Susan had no interest in getting involved in any sibling rivalry, so she merely smiled and changed the subject. "Are you girls hungry? I told your father that you all could eat dinner with Kathleen and myself."

"Who's Kathleen?"

"My houseguest. What about dinner?" she repeated.

"I guess so," Theresa said slowly. "If my father thinks we should."

"What are you having?" Tierney asked, dumping the bucket of crabs in a large pool of deeper water and then watching the crustaceans flee.

"We had been thinking of lobster if you wanted to go to the pound with me. Or there's always hamburgers."

"Hamburgers!" Theresa cried.

"Yes, hamburgers," her sister agreed. "I don't like eating things that have been alive."

"Hamburgers it is," Susan said, without explaining about the beef industry. "Let's head for the house. It sounds like your sister's there waiting for us."

"What do you mean?" Tierney asked.

"I can hear the dog barking. Can't you?"

"Yes, but it's strange," Theresa said.

"Why?"

"Because usually Karma doesn't bark when she's with Titania. Usually she only barks when she wants to be with Titania."

"Maybe something's wrong."

"We can hurry, but I don't think anything is wrong," Susan tried to reassure Tierney. "Kathleen is there, and she'd take care of any problem that comes up. I don't know about you, but I'm pretty hungry. Anyone like nachos—besides me, that is?'' she asked, hoping to distract their attention. That dog was making an awful lot of noise. . . . ''And I know there are potato chips and Fritos.''

''I love Fritos—and Titania does, too. She says they're made from corn.''

''You are so dumb. Everyone knows that—not just Titania.''

''I am not dumb and I didn't know that!''

''Maybe we should race?'' Susan suggested. Sure, there would be a winner and a loser, but at least all the quibbling would stop. The girls sped off and she hurried after them, thinking of kind phrases to use to comfort Tierney when she lost.

But Tierney didn't lose. The girl sped by her older and taller sister and almost leapt up the gentle slope of grass that spanned the distance from Susan's house to the water. Luckily Susan found she didn't have to say anything to Theresa either. The girl was knocked into the water by a very enthusiastic, very wet golden retriever. By the time Susan had caught up with them, both dog and girl were covered with the black mud that lined the bottom of the cove.

''Stop! Karma! Stop!'' the girl was crying out, but Susan was relieved to see that she was laughing. Susan grabbed the muddy orange bandanna that hung around the dog's neck, but it slid over the animal's head. Apparently thinking this was an exciting new game, the dog leapt up and dug her long teeth into the muddy fabric—and through it to Susan's hand. Susan screamed and dropped the scarf. Karma dropped it at the same time and sat down, her haunches sinking a few inches into the mud.

''She didn't mean to hurt you. She's not a vicious dog.''

''That's the way she plays.'' Theresa agreed with her sister. ''She's still a puppy, you know.''

Susan wasn't about to succumb to those droopy eyes with the feel of the dog molars on her fingers. ''How are we going to wash her off?''

''She loves being hosed down,'' Tierney suggested.

''And we should do something about your sister, too,''

Susan said. "There's an outdoor shower around by the kitchen door. I'll run inside and find some towels and something for you to wear. You run up to the house and get Titania—she'll have to wash her dog."

"Someone else is going to have to do that," Kathleen said, walking down to the group. "Down, Karma!" she insisted as the dog tried to leap up on her linen slacks.

"How did you do that?" Susan asked, amazed by the dog's instant obedience.

"Dogs always listen to a good trainer—I worked with police dogs when I was starting out in Philadelphia, so I know how to do it. You just have to show some authority."

"You'll have to show me," Susan said ruefully as the dog leaned against her leg, licking her knee. But she had more important things to worry about. "What do you mean Titania is gone? Where is she?"

"I don't know. She left the dog and an envelope with your name on it. I promised I'd take care of Karma until you arrived and give you the note. It's up at the house."

Susan frowned. "Then I guess I'd better go read it." She got the impression that the two sisters were making an effort not to look at each other. She didn't have time to think about what that might mean. The dog had taken off, running at full speed back to her house. "I hope it stays outside." But as she spoke, Karma leapt up onto the porch and, mud and all, pushed through the screen door and into her living room. The children flew after the animal, and Kathleen and Susan followed as quickly as possible. By the time Susan had arrived on her porch, Tierney was tugging the dog out the door. "Good thing you've got most everything in there covered up."

"Maybe you could tie her up out here?" Susan suggested, scowling at the animal.

"We can try," was Tierney's response.

"I saw some rope down by the water. The tide must have washed it in. Do you want me to go get it?" her sister asked.

"Good idea," Susan said, following the muddy prints the dog and children had made into her house. She stood in the middle of her living room and looked around. Except for the chair Humphrey Taylor had been found in, all the soft furniture was still covered with blankets, and now all the blankets were covered with mud and fur. "How did this happen so quickly?" she asked Kathleen, who was leaning against the wall, smiling.

"Apparently the dog leapt from chair to chair. She's just a puppy, you know. She has a lot of energy."

"So everyone keeps telling me. I'll sweep up later." She started for the kitchen. "The girls are staying for dinner. . . ."

"Don't you want to find out what Titania's message is?"

Susan pulled her hair back into a ponytail and groaned. "I really will forget my head next. Yes. Definitely. Where is it?"

"On the mantel. Are we feeding them lobster?"

"Hamburgers. I think one of us is going to have to go to the store. . . ."

"Why don't I? And I'll take the girls with me."

Susan had opened the envelope and was reading the note and didn't answer immediately. When she had done nothing but frown for a few minutes, Kathleen grew impatient. "What does she say?"

"She's disappeared."

"What?"

"Well, that's not quite accurate. Here. Read it yourself," Susan offered, passing her the sheet of paper.

Kathleen read quickly and handed it back. "I—"

"Is that Titania's letter?" Her youngest sister stood in the doorway.

"Yes, it is," Susan answered quietly. "Do you know what it says?"

"Not exactly," the girl answered slowly. "I know that she asked you to take care of Karma and that she's hiding. That's all."

"Hiding," Kathleen repeated.

"Do you know where?" Susan asked, leaning down to the.

child. "I know she probably told you not to tell us, but it could be important."

Tierney returned Susan's serious look. "I don't keep secrets very well. I try, but . . ." She stared down at the floor. "Titania said that she wasn't going to let me know where she was so I wouldn't have to lie. I really hate lying."

"But you know what the note says," Kathleen added.

"Yes. Titania read it to me. It says that she would like you to look after me, and my sister, and Karma—and that she is going to find out who killed Uncle Humphrey."

"And that she is going to be staying in some sort of secret place on the island," Kathleen added.

"Yes." Tierney nodded.

"And she really didn't tell you where?" Susan asked.

"No. And she didn't tell Theresa either. So you don't have to bother to ask her."

"Did—" Kathleen began.

"Do you know what?" Susan interrupted. "I think these girls are going to be hungry soon. And they're not going to get any dinner until you do the shopping. . . ."

"So why don't we all head to the store," Kathleen said, picking up on Susan's suggestion. "You can help me pick out things like soda. . . ."

"We're not allowed to drink soda at home."

"This is a vacation. Maybe your parents wouldn't mind," Susan said.

The thought seemed to perk up the girl. "Maybe not," she agreed. "Do you think we should take Theresa with us?"

"I . . ." Kathleen was uncertain about what, if anything, Susan had in mind.

"I think that's an excellent idea," Susan said quickly. "She's down by the water getting that rope. Why don't you help her, and then both of you should wash off before you leave, okay?"

"Okay." Tierney started to leave the room, but she turned back at the door. "You will look after Karma, won't you? Titania's depending on it."

Susan, who had just been thinking about shipping the dog back home, didn't answer immediately.

"Of course she will," Kathleen jumped in. "And we'll help her, won't we?"

"Sure," the girl called cheerfully, skipping out the door.

"And will we help clean up this mess?" Susan asked rather sarcastically.

"Worry about that later. We have to talk, and those girls will be back in a moment," Kathleen insisted. "The first thing to do is to call Janet Shapiro. There's going to have to be a search party organized. Can that be done on the island?"

"Probably better here than a lot of places. The islanders are always willing to help out someone in trouble. And tourists have gotten lost before. The volunteer firemen will organize a search, but it will be difficult to find Titania if she doesn't want to be found. This isn't going to be like looking for a child who wandered into the woods while his parents were stopped to look at seals lying on the shore."

"Where do you think she is?" Kathleen asked.

"Titania? How would I know?"

"You keep saying that it's a small island. You must have some idea where she is."

"None at all—but I suppose we should look around here. She couldn't be too far away."

"But you explored all over this area when you were a little girl. . . ."

"When I was a little girl, there were six homes on the cove and even fewer lining the ocean. There's been so much building. . . ." She paused. "Why, just in the eighties alone—"

"You thought of something, didn't you?" Kathleen interrupted impatiently. "Or someplace?"

"There was a cave at one time. Down at the end of the cove and around the corner . . ."

"Down by the Taylors' house?"

"Exactly. I don't know if it's still there. . . . Storms and time can change things a lot on the coast, you know. But if it's there, there is no way in the world those girls could have avoided stumbling across it.''

"Could Titania live there for a while?''

"Not comfortably. As I remember, it was mostly below water at high tide. . . . In fact, it could be dangerous. And the girls may not know that some tides are higher than others. . . . She might get trapped in it.''

"The tide is coming in. . . .''

"Let's tell the girls to skip washing up. Why should the inside of the car be cleaner than the living room? Why don't you just get the girls out of here, and I'll run down to the shore and check everything out before the water gets any higher.''

Susan hadn't planned on taking the puppy with her. In fact, she didn't. But halfway between the house and the sea, a very wet and very fuzzy ball sped past her, and she realized she had company. She grabbed the frayed rope hanging from the animal's collar and was surprised when Karma slowed down to trot by her side. She was thinking how nice a dog could be when the retriever leapt after a large blue heron that rose into the air in front of them. Susan felt like her arm was being ripped off. "Karma! Heel!'' she ordered. But either the dog was too young to obey or unwilling, so Susan wrapped the rope more firmly around her wrist and set off down the cove.

"Come on, Karma,'' she said, as the animal lunged into the water. "We're going to go find Titania.''

Whether the animal recognized her owner's name or whether she just happened to want to go in the same direction Susan was going, Susan didn't know, but they walked around the edge of the cove toward the spot where Susan remembered the cave was located. Unlike most things in her life, the hike to the cave turned out to be longer than she remembered it being in her youth. She climbed around boulders and tramped across tiny, sandy beaches before arriving at the tall, upended slabs of granite that guarded the entrance to the cave.

One of the most persistent of Maine legends is that Captain

Kidd buried his gold on one of the islands and took off, leaving the treasure to be found by the person who would spend enough time and effort digging for it. And, of course, each island's residents believed that their island was the island. When Susan was small, she had been convinced that this was the cave where the pirate had landed, and she and two of her cousins had spent much of one summer digging up the cave's sandy floor. About twenty years later, her children had done the same thing. No one had found anything more than a few sand dollars, some rusty tin cans, and numerous lobster buoys. Now she climbed into the cave and wondered if pirates concealed their treasure in Styrofoam ice chests—or if it contained Titania's provisions.

"No, Karma!"

But the dog ignored her and, pulling free, grabbed the plastic and began to worry it into small pieces.

Susan saw that she had been mistaken about the ice chest. Well-aged bait dripped from the holes that the dog was ripping in the plastic, and the resulting stench caused her to gag.

"Karma! No!" Susan accompanied the order with such a hard jerk that the dog almost fell over. She pulled the animal out into the open air. Happily, the beast had a short attention span, and a flock of eider ducks sunning on a rock was so distracting that Susan was able to start back across the cove. She knew Kathleen would have called Janet Shapiro by now, and a search was probably being organized at this moment. But Susan couldn't just wait and do nothing while people swarmed all over the island looking for the child. She had to help find Titania. And she knew that the girl's house was the place to start her search.

SEVEN

SUSAN AND KARMA WERE SEATED ON A LARGE ROCK, STILL warm from the afternoon sun. Susan waited to hear a car drive away from the Taylor house. Karma waited for a sea gull stupid enough to stroll within striking range.

Susan was the lucky one. "Come on, puppy!" she said, pulling the dog to her feet and heading up the steps to the house. "We might as well look around here while we have a chance—and maybe we can find you some dinner!" Apparently she had discovered a word the animal recognized. They ran toward the house together, crossing the patio while dust from the car's trip down the road still dirtied the air.

"Now, if only we can get in," Susan muttered, struggling to turn the knob on the large double glass doors.

Karma, less gentle and happy to be home, jumped up, thrusting muddy paws against the sparkling glass and shoving her way into the house.

"Hey, thanks." Susan would have patted the tawny head, but the beast was scampering toward the kitchen.

Susan headed straight to the winding stairway that filled the rear of the large entryway. Deciding to explore from the top down, she mounted smooth oak risers to the third floor, unable to resist pausing along the way to admire the spectacular view as she climbed.

Reaching the landing, she chose to explore the largest room first, assuming (correctly) that it was the master bedroom. She paused a moment to overcome her well-bred dislike of snooping, and then walked right in.

The room surprised her. While the rest of the house was unfinished, this place had been decorated to death—or to life; plant life, to be specific. A misguided designer might have called it a bower. Flowers were embroidered on bedspreads, curtains, and upholstery. Vines were carved in headboards and chairbacks. Honeysuckle was stenciled on walls near the ceiling and around windows. Pansies and roses were woven into the carpet. Needlepoint pillows adorned every available surface, each bearing a different blowsy bloom. Watercolors of improbably fabulous botanical specimens hung on the walls, and every lampshade had been pierced to give the impression of ivy joyously circling each light bulb. Susan wondered if anyone could enter the room without feeling a desperate urge to start weeding. This was Ted Taylor's dream bedroom? She thought not, guessing that the bedroom had probably been redecorated in honor of the new marriage.

The room had the same spectacular views out to sea that the rest of the house did. A quick inspection revealed a very modern bathroom attached; Susan was particularly taken with the six round brass portholes over the tub and the nautical scenes painted on the walls. The two walk-in closets were full of casual clothes. There was nothing of real interest, and Susan went off to check out the other two rooms on the floor: the guest rooms. At first glance, they were pretty much identical: double beds, double dressers, night tables with regrettable lamps, and Wyeth reproductions on the walls. Susan felt a little like she had wandered into two hotel rooms. Both rooms were neat and contained a minimum of personal belongings. Susan poked around, noticing that the room with the most flamboyant clothing (she assumed it belonged to the Brianes) was also overflowing with books. Each nightstand was piled high with literature. Susan paused long enough to be amazed by the number of reference works devoted to deep-sea fishing and then turned to the other side of the bed. What was Judy Briane reading before she fell asleep?

A couple of beautiful books by a European publisher with an international reputation for color plates sat at the base of the collection. One was a book of seaside homes in Finland;

one a tribute to Bauhaus. There were also a few books by or about I. M. Pei's work. Did this indicate a connection to Ted Taylor? Susan wondered. The rest of the collection was also interesting. Did people actually choose Alexander Pope for bedtime reading? she wondered, thumbing through the tall pile of Oxford paperbacks and deciding that either Judy Briane was doing graduate work or else she was the most unusual of intellectuals—one who wasn't addicted to a particular type of "junk lit."

Susan took a moment to check out the windows in these rooms, too. They looked into the woods behind the house, and it was even possible to see a corner of the Henshaw boathouse through the trees. Time, she decided, to head downstairs.

There were three rooms on the next landing also, but apparently the sisters had chosen to share the large room directly beneath their parents. Three pine beds stood against one wall. Five or six footlockers were scattered around the floor, and clothing peppered the place as well. Books and shells littered the windowsills, and posters of rock stars, sea life, and Einstein adorned the walls. Susan thought how pleasant it all looked and was glad she didn't have to be the one to suggest that it was time to clean up. As in all the bedrooms, the connecting bath was expensive and artistic. This one was mahogany and brass, like the interior of an old sailing ship.

Susan studied the bedroom. Despite the mess, each girl seemed to have her own territory staked out by posters on the walls and the small piles of possessions that encircled each of the beds. Susan assumed Titania's bed stood beneath a poster on which a photo of Einstein declared imagination to be more important than knowledge—and at this point in her life, Susan certainly hoped that he was right. She started her search there.

She was looking for something that might give her some idea of where the girl had been on the island, whom she might have met. The usual assortment of shells and pebbles stood on the trunk by the bed. Susan picked up a small bowl of sea urchin shells that smelled dreadful; apparently the shells weren't quite as empty as the collector had thought. Sea heather was drying in a tiny porcelain vase, and a collection of dark blue beach glass was arranged on a pile of well-read paperback classics. It looked like Titania was learning to knit. A length of knitting displaying a rough idea of a stockinette stitch hung from one of two needles stuck in a ball of yarn. That was all there was, except for a whirligig of a child on a pogo stick. Susan spun the blades of the construction and thought. There were some clues here; she only wondered if there were enough. That the trunk itself was locked didn't surprise her. Privacy was essential to most thirteen-year-old children. Susan didn't know how to pick locks and so, deciding that she had made a start, she got up to leave the room. Something tucked under the bed caught her eye, and she stopped to pick it up.

"Well, well, I wonder if this means something," she muttered, put her find in her pocket, and headed back into the hall.

The other two rooms on the floor were completely empty except for a few cartons that, opened, revealed books. Susan trotted back to the first floor, unable to decide what, if anything, she had learned from her snooping.

The dog, who had been waiting for her at the bottom of the stairs, attacked her Keds the moment she touched the main floor. Susan assumed the animal was hungry.

"Maybe you should spend more time with Kathleen. You seem to have a lot in common," she said. "Let's just hope that there's dog food in the kitchen." The animal skidded across the polyurethaned floors ahead of her, running smack into one of the tall cupboards. Susan decided it wasn't an accident. She opened the door, and a fifty-pound bag of puppy chow with an unpronounceable name and a repulsive odor fell out, spilling across the tiles. The dog was delighted. Apparently no one had ever presented her with an entire room full of kibble before.

Susan grabbed for the animal's collar, but a lot of food had disappeared before she regained control of the animal.

''You are going to get fat,'' she said, yanking the dog back to her house.

Kathleen had just arrived, and the girls were hopping from the Jeep as Susan and Karma got home. Tierney and Theresa were no sooner out of the car when Karma had leapt up and scrambled into the front seat, where she immediately began to drool.

''She thinks you're going to go for a drive,'' Tierney announced unnecessarily.

''I was actually thinking of doing just that,'' Susan said. ''If Kathleen doesn't mind getting dinner for the two of you . . . there are some things I'd like to check out.'' She gave Kathleen a look over the heads of the two girls.

''I'm sure we can manage dinner just fine without you. In fact, if you're heading back downtown, you could pick up some ice cream. We just realized that we forgot to buy any.''

''Fine. I'll be back in less than an hour probably—certainly in time for dessert. What flavor does everyone want?''

''Chocolate,'' Theresa requested.

''And peppermint,'' her younger sister added. ''I love peppermint.''

''That's enough of a choice for me,'' Kathleen agreed. ''Do you have your wallet?''

Susan patted the fanny pack she wore. ''I guess Karma's going with me,'' she said, getting into the driver's seat. She was anxious to start and didn't hear Tierney's comment as she drove off down the road.

''Maybe we should have told her that Karma gets carsick,'' she said to her sister.

''No. She'll be okay. She only barfs if she goes out right after she's eaten,'' Theresa answered as they helped Kathleen carry the groceries into the house.

''I am so sorry. I had no idea she was going to do that. She's not my dog—in fact, I just met her owners today, and no one told me that she gets carsick.'' Susan was apologizing profusely as she scrounged around in her belt pack for clean tissues. ''I really don't know anything about dogs.''

"Well, I do, and this one is jim-dandy—a real sweetheart." The woman Susan was visiting, the woman wearing the denim skirt that Karma had just vomited on, knelt down and smoothed the dog's fur back from her face. Karma's tail was wagging fast, smacking Susan's bare legs. "There's a bunch of rags just inside the kitchen door. You're welcome to use them to clean off your windshield if you want."

"Thanks, I . . ."

"I'll watch the dog. She can come into my studio with me."

"I don't think—" Susan began her warning.

"Don't worry. I understand dogs. And if she hurts anything, I'll blame only my stupidity for it."

Susan decided to stop wasting time. She hurried by a narrow flower bed of tall lupine and onto the porch of the tiny white cottage. The bright red back door was propped open with a chunk of white granite so that the large family of Maine coon cats living here could come and go as necessary. She found the rag bag and grabbed a holey T-shirt claiming to be from "lowstone National Pa" and returned to mop out her car. Karma had thrown up three times during the couple of miles they had traveled to get here, and it took a while to wipe everything down. When she was finished, she rinsed the rag at the outside pump standing in the side yard and hung it over the freshly painted picket fence. Then she hurried into the large old barn that leaned against the house.

A sign on the sliding door had only two words printed on it: YARN said one; the other was WEAVINGS. Susan walked in. She had been here more than once last summer when she knit sweaters for herself, her husband, and her daughter from the yarn that Beth Eaton dyed and spun from the island's sheep and goats, so she had no trouble recognizing the origins of the fluffy yarn Titania was using. And, having met Titania, she was fairly sure that whomever the girl met, she would have talked to about her life. Susan was only hoping that there might be some clues to the girl's hiding place and the reason she seemed to think it was necessary to hide.

Susan found Beth working at a large Swedish loom, one of three that filled the half of the barn that wasn't used to display items for sale. The dog lay on the floor at her feet, her head propped on her front paws.

"I think I know this dog," Beth said, throwing the shuttle through the warp and back again. "Doesn't she usually hang out with a redheaded teenager who's learning to knit?"

Susan was relieved. "Yes. And that's what I want to talk with you about."

"I was wondering why you'd appeared here. I would think that you'd be too busy to knit right now. Or doesn't finding a body in your living room make a big difference in a person's life?"

Susan wasn't too surprised; the island grapevine had always impressed her with its speed and efficiency. "A huge difference," Susan admitted. "Especially since Titania—the girl who brought the dog with her—has disappeared."

The shuttle flew across the loom and out the other side onto the floor, where Karma grabbed it in her mouth, refusing to let go until bribed with a shortbread cookie that Beth retrieved from a large jar standing on the end of her bench.

"I had no idea—that poor girl. Do you think she's been hurt? Or kidnapped? I hear that the man who died was her stepfather."

"He was, and I don't think she's hurt. She's hiding. . . ."

"Why?"

"I don't know. All I know is that she vanished—after asking me to take care of her dog."

Beth played with the shuttle, winding soft apricot wool around it for a few minutes before speaking. And when she did, it was in a voice so quiet that it was almost inaudible. "Do you think she had anything to do with killing her stepfather?"

"No, I don't. What have you heard that would make you ask a question like that?"

Beth chuckled quietly. "Those girls and their antics have kept the island amused since the week before Memorial Day. But it's difficult to tell what's the truth and what's exaggerated. Before this murder, the Taylor girls were well on their way to becoming legends in their own time. Do you want a cup of tea?"

"I'd love one," Susan answered. "But I shouldn't spend too much time. . . ."

"I have a thermos right here as well as an extra mug. Sit still and I'll tell you what little I know as well as what I've heard." She flipped another cookie at the dog, poured them both some tea, and began her story.

"Actually no one heard very much in the beginning of the summer. In the first place, neither Mr. Taylor came up with the family back in May."

"So you met the women in the family first?"

"I did, but that's not true of most people on the island. That house was built under the very close supervision of Ted Taylor—the first husband, as I understand it."

Susan nodded. "So he was up here earlier in the spring?"

"He's been up here almost every weekend since the middle of last summer, when they started work on the foundation. He's picked every workman, every piece of granite from the quarry, and every tree before and after the mill got through with it. He would have driven everyone crazy except for two things. . . ."

"Which are?"

"The recession has made people real happy just to get work. And he knows and appreciates good craftsmanship. Workmen like to be appreciated."

"So most people who know him like him?"

"Pretty much. He demanded the best from everyone, and one or two people thought that was being mighty picky. You know how it is. But I think you could say that Ted Taylor is liked and respected by those he came in contact with here." She nodded to herself and gave the retriever another cookie.

"And the rest of the family?" Susan munched on a cookie despite the pleading look in the dog's eyes. Was it her fault if the damn thing threw up at the drop of a hat?

"The three girls and their mother have been here since May, and no one has anything real bad to say about them. The mother seems a little high-strung, but nothing terribly unusual. If anyone thought about them at all, they probably just thought they were typical summer people. At least, I didn't hear anything different. In fact, I don't think anyone thought anything until their stepfather—I don't know his name. . . ."

"Humphrey Taylor."

"That's it. Until Humphrey Taylor appeared. There aren't a lot of people who marry their ex-husband's brother (although someone did mention that it was an ancient custom in some societies), and that got a fair amount of comment when it was known."

"And how did anyone find out about it? Or was it just the identical last names that tipped people off?"

"Humphrey announced it himself. In the post office one morning, of all places. He might as well have put it on a billboard in the town square—as you well know."

Susan did know. A lot of information went through the post office. It was a way of knowing who was on the island picking up their mail and who was off island having everything forwarded home. And the fact that the wife of the postmaster was one hell of a gossip helped the distribution process considerably. "He announced it?"

"You know how some of the high school girls help out when things get crowded? Well, one of them said there was mail for Mr. Taylor, and he said something like 'Mr. Humphrey Taylor or Mr. Ted Taylor?' and then went on to explain that he had married his brother's wife and requested that all the mail to Ted Taylor be sent somewhere else—I have no idea where. He wasn't on island then, as I remember it."

"And what happened then?"

"I think that's when the stories started. At least that's when I first heard anything." She scratched Karma behind her ears, and Susan waited for her to continue. "Less than a week later, most people on the island were talking about how Humphrey Taylor was in the supermarket when he put his hands in the pockets of his windbreaker and found that they had been filled with chocolate pudding." She chuckled. "More than a few people developed an instant respect for the man's vocabulary that day. There were contests among some of the coarser young men at the high school as to who could draw the most accurate picture of just what that man described at the top of his voice while waiting in line to pay for his cornflakes.''

Susan smiled. "And did he say exactly who he thought had put the pudding in his pockets?''

"There was no doubt in the mind of anyone in the store that he blamed his stepdaughters. And that's not all that happened. I heard various stories about the girls putting mud from the bottom of the cove inside the wet suit he wore kayaking, and one of my best customers heard that they filled the legs with strips of raspberry vines—and you know how full of thorns those things are. It sounds to me—'' she looked down at the dog ''—like they've been pretty busy. And then there's the story of the Zodiac.''

"One of those inflatable boats?''

"Yup. Humphrey's sank. There were holes in it.''

"Couldn't that just have been an accident?''

Beth shook her head. "Not a chance. There are numerous chambers in a four-man Zodiac. There were holes in each chamber. And you can't just poke holes in these things easily, you know. They're tough, double rubber. Someone would have to get out a drill with a large bit and spend quite a lot of time to turn the bottom of one of those boats into imitation Swiss cheese.''

"I gather Humphrey didn't go down with his ship,'' Susan said, thinking how much easier it would have been for her if he had.

"He didn't even get in it. The holes were discovered while the boat was still on land. It was a pretty amateur job.''

"Which, of course, is why everyone assumed that it had something to do with the girls. Right?''

"Right.''

"And they admitted it?''

"I have no idea. And remember, I'm getting everything thirdhand at best. Could be that a tree branch poked a hole in the side of his boat and he spent the day fishing before anyone noticed. People do exaggerate. I'm just repeating stories here.

"But I'd like to help that girl,'' Beth continued. "Her

name's Titania, right?'' (The dog lifted her head at the sound of her owner's name.) ''She's a sweet kid. And not very happy, it seemed to me.''

''How many times did you meet her?''

''I saw her with her whole family at a show down at the gallery on the pier. I probably paid attention because I'd heard so much about the family. She didn't stand out, though; in fact, I would have had a difficult time telling the three sisters apart. They look so much alike, and all have those dumb T names.

''But then she came here with her mother. She wanted to learn to knit, and her mother doesn't know how, so she stayed around for the afternoon and I tried to teach her. I've wondered how she was getting along and if she was practicing. She was making an easy stockinette scarf.''

Susan was able to report on the progress the girl had made before continuing. ''What was your impression of her?''

''Well, she didn't seem like a maniacal killer, if that's what you're asking. She's a sweetie. A little sad, though. She didn't talk much at first, and I just assumed she was shy. Later I realized that wasn't true. In fact, once her mother left, I had the feeling that she was desperate to talk. Poor kid.''

''Why do you say that?''

''She had a lot of feelings bottled up inside her—and some of them were awfully serious for a kid that age to be dealing with.''

''Like her mother's divorce and remarriage?''

''I think there was more to it than that—although that's pretty tough. We seem to think that just because divorce is common, it's easy. Titania kept talking about her uncle and how much she and her sisters didn't like him. I got the impression that they didn't like him before he was their stepfather.''

Beth stopped speaking for a moment, and Susan asked a question. ''Do you know why? Was it something he did?''

''I have no idea. You know kids—they're not all that artic-ulate about some things. Titania said that he was a jerk and added a few other insults. I didn't ask any questions, I just listened. If I'd known . . . Well, that won't help us now, will it? But she did say something interesting. She said that her father hated his brother. In fact, I think she said that they had always hated each other, ever since they were children.''

"Interesting, but she could have just made that up. Or else exaggerated something her father said in the middle of this divorce," Susan suggested. "Parents say a lot of things when they're under stress, and their children don't always take that into account. Children, I've found, have very literal minds, and Titania isn't that far from childhood."

"I'm not arguing with you. And I didn't question the girl at all. I just helped her knit and listened a little. Seemed at the time that was all I could do. Now . . . Well, if that poor kid was in the middle of a mess before, it's nothing to what she's going to have to deal with now. I sure wish I could help her."

"I just wish I could find her!" Susan exclaimed, and went on to explain what little she knew about Titania's disappearance.

"You don't think she killed her uncle?"

"I don't. Absolutely. But I don't think she's helping by running off, and I have to find her. Did she say anything about where she'd been on the island? Do you have any clues to where she might be?"

Beth shook her head slowly. "They've been up here over a month, and those kids have done the normal exploring that kids do. And you know the island. All the tiny coves—and there are lots of summer houses that are empty even in July. She could be staying in one of them. She could be anywhere. I sure wish I could think of something that would help, but . . ."

"I appreciate what you've told me," Susan assured her. "I'm going to do some more checking with other people that are like you—people who would have taken the time to talk with her. A friend is staying with me this week, and she's back at the house with the younger girls. Could you call there if you think of anything—anything at all?"

"Of course I will. And good luck."

Karma followed Susan back to the car.

EIGHT

THE DOG, AT LEAST, WAS COMPANY. IT WAS HARD FOR Susan to feel lonely with the animal drooling and throwing up all over her backseat. It was only a couple of miles to Susan's next stop, but the road curved around and bumped up and down, and Karma had lost all Beth's cookies by the time the Jeep stopped in the parking lot of the island's used bookstore.

"I'm going to have to tie you up outside, dog," Susan announced, urging the retriever from the car. "This is no place for you to be sick."

Karma responded with eyes that pleaded for company, and she licked her paws as though trying to clean up.

"Okay, but you have to be good. Come on." Susan tugged on the leash, and the dog happily followed her into the long, low, white building.

The sign on the door said TIME HAS CRITICIZED, and Susan smiled as she entered the large store. She thought this place was perfect. The many shelves were so stacked with volumes that they cascaded into piles on the floor. Old rocking chairs, painted light blue and made comfortable with red and white cushions, were scattered around so customers could always find a place to sit and read. A large library table near the door served as a sales table, and the woman behind it leapt up from the mounds of paperbacks she was sorting when Susan walked in.

"Susan Henshaw! I wondered when you were coming up this year. I have a pile of cookbooks put away somewhere that I've been saving especially for you!'' The tall woman with shoulder-length straight gray hair pushed her glasses up on her aquiline nose and looked down at Susan's feet. ''What a personable dog. I gather your son finally won the battle?''

''No way. This is not my dog, and living with this one is not encouraging me to dash right out and buy another. This is Karma, and she belongs to a neighbor. That's what I've come to talk to you about—if you have some time,'' Susan added, looking around at the half dozen or so customers browsing the shelves.

''No problem. I have help this summer. My nephew is home from college for the month, and I have no idea what I'm going to do when he leaves—he became indispensable his first hour in the store. Let me introduce you and then we can go outside and talk—before Karma consumes her weight in mystery novels.''

Susan looked down and was horrified to discover that the animal had an old paperback Agatha Christie dangling from her mouth. ''Karma! I'm so sorry. I'll pay for—''

''Don't think a thing of it. There probably won't be a customer for *Murder on the Orient Express* all summer long. People who haven't read it have seen the movie. But maybe you two should wait for me in one of the chairs back in the pine grove. Behind the building. I'll be out in a second.''

Susan took the hint, pulled the dog from the store, and went to find their meeting place. She wandered around until she spied the group of Adirondack chairs scattered under the trees. She wound the leash around the leg of the chair she was sitting in and stared off into the woods, absently patting the dog on the head.

''So why have you come to talk to me about your neighbor's dog? If it's a sitting service you need, you're going to have to find someone else. I won't stay in business long if she eats up the merchandise.''

Susan explained while the other woman sat down in another chair. ''The neighbor who owns Karma is Titania Taylor. I thought you might have met her.''

''Oh?''

"She has a small tower of books next to her bed," Susan explained. "It reminded me of the shopping I used to do when I was young, so I thought of you. . . ."

"You're talking about that little redheaded girl whose uncle was murdered, aren't you? I've been thinking about her all day," she added at Susan's nod. "Ever since I heard about his death.

"You're right about the books. She's been in at least once a week since I opened in May. She's an interesting one to watch. She really wants to read to improve her mind—she always picks out classics that she's heard about. She's bought *Jane Eyre*, *Wuthering Heights*, *David Copperfield*, and some Jane Austin, I think. Oh, and the complete poems of T. S. Eliot. And then she's seduced by writers like P. G. Wodehouse and Daphine Du Maurier—she knows they're not intellectual, but she can't resist and she buys them, too—and probably reads them first."

"And you give her a discount, right?" Susan guessed, remembering her own childhood.

"You have to encourage youth. It's an obligation."

"Have you spent much time talking with her?"

"Some. Things are pretty slow until July Fourth. And I can't resist spending time with the customers—especially ones as charming as that young girl. She gives me hope. I sometimes wonder if her generation reads anything besides Stephen King. I suppose he prepares them for the rigors of modern life, but still . . ." She shook her head, dismayed. "So tell me what's happening with that poor child and how you think I can help."

"She's disappeared," Susan said bluntly. "There's a search being organized, but . . ."

"Oh dear. But she's not a murderer, you know. That's not what you're thinking."

"No, of course not. I think she's a child who needs some help right now, and I'm hoping I can find her and . . . and help."

"You think she's on the island."

Susan was a little taken aback. "You know, it never occurred to me that she might not be."

"Well, you're probably right. If anyone had driven her off, we would have heard about it. And how far can she go in that little kayak of hers?"

"What little kayak?"

"She's got a little river kayak that she toots around the cove in. Didn't anyone tell you? It's not a sea kayak, not one of those imported technological wonders that you Henshaws paddle around in. . . ."

"Then she shouldn't be taking it out on the ocean. And she shouldn't be going out alone." Susan was worried. It was one thing to think that the girl had run away; it hadn't occurred to her that she might have drowned.

"Look, her mother bought her two of the best books I've seen on the subject, so the girl knows what she should be doing. Although she's probably pretty desperate right now. . . ." The woman's voice trailed off, a dismayed expression on her face.

"Because people might think she's a murderer," Susan said.

"Or that her sisters are. And I got the impression that she cares a lot about those sisters of hers. She may have run away to deflect attention from them."

Susan blinked. "Did she say anything that might lead you to believe that's possible?"

"I've been thinking about that all morning. You know, she talks a lot about her little sister."

"Tierney?"

"I suppose so. The other one has a less fanciful name, right?"

Susan nodded. "Theresa."

"Stupid names, much too unusual for nice girls like that. No wonder their mother has messed up her life. Anyway, Titania bought some books for Tierney, and she talked about her. Or, rather, she talked about how much she worried about the child and what the divorce was doing to her. I think, in fact, that Tierney's misery is the reason that Titania got the idea of carrying out all those pranks. It made the child feel better if she was doing something. At least that's the way she explained it to me.''

"You talked to her about it? About the pudding in the pockets and everything?''

"Not much. I didn't approve, and I let her know the way I felt about it. I thought that the sooner those girls got used to their new situation, the happier they'd be. But she's a teenager, and she sure didn't see it like that. I suppose you've got to admire the child; she really thought that she was going to break up that marriage and get her parents back together. It may be something that most children fantasize about, but she set out to make it happen—and to cheer up her little sisters at the same time.''

"We think Humphrey was hit with a rock in a bait bag. I don't think Tierney could have done something like that. She's pretty small.''

"What about Theresa? I know she's younger than Titania, but they're close to the same size. Sounds like either of them could have done it that way.''

"True. And if they didn't do it, why would the girl run away?''

"I don't think it's that simple. Titania is very fond of her mother, and she's crazy about her father. She could just as easily be protecting them—if she ran away to protect someone. Maybe the whole thing just got to be too much for her. Maybe she took off because she just couldn't bear to stay around any longer.''

Susan was thinking so hard that she didn't notice the dog had eaten one of her shoelaces and was removing the other with an amazing delicacy.

"I sure hope you find her. I'd hate to think that something might happen to that kid.''

"I felt better before I knew about the kayak,'' Susan admitted, standing up.

"I wonder if my nephew knows something about this. Why don't you go in and talk to him?'' She reached out for the leash. "I'll keep the dog out here with me.''

Susan headed back to the store and leaned against the door while waiting for the young man with the long ponytail to have a free moment. He was a good-looking boy, Susan thought, and three high school girls were working hard to develop an interest in the shelves closest to the desk, which happened to be where books on gardening were kept. Susan wandered over to the nearby shelves labeled building and architecture, thinking of the volumes she had found in the nearly empty rooms at the Taylors' house. She opened a large tome on Frank Lloyd Wright and admired the pictures. In a few moments the young man was free to speak with her.

"Can I help you?"

"I just wanted to ask you a question or two if you don't mind. Your aunt is outside taking care of the dog."

"She's beautiful," he commented.

Susan didn't know if he was talking about the dog or his aunt, but she agreed politely. "I was wondering if you've noticed a teenage girl who comes in here a lot." She saw him glance at the three students who were now giggling over art books in a corner. "The girl I'm talking about is a lot younger than they are. Her name is Titania Taylor and she has short red hair and—"

"I know who she is. We've had some good conversations. She's interested in poetry. I think that's probably pretty rare in someone her age."

Susan, out of college for over twenty years, knew that it was "pretty rare" in most age groups. "She's gone off someplace. No one seems to know where, and I'm trying to find her. You don't happen to have any idea of where her favorite places are on the island, do you? Of course," she added, remembering her conversation with the young man's aunt, "she might have left the island."

"Oh, I don't think she would do that. I don't think she's the type of person who would leave the people whom she loves stranded in a crisis. She strikes me as having a lot of integrity. You know—" he paused and looked back at the desk for a moment "—she came in the day before yesterday and bought a survival guide."

"What?"

"One of those books about how to survive in the wilderness. You know the type of thing. How to make a temporary shelter, how to catch a fish on a pin, how to start a fire if you don't happen to fancy sushi. I think the book she bought was a pretty serious one—if she's out there all alone, I sure hope it helps out."

"So do I," Susan agreed quietly. "So do I."

Susan steered her car down the narrow dirt road through the woods toward her next stop. Despite the way her car smelled, she was hungry and not terribly anxious to arrive at her destination. She owned more than one set of bowls made by this potter, one of many on the island, and while she loved his work, she found him arrogant and disagreeable. She wasn't quite sure what to ask him, and she didn't know if he would bother to answer. "Maybe you should stay in the car, Karma," she called back over her shoulder. "He probably doesn't like dogs."

She barely had the words out of her mouth when two huge black monsters flung themselves out of the woods and at her car. She drove even more slowly than before as the two animals escorted her to the wooden studio attached to the modern timber house nestled in the woods. Karma bounded from one side of the seat to the other, nearly hysterical by the time they arrived.

As the engine noise died, Susan rolled down her window and wondered what to do. She didn't know these dogs, didn't have any idea whether the looks on their identical black faces were threatening or welcoming. Karma, apparently unsure herself, stared intently from one to the other, drool pouring on her front paws.

"Are you going to stay there or get out?"

The greeting, or lack of such, didn't really surprise Susan. But she watched, amazed, as the tall, dark man waved his right arm in a small circle and both dogs instantly dashed to his side. "You're here, aren't you? Are you going to get out?" he repeated.

Susan tried to smile and opened the car door. "I wanted to ask you some questions, if you have the time."

She didn't expect a helpful response and she didn't get one. "This is a potter's studio, not an information booth. There's one of those over by the bridge. You've come to the wrong place."

He turned and walked back into the building, dogs trotting by his side. But as he entered one door, another opened and a beautiful, slim woman in a denim jumpsuit, one burgundy scarf covering her head and another tied as a belt around her slender waist, appeared. She was smiling warmly. "Good evening," she said, walking up to the car. "My husband has had a terrible day. There was a lot of breakage in the kiln, and he's not really the most personable man under the best of circumstances. But I'd be happy to help if I can. Did I hear you say that you needed some information?" She tapped on the window at the golden retriever. "Beautiful dog. Don't worry. They outgrow car sickness."

"She's not mine," Susan admitted. "But she is cute, isn't she? Although she looks better when she's cleaned up."

"Why don't we go into the showroom to talk? If you can leave her in the car."

"Of course. I'd really appreciate that—if you have the time."

"I do. We're going out for drinks at a friend's house later— we try to celebrate the sunset with white sangria on Friday nights in the summer, but a night as clear as this is pretty rare in Maine, as you may know."

"I sure do. We have a house over on the other side of the island, and I've been coming to Maine since I was little." Susan offered her credentials.

"It's been a great summer so far, hasn't it?" She opened the screened door for Susan as they chatted.

"This is my first trip up this year," Susan admitted. "That's good to hear, though. I hope it lasts through the holiday weekend." She looked around the room. One wall was window from the slanted ceiling to about three feet above the floor. From there down, wooden shelves were filled with cups, mugs, teapots, coffeepots, bowls of all sizes, and other utensils. The opposite wall was painted white, and platters and plates of all sizes hung on it. Tables in the middle of the room also displayed the artist's work, and in the middle of it all, a large pottery fountain sprayed water into the air. "Have you sold a fountain yet?" Susan asked, wandering between the tables.

The potter's wife chuckled. "You have been here before. And, for the very first time, this year the answer is yes. An ashram up in Vermont bought three. They're using them in their meditation rooms. I haven't been there, but my husband and a friend spent a week doing the installation, and they were both very enthusiastic."

"That's fantastic." Susan continued to wander.

"Are you looking for something in particular? I thought you came here for information."

"I did, but I think there's something of a needle-in-the-haystack situation here." She reached out and picked up a small, round pot about four inches high with a tiny hole in it. "Do you sell many of these?"

The other woman took it from her and turned it over in her hands while answering. "Actually, we do. It's one of those things that people buy because they've come all the way down that drive and they've gotten us away from whatever we were doing, and what with the person who made all this standing around, a lot of people feel that they must buy something. Naturally, most people aren't going to dash out and buy a set of dishes on impulse, and the platters and large bowls are difficult to transport and expensive, so these just fit the bill. They cost less than twenty dollars, they come in a variety of colors, and people can stick a twig or two in them and feel very artistic and remember the vacation they spent in Maine."

"Then you probably won't remember a young girl—thirteen years old—with red hair who bought one. It's light turquoise," Susan explained, not feeling very hopeful. "She must have bought it recently. She's new to the island this summer."

"No." The answer came slowly after some thought. "I don't remember anyone like that. And my husband—"

"He's probably too busy to pay attention to that type of thing," Susan interrupted tactfully.

"That's one way of putting it." She frowned. "But, you know, he just created that color." She picked up a plate with a heron painted on it. "Are you sure about the customer? There were two women—city types; I should say, the very worst city types that we see here—who bought a vase like you're describing. It was just a few days ago. And I understand it was a gift. The daughter of the person they're staying with is what they said, I think."

"That's possible." Susan described Judy and Sally as well as she could. "Were they alone?"

"They were. They complained all the time they were looking around that their husbands were doing nothing but fish. As far as I could tell, these women were doing nothing but shop. And they weren't on the outlet trail either. The blonde bought one of my favorite oblong platters, and the other one bought a set of flowerpots. Those aren't inexpensive purchases. And they're awkward to send. And then, as they were getting ready to leave, the blonde picked up a little vase like this and suggested that it would be a pretty gift for the daughter of the house where they were staying."

"That was nice," Susan commented casually.

"Not all that nice—in fact, that's why I remember them. The one who suggested the gift was really put down by the other, who felt that there was no reason to give the girl a gift, and made her feelings very plain. She was really rather snotty, in fact. Obviously there was no question that she could afford the gift and they were staying in their house. But maybe the people you're talking about wouldn't act like that? I hate it when my husband's pieces go to dreadful people. I know it's silly, but I always think people who act like that don't deserve to have beautiful things."

"These people would act exactly like that. But the child is nice, and she evidently treasures the vase. It's sitting right next to her bed with a sprig of beach lavender in it. It's very pretty.''

"It's none of my business, but why are you interested in these people? Aren't they the type that it's better just to ignore?''

"I'm concerned about the girl. You see, she's disappeared,'' Susan explained. "Did you hear about the murder on the other side of the island?''

"No. I've been at home all day. I'm a writer, and my friends know not to call me during the day, when I'm working. I'm sure I'll hear about it toni . . . The girl—it wasn't a child that was killed?''

"No, her stepfather,'' Susan answered, and then explained briefly what had happened and the family history.

"Wow.'' The woman put down the large vase she had picked up while Susan was speaking. "How terrible for the children. I always feel for the children. How can they possibly comprehend how much of what is happening is their fault and how much is the responsibility of their parents? And now that the child has disappeared . . . What did you say her name was?''

"Titania.''

"What are the other two little girls going to do now that Titania has vanished?''

"I really don't know,'' Susan said. "I've been wondering the very same thing.

"In fact, I'd better get going. I have one more stop before home. The girls are probably still at my house, but I haven't spoken to them about their sister. I was hoping to find out where she is without causing any more upset, but it looks like that isn't going to be possible.''

"They must be terribly distressed.''

"In fact, they seem fine.''

"Then, if they're as close a family as you think they are, they must have a reason to believe that their sister's safe. No?''

"I wish I were sure that was true,'' Susan said, starting for the door. "It's her dog that I'm taking care of.''

"Too bad she's just a puppy. If she were older, she might be able to lead you to the girl."

"Do dogs really do that type of thing?" Susan asked skeptically.

"They're supposed to. Maybe I read too much Jack London when I was young. Good luck," she added, getting ready to close the door behind Susan. "And feel free to call on me if there's anything else I can do. I'd like to help the poor kid."

Susan expressed her appreciation and got back in the car. She hoped Karma was running on empty. She had no intention of taking the time to drive slowly just for the sake of a dog's stomach.

But either the dog was growing accustomed to the bumpy Maine roads or she was just too tired to make the effort necessary to empty her stomach; the trip was entirely uneventful. And, as no one was home at her last stop, Susan, forgetting her promise to pick up dessert, entered her own driveway just as the sun was beginning to slide behind the pointed white pines in the distance. She had been thinking about Tierney and Theresa and was surprised to see them kneeling together on the lawn beside her house. There was a large pile of lumber and what looked like an old wagon on the ground between them. Susan stopped and got out, with the dog following close behind.

"Hi!" Kathleen must have been watching out the window, as she appeared almost immediately. She waved Susan over to the house. "Are you hungry?" she called out when they were closer together. "Did you find her? Or anything that might help?"

"No." They watched Karma run over to the two girls. "I learned a few things that are interesting, though. I'll tell you in a bit. What are they doing?"

"They're building a float for the parade."

"What?"

"Evidently there's a Fourth of July parade in town. . . ."

"I know. There is every year."

"Well, they said that anyone could march and that anyone

could make a float and be in the parade. Apparently their older sister suggested that they do this. They're making some sort of cart that the dog is supposed to be in. I didn't ask too many questions. I was just happy to see them occupied and busy. You don't mind that they're using those old boxes and things that they found in the boathouse, do you?''

"I guess not. I didn't even know they were there. Jed always leaves the place immaculate over the winter. After we get the kayaks out in the spring, I try to avoid that place. It's usually full of spiders.''

"Want some dinner?" Kathleen asked as Susan paused for a moment.

"I'd love some.'' She waved to the girls and accompanied Kathleen inside. "Do they seem at all distressed to you?''

Kathleen paused on her way to the stove. "I've been wondering about that myself. Tierney—that's the youngest, right? Well, she's worried about her mother and father, and she does seem to feel a certain amount of chagrin that someone she didn't like died," Kathleen explained. "She acts as if she doesn't know how to act. But Theresa seems almost unnaturally calm. She's not talking about the murder, and she tries to keep her younger sister from even thinking about it. She kept up a stream of strained conversation throughout dinner. Ever since you left, in fact.''

"That's interesting, but it's not what I meant," Susan explained, removing a beer from the refrigerator. "I was wondering if they were worried about Titania.''

"Not at all as far as I can tell.''

"Doesn't that strike you as odd?''

"Very. But it also strikes me as positive. They may know something that we don't—they may know that she's safe," Kathleen suggested.

"I'd sure sleep better if I thought that was true," Susan said.

NINE

KATHLEEN GOT OUT OF BED, WALKED ACROSS THE ROOM, and peeked into the hall. "What is that damn dog barking at?"

"I don't know. She started when I brought her inside, and I can't get her to stop. And I had to drag her in." Susan joined her friend in the hallway.

"Don't the girls have any idea what she wants?"

"Look," Susan suggested, pushing gently on the door of the children's bedroom.

Kathleen was amazed. "They're asleep! I can't believe it."

Susan pulled the door closed. "It's been a big day for them both. And they're young." She yawned. "I, on the other hand, am not going to get to sleep tonight unless that miserable animal shuts up." She glared at the dog, who was trying to merge with the windowsill and yapping loudly. "You don't think she's sick, do you?"

"You think it's pain?"

"I have no idea what it is. I don't know anything about dogs!"

"When was the last time you took her out?"

"She came in less than an hour ago."

"Did she visit a tree or anything before she came in?"

"How should I know?" Susan asked indignantly.

"You're going to have to pay some attention to these things if you're going to take care of dogs."

"I'm taking care of a dog. One dog. Once. And that's all!"

"Still . . ."

"Okay. I'll take her outside. She can do what she has to do. And the way things are going," Susan added, putting the rope around the dog's neck, "I'll probably step in whatever she does first thing tomorrow morning!"

"I'm going to go back to bed," Kathleen said, too tired to be amused.

"Enjoy. Come on, dog." Susan pulled the animal after her down the steps to the first floor. "You know, if you have to go out, you might act a little more enthusiastic about it. This isn't my idea of fun. I'd rather be asleep in bed."

Karma yanked on her leash, and Susan followed the dog through the hallway, out the front door, across the porch by the large pile of flotsam and jetsam that evidently was to become the Taylors' parade float, and down to the lawn. There Karma began to wander anxiously, nose to the ground. Susan trotted behind, not really distressed at being outside on such a beautiful evening. Stars flooded the sky, and the moon was so bright that it was possible to walk around without fear of colliding with anything.

"Nice night. Right, Karma?" Now that they were outside, the barking had stopped. Susan took a deep breath of the sweet night air, scented with wildflowers and sea spray, and was happy to follow Karma across the lawn and down to the water.

The light from the moon flickered on the cove, making waves of small ripples on the tide, causing impossible images in the water. Just for a moment, Susan imagined that she had seen an Indian in a canoe skim across the water. No, an Eskimo . . . someone in a kayak cutting straight through the water on an imaginary line leading out of the cove and into Penobscot Bay. But dogs don't have imaginations—or do they? Karma barked twice and flung herself into the freezing water. Susan dropped the lead before she fell in. It was time, she decided, to go for her first kayak ride of the year. Leaving the dog to paddle around in the shallows, Susan ran across the lawn to the boathouse.

There was a light switch right inside the door, and Susan flicked it on as she entered the long, narrow building. By family tradition, the kayak on the rack closest to the door was her sixteen-foot Orion. Giving more than a little thought to her forty-three-year-old back, she lifted it down and carried it out to the lawn, returning to the building for her paddle, life vest, and spray skirt. She slipped the vest on, zipping it over her nightgown, and tucking the paddle and the elastic skirt into the boat, she lugged it down to the water.

To get launched, she was going to get wet. Icy water filled her slippers and froze her feet, but she plunged in, tightly holding on to the boat. Bracing the paddle behind her, she struggled to get into the kayak's cockpit without flipping. After a few precarious seconds, she was in. Unfortunately, she had forgotten to don the spray skirt first. Well, she wasn't going to be out that long; she'd be careful and keep her paddle low to prevent water from sliding down the long wooden blade and into the kayak with her. She scrunched up the spray skirt and tucked it down between her wet legs.

Pushing gently against the shore, Susan headed her boat out into the water with a few sweep strokes to point her in the right direction. The other kayaker had disappeared. Karma was out of sight. Susan was having a wonderful time.

Susan always thought of porpoises when she was kayaking, slipping through the water quietly, efficiently, quickly; she loved the sport. She had never been out after dark before, and she immediately appreciated the height of the tide. The moonlight was beautiful, but it was difficult to distinguish between small waves and large rocks. Luckily, she was familiar with the few barriers inside the cove, and the water quickly became deep enough to keep her from crashing.

The last time Susan had seen the other boater, he or she had been heading south, so Susan made a similar decision when she arrived at open water. Staying as close to land as she dared (she didn't want to risk being capsized by hitting a rock), she paddled through dozens of lobster buoys, peering ahead for a glimpse of the person she was following. She stopped paddling every few minutes, hoping to hear the gentle splash as the other person sped though the water. She couldn't hear or see anything, however, and she was fast becoming aware of the fact that she had not taken the time to rinse out her vessel before sailing. The winter's population of bugs was having a field day on her bare legs. The lumps of wet fabric were also uncomfortable, but Susan's kayak had been designed to turn with a mere shift of her weight, and any unnecessary activity could take her out to sea.

Just when she thought she could bear it no longer and was going to have to turn back, she heard voices nearby. She pulled her paddle from the water and rested it on the coaming. The drips of water were almost as loud as the voices, and she strained to hear, reminding herself that it was as likely to be a party on land as the person she had followed. In fact, she would have continued on if she hadn't heard the words "Henshaw" and "bitch" so close together that it was impossible to believe that they hadn't been used in the same sentence.

"At least she's gotten the girls out of our hair. I never felt comfortable with them pulling those stupid pranks. Who knows what they might have overheard while they were sneaking around? One of them was hiding in the linen closet after midnight the other day. Apparently she planned on jumping out and scaring old Humphrey, but she fell asleep."

Susan heard a chuckle. "You know," a voice answered, "sometimes I feel awfully sorry for those kids. They're too young to be involved in this mess."

"Don't waste your compassion. Those girls would kill us if they knew about this. I wouldn't be terribly surprised to find out that they killed Humphrey. . . . Well, someone did. You can't ignore facts. And they've got this warped belief that they could break up a marriage. . . ."

Either the woman speaking had lowered her voice or Susan had drifted out of range; she could no longer make out what was being said. She paddled in toward land.

"You don't have to worry. We'll be safe. No one is going to think of looking in the house. It's too obvious. Believe me, there's no way we're going to get caught."

"Speaking of that house, we'd better be getting back. You're supposed to be on a trip to the store, right? There aren't a lot of all-night groceries in Maine."

"No problem. I'll tell them that I went to the grocery in Blue Hill and took a wrong turn on the drive home. It's easy to do something like that on these damn country roads."

"Maybe." He sounded doubtful. "Just don't elaborate. It's easy to get caught in a lie."

"I'm fine. I never get caught." Susan heard the misplaced pride of a habitual liar in the voice. "What about you? Most people don't kayak close to midnight, do they?"

"No problem. I stopped at the lobster pound right after dinner and bought six giants. I'll give them to my dear wife. She'll think I was out robbing the traps at the head of the cove. She'll get a kick out of it, and no one else will notice— or care."

"You can pull up heavy traps in a kayak?"

"Not without tipping over. But she won't know. She wouldn't be caught dead in one of these things. She's more the fifty-foot-sloop type—as long as there's a full crew aboard to do all the work."

"Exactly how long have you two been married?"

"Nineteen years. Why?"

"I just wondered how many years it took to build up all this hostility."

"It took about nineteen days. No, wait. About nineteen hours. Do you know how my dear wife spent the first morning we were married? She shopped. She had brought five suitcases stuffed full of clothing with us to Hong Kong. The overweight charges almost bankrupted me at the airport. And then she went out to buy things to tuck into the odd empty corner. Things like pearl necklaces and jade bracelets. Not ordinary green jade, mind you. Judy's taste runs more to the subtle and rare ivory and lavender jade. Took me years to pay off those American Express bills. First-year psychiatrists don't make much money."

"So why didn't you just get a divorce?"

"First-year psychiatrists don't get divorced the day after they get married. It might be construed as a lack of good judgment. I was too young to realize that time erases many mistakes. I don't know how I would have made it through these last few years if I hadn't run into you.''

''What's that they say? There are no accidents?''

''So maybe they're wrong.''

Susan heard footsteps and had a moment of panic. Paul was apparently returning to the shore, to his kayak.

Kayaks are meant to travel forward with speed and grace. Turning them around is another matter. Susan struggled to change direction, succeeding only in bumping the shore. She braced her vessel against land and waited for Paul to leave. Happily, he slipped, and his angry splashing and cursing covered up any noises she made.

Half an hour later she was sliding her craft back into the cove. She was cold, wet, and, she feared, completely covered with bug bites. The mosquitoes had decided to attend her wait by the coastline. Her legs were getting numb, and she was unable to determine what damage had been done to them inside the boat. In a while, she promised herself, she would be back on land, in a warm shower, where she could think over what might be hidden where in the house. She had visions of going through that pile of boxes in the room on the second floor. But what was she looking for? Would she know if she found it?

The tide was beginning to go out, and she realized that she was going to have to cross the current to return home. Crossing a current is difficult to accomplish without having two points in view to use for spotting. Susan could see the lights left on in her bedroom, but no other landmark was visible. The moon was behind her, and she was wondering how she was going to manage when she heard angry voices. There was no mistaking these two. Ted and Tricia were reliving the conflicts that had destroyed their relationship. Apparently, Susan thought, their marriage had included many arguments: they had become so good at them.

Accusations of sexual infidelities, financial irresponsibility, incompetent and inadequate parenting, were volleyed through the soft night air. At one point, Susan heard Tricia complaining about her husband's dedication to his craft, over his insistence that he design their homes. Probably not enough closet space, Susan thought, paddling hard against the current. She didn't bother to stay quiet. They were making too much noise to notice the rhythmic swoosh, swoosh as she passed below them.

She might have made it to her house without notice if Karma hadn't appeared, bounding enthusiastically out of the woods and leaping at her kayak as she touched shore. A mistaken shift of weight can cause a sea kayak to capsize. Eighty pounds of dog works well, too. Within seconds, Susan was underwater, struggling to get out of the cockpit without damaging herself or her boat on the bottom of the cove. The dog didn't surprise her by not helping. In fact, Karma's teeth fastened on to her soaking cotton gown as though she had no intention of ever letting go.

"Can I help?"

Susan was thrilled to hear Kathleen's offer. "Yes. Please. Can you get this dog away from me without falling in yourself?"

"Sure." Kathleen's voice was cheerful. "Come get a cookie, Karma."

Magic. The dog flew to Kathleen, and Susan was left to struggle to shore and stash her kayak under some nearby trees.

Susan wasn't surprised that she had trouble going to sleep that night. There was a murderer loose, a thirteen-year-old girl was missing, and a damp dog was snoring beside her in the old-fashioned double bed.

It was a relief how quickly the animal had dropped off to sleep, and Susan wasn't anxious to awaken her. But she couldn't rest with so much going around in her head. She reached out from under the toasty wool blanket, still necessary in Maine during the cool summer nights, and turned on the bedside light. The switch seemed to make a loud noise, but Susan was relieved to see that Karma didn't stir. She picked up the pen and notepad that she always kept nearby, and tried to get organized. The first thing to do was figure out what had to be done in the morning.

Susan loved making lists. They gave her the illusion of control, organization, and progress. She took her pen and made a strong line down the center of the page. On the right, she would list everything she knew about the murder; on the other side, she would list everything she knew about Titania's disappearance. Fifteen minutes later, she had dozed off, the still empty sheet in her lap.

When she woke up, the room was completely dark. After a moment, Susan realized that coastal fog had moved in, eliminating the light from the moon, causing the low wail of an automatic foghorn somewhere at sea to enter her consciousness. Karma rolled over and growled in her sleep.

Susan got up, slipping on her robe in the dark. The dog could growl all she wanted; Susan wasn't going to be impressed with the fierceness of a canine who was sleeping through what sounded like a meteorite landing on her porch. Barefoot on the chilly wood floor, she ran out into the hallway and down the stairs, pausing only to grab an iron doorstop on her way outside.

The doorknob, rusty from years in the sea air, screeched as she turned it, and she lifted the heavy weapon above her head as she flipped the switch that turned on the porch lantern.

"For God's sake, don't kill me! I haven't done anything!"

Susan squinted down at Halsey Downing, who had apparently chosen her porch as a likely place for a brief nap.

"I fell. . . . I guess I tripped over this pile of stuff," Halsey said.

"What time is it?" Susan asked, not bothering to explain about the construction of the float.

Halsey rubbed her head. "A little after three. I wouldn't have bothered you in the middle of the night and all, but I thought this might be important, even urgent." She handed Susan a folded sheet of lined paper. "I just read the first few sentences . . . and the end to see who it was from," she explained. "I heard at the restaurant tonight that the little girl is missing. The whole island is talking about it. A lot of people have joined the search party, but others figure that she can take care of herself, and one or two people think maybe she's the murderer—accidentally, though. I mean, that she killed her stepfather accidentally. I can shut up until you finish reading,'' she ended, apparently recognizing the look of annoyance on Susan's face.

Susan scanned the note down to its signature, then started at the beginning and read it through again before speaking. ''Who gave this to you?'' she asked.

''No one. I found it in my pocket.''

''Your pocket?''

''The pocket of the jacket I wore today. The one I wore to work. I didn't wear it during the day, but I stuck my hand in as I was walking out the door tonight, and there it was. I started to read it before I realized it wasn't for me. That girl must have thought my jacket was yours.''

''When did you leave The Blue Mussel tonight?'' Susan asked, thinking that Titania had probably made no such mistake.

''About twenty minutes ago. We're short a cook for the weekend, so I stayed late and did a lot of baking. Pies, cakes, puddings. You know.''

It was a measure of Susan's interest in the note that she didn't think to stop and request The Blue Mussel's recipe for raspberry cream pie. ''And you wore your jacket there today?'' she continued her questions.

''Yes. I got to the restaurant around eleven this morning,'' Halsey added without being asked.

''And you hung it up right away?''

''Yes. It was chilly for a while, but it's new—that jacket— and I didn't want to get it dirty. Everything gets filthy in the kitchen.''

''And you don't think the note was in it when you arrived?'' Susan thought that was unlikely, but she had to ask.

''I'm sure it wasn't. Like I said, it's new. I just cut the tags off this morning, and I looked in the pockets then. For those little cardboards with extra buttons. You know.''

Susan nodded. ''And where did you hang it? On the coat-rack by the front door?''

"No, that's just for customers. We have our own hooks in the mudroom outside the kitchen entrance."

"I've never been back there. It's around the side of the building, right?"

"Yes. There's a sort of dirt road where trucks can park and unload stuff right into the kitchen. The mudroom isn't very big—maybe five feet square or so—and there are hooks on the wall right next to the inside door so we can hang up our clothing and dump our boots. It's very convenient."

"Is the door kept locked?" Susan asked, knowing how unlikely that was.

"No. And anyone could just walk around the side of the building, open the door, and stuff something in a pocket. That's what you think happened, don't you?"

"Uh-huh."

"But why? Why not come to you? Or at least, if she doesn't want to see anyone, why didn't she stash the note somewhere here? Say, do you think she's hiding somewhere near the restaurant, so it was easier for her to leave the note there?"

"She could be, but I think she didn't want to come this near home. She knows that we know you—remember, she came into the restaurant last night while we were talking— and she probably figured that you were a nice person who would deliver the note. But," Susan added, "you might also be right. She may be hiding near there. Can you think of a likely spot?"

"Do you think she'd be hiding so near downtown? After all, there are lots of people around. Although I suppose she could be staying in someone's house—a summer person who hasn't arrived yet. But most of those houses are on the water—and it would be safer to stay farther away from people. Unless someone is hiding her."

"Did she have any friends on the island?"

"None that I know of, but I wouldn't have necessarily heard. You're not going to tell me what the note says, are you?"

Susan thought for a moment. Halsey had certainly read part of the note, possibly more than she admitted. There was no real reason not to trust her to be discreet with the entire thing. Susan passed it over without a word.

"I read the first part already. Where she asks about her Karma."

"That's the name of her dog," Susan explained, hoping the animal didn't hear the word and wake up. Kathleen, wearing a pair of flannel pj's printed with flags, had joined them. Susan smiled at her. "Titania has sent us a message," she explained. "Why don't you read it out loud?" she suggested to Halsey.

"Okay. 'Dear Mrs. Henshaw, How is Karma? Her food is under the microwave in my mother's kitchen. Her chew bones are there, too. She gets one each day.' She really cares about that dog, doesn't she?"

"Yes. It shows distinctly poor taste. Keep reading," Susan ordered.

"Okay. 'I don't think my mother's friends are what they are supposed to be. There is something strange about the house—I know that. Maybe the mantel in the living room? Please take care of my sisters, and don't forget the mantel. Titania. P.S. Thank you.' "

"It's hard to resist a child with such nice manners," Kathleen said quietly.

"Impossible," Susan agreed.

"So how are we going to get into the house to look at the mantel?" Halsey, with the impatience of youth, wasn't going to be distracted from the central issue. "Now, wait!" She jumped up. "Maybe I could start a brushfire, and everyone would run out of the house to help fight it. Or, better yet, I could just pretend there's a fire and yell, and everyone would leave the house, and one of us could sneak in and look at the fireplace—if only we knew what we're supposed to be looking for—"

"I think," Susan interrupted, "that we should all go to bed and worry about this in the morning. I can't tell you how glad I am that you brought this right here," she added, seeing the disappointment on Halsey's face. "I was beginning to have visions of that poor child's body floating in the bay. At least now we know she was okay sometime today. But it's late and we're all tired. I think we should let Janet Shapiro know about this and then go to bed. There'll be plenty of time to get into the Taylor house and look at the mantel tomorrow.''

"You're probably right," Halsey agreed, ostentatiously yawning.

"She's absolutely right," Kathleen said. "Murder investigations are long and exhausting. We're all going to need our sleep."

"Maybe I could come back in the morning—I was going to help you set up the house," Halsey added. "Remember?"

"That's fine," Susan said. "About seven-thirty?"

"Isn't that a little early?" Kathleen asked.

"People on the island get up early," Halsey commented, standing up and heading for the door.

"They certainly do," Kathleen agreed. Between dead men and exhaustion, she was going to need another vacation to recover from this one.

"I don't suppose you could stop and get some doughnuts on the way here tomorrow?" Susan asked, following Halsey to the door. "Theresa and Tierney are going to wake up hungry, and all we have is granola and eggs."

"No problem," Halsey assured her, hurrying out to the beat-up Volkswagen bug that was sitting in the drive. "I'll bring a lot."

Susan waved and returned to the house as the tiny engine sputtered to life.

"Where are you going?" Kathleen asked, starting up the stairs.

"The kitchen," Susan answered cryptically. "I'm going to make some coffee."

"Coffee? Are you nuts? Aren't you going to bed?"

"Not until I stop Halsey from doing something stupid. You don't believe that she's headed back home to sleep, do you?"

* * *

"I don't believe that we're doing this!"

"What could we do? There's a murderer around. We couldn't just leave Halsey alone out here."

"We could have locked her in the basement—that way she'd be safe until morning, and we wouldn't be risking death from millions of bug bites."

"I don't think you can die from bug bites," Susan insisted.

"I would have agreed with you before spending the night outside on a Maine island," Kathleen said, slapping her neck.

"You could go back to the house. There's really no reason for the two of us to be out here. You'd hear me yell if there were an emergency."

"And miss all the fun?"

Susan grinned. They were creeping through the edge of the forest between the two houses, watching for Halsey.

"Maybe she's not going—"

"Shhh! I think I hear her . . ." Susan began, praying that the dog hadn't managed to escape from the house and follow them. She thought she'd closed the bedroom door carefully. But in this fog, it was impossible to recognize anything—without getting close enough to be seen. Susan was here to stop Halsey from breaking into the Taylor house, but she was hoping Titania might come around. She couldn't believe that the child would completely abandon her sisters—to say nothing of that damn dog.

"Get down," Kathleen ordered, shoving Susan to the ground.

Susan held her breath as heavy hiking boots passed not fifteen feet from the women. "Can we get up now?" She whispered the question as the footsteps disappeared into the fog.

"Shhh!"

The women lay on the ground for ten minutes more as someone following the first person walked by, circled back, and then disappeared.

"I—"

"Doesn't anyone sleep around here?" Halsey asked loudly, interrupting the silence.

TEN

"I THOUGHT I WAS GOING TO HAVE A HEART ATTACK."

"I wondered why you had stopped complaining about your bug bites," Susan said, refilling her friend's coffee cup.

"Don't remind me. I'm trying not to scratch," Kathleen said, clasping her hands around the beverage.

"There's some stuff that's supposed to stop itching in a tube in the medicine cabinet—Jed bought it last year. I don't know whether it works or not, but—"

"I already tried it. In fact, I think maybe I'm allergic to the stuff. If anything, I feel worse. Maybe Tylenol would help," Kathleen said.

"I sure wish I knew who was wandering around the woods last night—besides us," Susan said a little impatiently. She liked Kathleen, but she had listened to her hunger pains and car sickness all the way to Maine; she hoped she wasn't going to have to hear about her skin for the rest of the trip.

"Did Halsey have any idea who it was?"

"None. She says she didn't even know there was anyone outside, besides herself, until she almost tripped over us."

"Then she probably scared away whoever else was there." Kathleen picked up the last piece of French toast, swirled it around in the syrup on her plate, and popped it in her mouth.

"I wonder when the girls are going to get up," Susan said.

"Theresa and Tierney? They've been up for hours. I'm glad you convinced Halsey to spend the night. I heard her feeding them sometime before six this morning. They're out on the porch with that cage they're building. They tried to put Karma in it and discovered that they needed to do some readjustments—or find a smaller dog.''

''A smaller dog is a good idea. That animal's awfully big,'' Susan commented, sitting down to her tiny bowl of cereal and wondering, not for the first time, where Kathleen hid all the calories that she consumed daily. Certainly not anyplace that showed.

''Apparently Ted Taylor had a golden retriever when he was a boy, and he loved it so much that he just automatically assumed it was the perfect breed for his children. At least, that's what Theresa said.

''Do you have any plans for today?'' Kathleen continued. ''Tierney said that you had promised to take the girls to a dance tonight. They were anxious to ask their mother, but I told them to wait. I thought she might be mistaken. . . .''

''It's a tradition,'' Susan interrupted.

''A Fourth of July sock hop? Or maybe a formal ball?'' Kathleen joked.

''Square dancing. On top of Cadillac Mountain. In Acadia National Park. It starts at midnight.''

Kathleen opened her mouth and closed it again without saying anything. It was absurd enough to be true.

''But that's not until tonight,'' Susan continued. ''There's a baked-bean supper down at the community church that we always go to, and we should check out the finish line of the marathon around the island and the kayaking races, but that still leaves us a lot of time, doesn't it?''

''To do what? Go to Humphrey's funeral?''

''That's going to have to be put off until after the autopsy. We have other things to do. We have to get a look at that mantel, to set up this house, to talk with Janet Shapiro, to help the kids with their float, to do whatever else needs to be done to prepare for the holiday. I always feel like there's so much more time in Maine than at home,'' Susan concluded happily.

''You do?'' Kathleen looked puzzled.

''I think we should go check with Halsey first,'' Susan

added, putting her plates in the dishwasher. "Is she still up in the attic?"

"She was the last time I looked. I'll go sit with the kids. They seem to know a lot more about building than I do, so I can't really help them, but maybe they'll talk about their sister or their stepfather—or something," she added, scratching her ankle with a syrupy fork.

"Good idea." Susan started from the room. "You know," she said, turning back, "I want to go visit an artist on the island this morning, too. Why don't you and the girls come with me? You'll enjoy it, and they might learn something." She hurried off to the third floor.

The attic was in considerably more disarray than yesterday. The women, with Halsey's help, had removed the shutters from the first floor. The girl had spent the night in the spare bedroom and had been up before daylight pulling blankets off the living room furniture and lugging them upstairs. She was now standing in the middle of the attic, arms across her chest, staring at dozens of framed photographs leaning against the large brick chimney and scattered about on broken lawn furniture and an ancient wicker divan. She spun around when Susan appeared at the top of the stairs. "Who are all these people?" She waved her arms at the pictures.

"Relatives, friends; a few are even strangers. It's the history of the house. Look." Susan knelt down and moved a few small sepia prints aside. "These are the workmen who built the boathouse." Together, they stared at the photograph of seven solemn young men.

"That's the front porch," Halsey cried with the thrill of recognition. "Look how tiny the lilac bushes are. And that dog on the lawn looks a lot like Titania's pet, doesn't it?"

Susan nodded. "Hard to believe, isn't it? I've always wondered if they got dressed especially for the photograph or if they came to work in jackets and hats every day."

"These belong on the wall going up the stairs, right?"

"Yes. There's even an order. They're arranged chronologically." She turned over a picture of three skinny boys swimming beside a wooden canoe and pointed at the tiny number that had been handwritten on its reverse side. "See? This is fourteen. It's near the beginning of the series. These are my uncles when they were children." She turned it over and ran her finger over its surface. "Two of them are dead now. . . ."

Halsey stood back and gave Susan a few minutes alone with her thoughts before asking another question. "Do I hang them from the top of the stairs down or from the bottom up?"

Susan put down the photograph. "They go from the bottom up, but why don't you not worry about it? I think I'd like to hang them this year. Just pile them on the floor of my bedroom, and I'll get to it later." She glanced at her Swatch. "You have to be at the restaurant in half an hour, so why not get the shutters off the windows of the boathouse and leave the rest of this. I don't suppose you could come back tomorrow morning?"

"I'm helping serve at the red, white, and blueberry breakfast at the Grange hall, but I could come here for an hour or so after that," Halsey offered. "Before the parade?"

"Then you'll miss the dinner on the pier. . . ."

"I don't mind. And I really do need the money."

"Okay, it's your decision. I'll probably see you at the breakfast."

"Then I'll get to work on the boathouse now. You don't want those shutters brought up here, do you?"

"No, just stack them right inside the door—there's a space where my kayak is usually kept. They normally slip right under the kayak racks on the back wall, but since there's no one here to use those boats, we may as well make things easy for ourselves."

"Great."

Susan smiled as Halsey bounded down the stairs. Oh, to be young and energetic after a night of less than sufficient sleep! She picked up an armload of pictures and carried them down the stairs and to her room. She heard male voices as she was placing them on the floor beside her dresser, and she headed straight down to the kitchen, wondering who was visiting so early in the day.

She was surprised to find Paul Briane and Ryan Harter sitting at the kitchen table and being served coffee by Kathleen. "If we get confused, we figure that we can just follow everyone else—there's no way that Paul or I are going to be in the lead," Ryan was explaining. "We're not that good. We just thought it would be fun to try. . . ."

"Here's Susan," Kathleen announced, looking up at her entrance. "You'll have to ask her."

"Ask me what?"

"We're wondering if you would loan us a kayak for the race this afternoon," Paul Briane said.

"The Taylors had two, but one was damaged recently, and Paul and I wanted to join the race around the island today—and we were hoping to travel as a pair," Ryan Harter explained. "I know it's a lot to ask, but we're both competent paddlers and we'd certainly pay for anything that we damaged if an accident happened."

"Actually, I'm the person who would be using your boat, if you'll let us borrow it," Paul explained. "And I really do know what I'm doing. I've been paddling for years."

He continued to list his qualifications, but Susan, who had witnessed his skill last night, didn't bother paying attention. In Maine, neighbors help one another, and she couldn't imagine any reason why she shouldn't follow the tradition. "My boat's out front. You're welcome to use it if you want. Come on out and take a look."

The men greeted Tierney and Theresa as they walked to the tree where Susan had left her kayak the night before. "This is it," she offered, proud of her craft. "Everything is inside it except the life jackets, but you must have some at the Taylors'. The paddle is leaning against the wall there, unless you want to use your own. . . ."

"I will," Paul answered her.

"Are you going to paddle to the starting line? It's just outside the cove—at the yacht club. It's visible as you get into the open water. You should be there ahead of time. They'll be giving out directions and explaining about the temporary buoys that are set out for the race. The starting time is noon, right?'' Susan asked.

''Yes. You've never entered?'' Ryan Harter asked.

''No. My son has talked about it, and my daughter has run in the island marathon that takes place at the same time, but no Henshaw has done this. We always show up at the finish line, though—to cheer on the winners and the losers.''

''Well, I don't suppose Ted or Tricia plan on doing anything today. Janet Shapiro is there now talking with Trish, and I don't have any idea what old Ted is doing. After the fight he and Trish had last night, I don't think we'll be seeing much of him today.''

''A fight?'' Paul had walked on ahead, and Susan hoped Ryan would keep talking.

''They decided to do a review of great disagreements of the Taylor family on the patio around midnight. I suppose Paul may have found it interesting professionally, but the rest of us were a little embarrassed. The house isn't air-conditioned, so we were pretty much forced to listen. I'm glad the girls were over here.'' He looked at the two heads, bent over their work on the porch. ''They really didn't need to hear the details of their parents' sexual dissatisfactions.''

''But they didn't mind that their guests heard?'' Susan asked.

''I don't think they were in control enough to worry about who heard what. They were furious. Ted accused his ex-wife of being frigid—and then flirting with every man in sight at the same time. And Tricia explained in detail how Ted had caused her to lose interest in sex over the years and how his philandering had destroyed their marriage.''

Susan nodded. This didn't sound like the part of the argument that she had overheard, but at the time, she had gotten the impression that it wasn't a short fight. ''It must have been embarrassing for you. Have you been friends of the Taylors' for long?'' She asked a question that she had been wondering about since yesterday.

''Since Sally and I got married. Sally and Tricia were

roommates in college—in fact, Sally introduced Trish to Ted.''

"Really?''

He chuckled. "Yes, in fact, Trish says that if Sally hadn't been such a pig, she and Ted would never have met. They were eating lunch in the student union, and Sally had ordered a huge hot butterscotch sundae for dessert and was in the middle of it when Ted appeared and asked her about an assignment for a psych class they were in together. Well, Sally introduced Trish to him, and he called her later in the day and asked her to go to a movie—but Trish was going with some other guy and refused. Then, over spring break, Trish and her boyfriend broke up and Trish went home with Sally—and guess who appeared?''

"Ted Taylor?''

"Yup. They started dating and were married the summer after their senior year. Sally was maid of honor at the wedding. Sally then went to New York to work as a junior copy editor at a publishing house—and that's where we met. Ted and Trish were living in Denver at the time, so we didn't meet right away. They came to our wedding a year later. But you know how weddings are: we met, but we really didn't have time to get to know each other. And then Sally and I went skiing at Breckenridge the next winter and visited the Taylors for a few days. Sally and Tricia spent a lot of time reminiscing and catching up, so Ted and I had a chance to get to know each other pretty well. . . .''

"And you liked each other right away?''

Ryan shrugged. "Sure. Why not? We've never lived that close to each other, but Trish and Sally both go to all their college reunions, so we've become pretty good friends.''

"But you seem to have stayed closer to Tricia than Ted after the divorce.''

"Let me tell you, it's not easy to stay friends with both members of a couple who are in the middle of a divorce. Tricia would bitch about Ted to Sally, and Ted would complain about Tricia to me, and then, worst of all, Sally and I would talk about them and end up arguing about our own relationship. Divorce is contagious, and don't let anyone tell you anything different.''

"But . . .''

"But it was a lot easier after Tricia married Humphrey. Old Humph was dull, but his presence seemed to keep things calm. Otherwise we would never have agreed to come on this vacation. I was more than a little skeptical about it, I can tell you. But Sally said it was very important to Trish, and frankly, we've had a difficult year. The recession really knocked the cable industry for a loop, and I've been working eleven- and twelve-hour days, seven days a week, for a long time. I was even out of work for a while—and finding a job is harder than working these days. I thought I owed it to my wife to let her select the way we spent this vacation.''

Susan thought about what she had heard between Sally and Paul the night before and decided that Ryan's wife certainly hadn't been as bored in the past year as he thought. And, anyway, he had spent the vacation fishing rather than courting his wife. Ryan apparently realized she might be thinking along these lines.

"Sally wanted to be here to help Trish more than to be with me. Sally and Judy have been worried about Trish. Those girls have been driving her crazy ever since Humphrey appeared on the scene. . . .''

"So you knew about the pranks that the girls had been pulling before you came here?''

"Sure did. In fact, we were at the house the weekend after Tricia and Humphrey got back from their honeymoon and got to see old Humphrey's face when he tasted what he thought was his precious Laiphroing. He looked like he was going to die right there—like he thought he had been poisoned. Of course, I think everyone there thought about the possibility of weed killer in his drink—or some other domestic poison. Titania was standing in the doorway of the room with a smirk on her face. But it turned out to be food coloring and root beer or some other bloody childish concoction.'' He chuckled. "Old Humphrey was furious, I can tell you. I think it was a good thing that Ted kept the girls at his new apartment for a few extra weeks. The excuse was that their rooms were being repainted at their old house, but I think Trish and Ted agreed the girls were safer where they were—or that Humphrey was safer with them someplace else. To tell the truth, I'm not sure which.''

"You think one of the girls might be a murderer?''

"No. I didn't mean that. I certainly don't think any of them would intentionally kill Humphrey—or anyone else, for that matter. But they're kids and they might not understand. I was talking with Paul about it the other day. He's a psychiatrist, you know. And he was telling me that children don't understand mortality—that they even believe that death isn't permanent. He said that sometimes children kill their baby brothers and sisters but that they have no idea how serious a thing murder is.''

"I think that might be true for some very young children,'' Susan said slowly. "But certainly even Tierney understands that death is final. And I don't know any of the girls well, but none of them seems to have anything wrong with her psychologically—at least nothing so serious that she might murder her stepfather thinking that it didn't matter. Surely Paul didn't imagine something like that could happen.''

"No, I . . .''

"Does he see children in his practice?'' Susan asked, thinking that she might talk with Paul Briane and get an expert opinion since one was easily available.

"No. He doesn't see patients.''

"Then what does he do?''

"He runs a clinic. It's designed to help people eliminate compulsive behavior from their lives—or something like that. I think he was expecting a lot of nymphomaniacs to sign up for the program when he opened the clinic, but apparently what most people do compulsively is eat. Judy says that when he got involved, he didn't realize that he was going to be spending most of his working hours with fat women.'' He grinned.

"But if the clinic works, wouldn't they be getting thin?'' Susan asked, momentarily distracted.

"They just get them on the road to recovery while they're residents. Apparently they thin out when they get home—if the program works at all. I suppose it must. He sure seems to be raking in the money."

"Even in the recession . . ." Susan began, remembering how Ryan had said his own business had been doing in the past few years.

"Even in a recession, people will pay to improve their lives. Self-help is the wave of the future. Lots of good businesses there." He spoke with approval.

"So you came to Maine because Tricia wanted Sally to be here."

He nodded. "I think she thought that the girls might lay off if there were other people around. I don't think she thought anyone was going to murder Humphrey—don't get me wrong. But I think she hoped it might make things easier if we were here. At least that's the impression I got."

"Do you think Humphrey thought so, too?"

"I thought old Humphrey was a little nervous, to tell the truth. I suppose picking up a glass and not knowing what's in it could do that to anyone. And just the thought of finding my pockets full of pudding or thorns gives me the heebie-jeebies, to tell the truth."

"How long have you been here?"

"Since last Saturday. Humphrey and Tricia had been doing better, come to think of it. When we got here, they were pretty nervous, but as the week's gone on, everybody relaxed. Until you found Humphrey in your living room, that is."

"Tricia thought he had gone back to Boston?"

"Yes. We all did. Some sort of business emergency. Humphrey got a call from the office sometime on Thursday and had to leave immediately. He was supposed to be back before the Fourth. I'm sure of that because he mentioned how terrible the traffic was going to be leaving the city during the holiday weekend."

"What business was he in?"

"Oil and precious minerals exploration. Humphrey was a

geologist. That's what he was doing in Alaska and the Mid-east for all those years.''

"I didn't know—" Susan began.

"You know, that's a wonderful kayak you've got. I just might win the race in that." Paul Briane had returned. "We'd better get going," he added to the other man.

"What time is it?" Ryan looked at his watch.

"Time to get into the water and find that yacht club. You said you'd be at the finish line?" he asked Susan.

"We sure will," she answered, wishing he had waited a while before joining them. She had been learning so much from Ryan.

"Then we'd better get going," Paul said. "Besides, it looks like you've got company." He nodded over Susan's shoulder.

Susan turned and saw Janet Shapiro coming around the corner of her house. She waved as the men, walking her kayak down to the sea, thanked her for the loan.

"Do you have a few minutes?" Janet Shapiro asked, nodding to the girls and Kathleen, who were still on the porch. "I'd like to talk with you."

"Of course. Do you want Kathleen, too?"

"Sure do. I can use all the help I can get."

"Then why don't we go in and get some coffee or tea? I gather you have a problem?"

"You could say that." The deputy waited until the three women were alone in the kitchen before explaining. And when she did explain, it was a surprise. "They're fighting over the body."

"What?"

"Tricia and Ted Taylor are fighting over custody of the body of Humphrey Taylor. Neither wants it. I called the man in charge of the morgue to tell him that I was going to sign the forms that would release Humphrey's body to his wife right after the autopsy was completed—and it turns out she and Ted Taylor have been fighting over it.''

"Why?"

"Who knows?" Janet shrugged. "I suppose you could

say that Humphrey was closer to Ted than to a woman that he'd been married to for less than a year. I suppose an argument could be made for Ted Taylor's rights to his brother's body here.''

''And you agree with that?'' Susan thought that Kathleen sounded skeptical.

''Not really. No. But I don't want to get in the middle of a family feud—or a lawsuit, for that matter. I'm letting them fight it out among themselves right now. But there's only so long that I can put off handing the body over to someone. It's a holiday weekend, and I can use that as an excuse till Tuesday, but I sure hope those two find that they can agree to something before then. The morgue isn't so big that we can store bodies indefinitely.''

''How's the investigation going?'' Susan asked, passing mugs of steaming coffee.

''The weekend may be making it easier to keep Humphrey Taylor, but it isn't making it easier to find out anything about him. I have calls in to a few contacts in Boston, but everyone is promising to call back—on Tuesday. And people here on the island don't know much about Humphrey Taylor. It was Ted Taylor who had been spending so much time on the island since last spring. He's practically got his own personal room at The Landing Inn—they even let him stay there over the winter, when they're usually closed. He loved that house.''

''He still does,'' Susan said. ''I wonder why it went to his wife in the divorce settlement.''

''I don't know. Do you think it might have any bearing on the murder?'' Janet asked.

''Probably not, but we should try to find out everything that we can about that house. It may hold a clue to the murder,'' Susan mused.

''You're thinking of the note from Titania,'' Kathleen said, nodding.

''That's the note you mentioned in the message on my answering machine last night?''

Susan nodded. ''Titania left a message in Halsey's coat

yesterday. It's right here in the drawer under the phone. I was going to bring it over to your house first thing this morning, but I didn't get to bed until awfully late, and frankly, I forgot." She got up while talking and retrieved the letter, handing it immediately to Janet Shapiro. "I know I should have given it to you right away, but . . ."

"It's good to know that she's alive," was Janet's first comment. "The search is going full blast. Every volunteer fireman is out in the woods, and a bunch of high school kids are knocking on the doors of each house on the island. I sure hope they find her soon. I have a feeling she knows something about all this."

"And it's interesting what she says about the mantel, isn't it?" Susan insisted on returning to the topic.

"Sure is. I guess we'd better go right over there and check this out."

"Just like that? Just walk in and ask to see the mantel?" Susan was surprised, thinking over the plans she had made, most of which included breaking and entering.

"Just like that." Janet stood up, smoothing the white T-shirt she wore down over her ample chest. "That's one of the advantages of being a police person."

ELEVEN

"More questions?"

"Yes." Janet Shapiro was blunt. "I don't think it will take more than a few minutes."

"Well, I'm glad you're here," Tricia Taylor surprised Susan by saying. "You can pick up some clean clothing for the girls. I'm glad they're staying with you. I feel much better about all this knowing that they're out of harm's way."

"They're very nice girls, and I'm enjoying having them. They're busy building a float for the parade tomorrow," Susan explained.

"Then we'll all have to go see it," Tricia assured her, before turning her attention back to the policewoman.

Susan thought that was the very least she could do, but she didn't say anything.

"I'd like to look at your mantel," Janet explained. "I understand that there's a history of the family carved on it."

"The history of the family according to my ex-husband is carved on it," Tricia corrected her. "Feel free." She waved toward the living room. "I'll just run upstairs and get some things for my daughters." She left them to find their own way.

"She doesn't seem terribly concerned about Titania's disappearance, does she?" Susan asked quietly as they walked to the living room.

"I'll say. I'd be frantic if Bananas vanished. And I keep thinking that she should want her other daughters with her

134

in this crisis. She doesn't seem terribly concerned about any of her family members.''

''True.'' Susan followed Janet across the large, open space to the huge mantel. Made from what looked like chestnut, it was elaborately carved beneath the mantelpiece and halfway to the floor down either side.

Janet bent down and examined the carvings, apparently deciding to move from left to right. Susan wasn't so sure this was the correct order. In the middle of the design, centered, was what looked like a modern nativity scene. A woman, recognizably Tricia Taylor, sat under a tree with a baby in her lap, while two other children leaned over to get a closer look at the child. In the background of this tableau, a man peered from between three evergreens. To Susan, it looked like an idealization of the entire family—minus Humphrey.

She continued on across the top and down the left side, wishing she could take notes. The images seemed, except for the centerpiece, to be in chronological order beginning with a recognizable view of the Statue of Liberty and Ellis Island on the left and ending with an imprint of the house itself. In between were pictures of children playing, pets, universities, towns, vacations (unless the Taylors had lived in Paris at one time), holidays, wedding (Ted and Tricia, *not* Humphrey and Tricia), christenings, birthdays, and the normal celebrations of everyday life. If there was a clue here to why Humphrey died, it wasn't immediately apparent to Susan.

Nor to Janet Shapiro. ''I don't see what Titania was talking about,'' she said. ''Unless it's this man back in the trees.'' She pointed to the middle carving. ''It could be Ted Taylor, of course. Or maybe . . .''

''You think it may be his brother,'' Susan said, looking more closely. ''It's an interesting idea. And if this was designed by Ted—''

''Oh, it's Ted's work, all right.'' Tricia had returned, a boat bag of clean clothing in her hand. ''Who else would think of his own life as a series of publicity shots—with significant buildings in the background?''

"We were wondering about the man hovering in the background of the middle picture," Janet explained.

"In the trees? Everyone asks about that. It's Ted. The person who carved all this was given a pile of old photographs and asked to do a sketch for approval before he started. And Ted loved everything except the middle image. It was taken from a family portrait done after Tierney was born, but the photographer had us all stand in front of one of those fabric backdrops. In the sketch it was fine, but carved in wood, it looked like we were seated before a waterfall. Ted suggested that the carver add trees—which he did. And you can see the result. Paul says it looks like Ted is a mugger waiting for his victims. Oh, well." She sighed. "I was going to have this replaced when Ted and I broke up, but Titania became hysterical at the thought, so I just left it. I suppose it will be there forever. Years from now, someone else will own this house, and they'll be able to while away the hours wondering why anyone would choose their fireplace as an appropriate place to immortalize a psychopath stalking his victims."

Janet chuckled. "There are pictures here of you and Ted as children," she said.

"There's even the immigration of Ted's grandparents from England—that part wasn't from photographs, of course. The girls love all this, but to be honest, I think it's more than a little tacky. And that's very unlike Ted. The man's life is practically a monument to good taste usually. I think he got carried away here.

"Is there anything else that you want to talk to me about?" Tricia added as Susan continued to stare at the mantel, and Janet Shapiro said nothing.

"No, we—"

"Then I have to get going. I promised Judy and Sally that I would show them around some of the galleries in town before we head over to the finish line of the race. For all the problems in my marriage, I'm thankful that I never married a sports fanatic. Those two men are never home."

"And you will remember to get together with your ex-husband and make a decision about Humphrey Taylor's body?'' Janet urged.

"Yes. Of course," Tricia agreed coldly.

"Then we'll see you later at the yacht club," Susan said, taking the bag of clothing and determining to act as though nothing were out of the ordinary here.

"There's a box of dog food in the bottom there," Tricia explained, seeing her guests to the door. "It's typical of that damn dog that she moves out when Humphrey is no longer around to sneeze at her."

"Humphrey was allergic to dogs?" Susan asked.

"Terribly. He was asthmatic from birth. I think that's the only reason Ted gave that hairy beast to Titania. He wanted to make his brother miserable."

Karma was asleep in the sunlight on Susan's lawn when the women strolled back to the house. "Seems to me," Janet was saying, "that woman is working real hard to make us think that what we have here is a case of fratricide."

"And you don't think Ted did it?"

"Nope. What did he have to gain? He's already lost his wife, and it doesn't look like she's going to return to him whether she's married or not. The two of them don't seem able to agree on much of anything, and they sure don't act like they're in love. And he's not going to get that house back."

"And he sure loves that house," Susan agreed. "You know, looking at that mantel has started me thinking. Is it possible to do some checking into Ted Taylor's past?"

"And Humphrey Taylor's and Tricia Taylor's." Janet nodded. "I've already set that ball in motion. I included the Brianes and the Harters on the list, too. It shouldn't take long to find out what information is available on various computer systems. I'll let you know. . . . Are you thinking of something specific?"

"No, I wish I were," Susan said, lowering her voice as they approached the children.

"Hi!" Tierney spied them first. "Mrs. Gordon is inside.

She said to tell her as soon as you came back. We're all going to an art gallery, aren't we?''

"Sure are. And we can watch the end of the kayak race around the island, if you want.''

"We'd love to," Theresa said politely.

"Are you coming, too?" Tierney asked the deputy.

"No, I have to head back home. I have some work to do. But I'll probably see you later today. I'll be around—checking out things and trying to discourage children from playing with fireworks. It's been a pretty dry summer. Last year more than one fire was started by people fooling around with those damn things. You two have better sense than that, don't you?''

The girls nodded solemnly, apparently impressed with her warning. "We had some sparklers," Tierney admitted. "But Karma ate them.''

"You're lucky they didn't make her sick," Susan said, astounded at the dog's ability to digest the undigestible.

"Oh, Daddy just took her out for a ride in the car and she barfed them right up. It was Uncle Humphrey's car," Tierney explained, grinning at the memory.

Susan heard Janet snicker behind her. "Why don't you call Kathleen and tell her that we're ready to go. I think we should leave the dog here," Susan started, then wondered if that was such a good idea. There was so much in the house to chew up. . . . "Do you think it would be all right if we left Karma in the boathouse? It's clean and dry." It's pretty difficult to consume fiberglass, and the paddles were hanging near the ceiling, she added to herself.

"We should put bowls of food and water in there for her," Theresa said. Tierney nodded.

"Good idea," Susan said enthusiastically. "If your girls would take care of that . . ." She turned, but she didn't speak to Janet until they were alone. "I've been thinking," she said. "Maybe Titania's wrong and it's not the mantel. Maybe it's something else in the house." She explained about the boxes of books that she had found.

"It could be anything at all. For all we know, someone

left a message on a fogged-up bathroom mirror. I certainly wish that child had been more specific in her note.''

''I hope she's safe,'' Susan said, waving as Theresa and Tierney came toward them, bowls of food and water in their hands. The dog trailed close behind.

Kathleen came out while Karma was surprising Susan with her willingness to enter the boathouse (possibly she liked to eat spiders?), and they were soon in the car on the way to the artist's gallery.

''I assume there's some reason why you feel the need to see this artist right now?'' Kathleen asked, knowing that Susan would understand the unspoken question.

''I think we might find something that we're looking for here,'' Susan replied carefully, conscious of the children in the backseat.

Kathleen raised her eyebrows, but no one said anything until they parked beside a large white house that had been extended over the decades with one or two sheds and a substantial barn. ''This is where that funny man with the mustache lives!'' Tierney cried out happily.

''Then you've met Monsieur Touve?'' Susan called back over her shoulder.

''Yes. We love him. He's going to give us art lessons. I'm going to take mask making, and Theresa wants to do collages, and Titania's going to make porcelain beads.''

Susan was interested in Tierney's enthusiasm, and in her older (and wiser?) sister's apparent lack of such. Could Theresa be hiding something? She stopped the car and everyone got out.

''Look at these things,'' Kathleen said, reaching out and spinning a little wooden figure of a man riding an old-fashioned bicycle. It was more art than craft. The thin legs pumped and the wheels spun as the rider turned his head from one side to the other. Kathleen was enchanted—even more so when a man looking remarkably like the bike rider, from his striped polo, skintight black jeans, and fabulous long black mustache to the red beret tilted on his head, appeared in the doorway of the barn.

"Greetings, *mes amis*," he called out in an accent that was more Bronx than Bordeaux. "Good to see you, although—" he paused dramatically "—I believe one of you is missing. And you've added a most charming nanny." He stared at Kathleen. "A most charming nanny," he repeated with a stage leer.

"And *bonjour* to you, Monsieur Touve," Susan greeted him. "This is Kathleen Gordon. She's staying with me for the weekend."

"And we are too old for a nanny," Tierney protested indignantly. "Nannies are for babies!"

"You're absolutely right," he agreed. "Why don't you young ladies go into my studio? I have some interesting new masks that just arrived—sent by a friend in New Orleans. They're laid out on my worktable. And help yourselves to the lemonade in the green pitcher. But don't touch the pink bowl—it contains punch that's mellowing for my party tonight. I don't know if it's lethal, but it's definitely not for little girls. Or young ladies," he added as Theresa scowled at him.

"Masks! Come on, Theresa!" Tierney tugged on her sister's arm. "Let's go."

Theresa made a point of smiling politely before following her sister into the barn.

As they left, Monsieur Touve became less French and more serious. "I'm very glad to see you. I've been worrying about Titania. I heard that she's missing," he commented.

Susan nodded. "Actually that's why we're here," she explained. "I was wondering if you knew anything about her—or where she was."

"I have no idea—not that I don't wish I did. That girl is enchanting, and the island may be safer than the big city, but in this world no one should leave a child like that alone. Terrible things happen in this world."

Susan had often speculated on what particular event had led this man to leave a successful and lucrative life designing stage sets in Manhattan and settle down on an island in Maine, but this wasn't the time to pursue that.

"Apparently you thought I might know something about this?" Susan recognized that it was a question.

"I found one of your whirligigs in her room," she answered. "One of your best ones. And since she couldn't possibly have afforded to buy one, I knew you must have given it to her. So I assumed that you knew her well."

"Why don't we go into the house to talk? I could get you some coffee or something."

Susan glanced at Kathleen; she couldn't possibly be hungry again. "We're fine, thanks. But it might be better to talk someplace a little more private."

They were seated in Monsieur Touve's elegant living room before he explained his relationship with the girl. "We met in a very Maine way," he said, the accent no longer in evidence. "We were clamming in the same cove," he explained. "I won't tell anyone about it. It's the best place on the island, and I don't want it dug by people who don't respect the size limits on clams. Anyway, I was clamming there, and Titania appeared with a brand-new basket and shovel. I don't usually like children, but she seemed quieter than most and she listened to what I told her, so we got along fairly well."

"Was this early in the summer?"

"Before Memorial Day. She explained that she and her sister attended a private school with a very long summer vacation. It was still cold. She had brought along a thermos of ginseng tea and offered to share it with me. I appreciated the sophistication of her choice, although I didn't accept. We met at the cove a lot in May. The tide was out in the afternoons and the sun was getting warm. We talked some and dug a lot of clams. She's a nice girl—appreciative of the beauty of things and interested in ideas. To tell the truth, I had a hard time understanding the stories that were being told about her on the island—about how she was working to drive her stepfather crazy. She seemed very sweet to me. I suppose I just don't understand children."

"Did she talk to you about that?" Kathleen asked, accepting the chocolate croissant that Monsieur Touve offered.

"Not really. I didn't ask her, though. I didn't see any reason to pry. When she talked about herself, she talked about her sisters and her father—not her stepfather—and that beautiful beast that she adores." He glanced lovingly at a bronze setter who had been sitting quietly in a corner of the room ever since they had entered. "And my own opinion is that the man who died must have been a pig. She wouldn't have disliked him so unless he was. She is a young lady with natural discernment."

"Is she here?" Susan asked quietly.

The man snapped his fingers, and the Gordon setter leapt to his side. "No," he answered, scratching the dog behind the ears. "In fact, I was hoping that you were hiding her."

Susan stared at him.

It was Kathleen who spoke. "You don't think she is hiding herself?"

"Why would she hide?" he asked, apparently surprised. "You certainly don't think she killed her stepfather? That child is not a murderer. She's not even a child who would accidentally kill someone. She is an intelligent creature with an amazing amount of control for someone her age!"

"We're not arguing with you," Susan insisted. "But we know that she's hiding. She even sent a note."

"What?"

Susan explained about the message that Halsey had delivered. His reaction was not what she had expected.

"How do you know that someone didn't make her write that? For that matter, how do you know that someone else didn't write it?"

"Well, I . . ." Susan began, not knowing the answer to those questions.

"But her sisters say that she had planned on hiding. She told them not to worry about her," Kathleen explained.

"Then it's possible that you're right and she's hiding, but there's still a worse alternative."

"Which is?" Kathleen asked. Susan was silent, hoping not to hear anything worse than the alternatives she had already considered.

"What if she is hiding hoping everyone will then think that she's guilty? What if she is hiding because she knows who the murderer is and she is protecting him or her?"

"That would be dangerous," Kathleen said slowly, putting down her snack.

"Definitely."

"Now, wait," Susan insisted. "Did she ever say anything to you that would make you think that?"

Monsieur Touve spoke slowly. "She is loyal. She is responsible. People that she loved are under a tremendous strain. I think it is more than possible. What did the note actually say?"

"She wanted us to look for something in the Taylor house—something that would solve the murder," Susan explained.

"I gather you don't know what you're supposed to look for? Or don't you want to tell me?"

Susan explained about the mantel.

"But the only part that seems unusual is the center scene, where Ted Taylor is standing in the middle of a group of trees," Kathleen added when Susan was finished.

"Oh, God, the famous family scene. I've heard about that before—more than once." He looked at his two puzzled guests and continued. "Let me explain. Ted Taylor found a worker over near the park to create the mantel and a few doors. To be more accurate, Ted Taylor came to me and asked if I would accept a commission to do the work for him. I don't do that type of work—purely decorative. I did enough of that years and years ago before I could make a living creating things that I love. I suggested a friend. . . ."

"The man who lives by Acadia National Park?" Susan asked for clarification.

"Yes. And Ted liked the work my friend showed him and gave him the job—with the condition that he do the work on the island."

"Why?" This from Kathleen.

"So he could keep an eye on how it was going—as least that's what I assume. Ted Taylor isn't a bad person to work for if you don't mind someone looking over your shoulder. Fortunately, my friend could care less. I don't think I'd like it." He gave a little Gallic shrug. "People are different.

"Anyway, everything went fine. Ted arrived here with piles of photographs of designs that he wanted included in the mantel. He delivered the wood. He approved the initial sketches. The work was done in the large shed that's behind my studio. The doors were done first, and then the mantel. But the middle of the mantel—the keystone, I suppose you could call it—was supposed to be a duplicate of a rather sentimental portrait that had been done of the family back when the youngest girl was a baby. It was dreadful. The pose was artificial and the background indistinct. Ted Taylor was upset. My friend was distraught, and I was getting bored with the whole thing. The only people who were enjoying all this by that time were the girls, who were coming to the island on weekends and school holidays and, I think, having some fun.

"To get back to the woodwork: There weren't a lot of possible remedies. The entire section could be cut out and replaced with another piece the same size. That's what I would have done and that's what my friend wanted to do, but Ted Taylor wanted a mantel carved from a single piece of chestnut, and he wouldn't accept anything else. We discussed shaving off the entire background design and having the figures stand out in bas-relief, as it were, but then Ted Taylor came up with another idea. He decided that he wanted trees— balsams, to be exact. He thought it would represent the family's relationship with Maine or something. So my friend carved trees around the family, and that's it. If that has anything to do with Humphrey being killed, I sure don't see it."

"Are you sure you know the whole story?"

"The whole thing was enacted in my house and studio— believe me, I know the whole story. I got to hear my friend's side and then Ted Taylor's side more times than I care to remember. I didn't get a lot of my own work done during that time."

"Could anything be hidden behind the wood?" Kathleen asked.

"There could be, but there isn't. I was there when the mantel was installed, and I can assure you that it was installed right over concrete—solid concrete, just like the stuff that was used to keep the rocks up. And I don't think any of those rocks are hollow either. Don't secret hiding places in the chimney strike you as a little too Nancy Drew to be true?"

"Hmm. The Clue in the Woodwork. I think I read that one when I was a girl," Janet Shapiro mused, shading her eyes with her hands and looking out to sea. "I'm just kidding," she added. "I think Nancy Drew had the good sense to stay away from cases as complicated as this one."

"Smart lady," Susan agreed.

"Let's go over there and try to discourage those boys from blowing their heads off with bottle rockets and Roman candles. I don't know what there is about boys and things that explode, but half the male population of the island finds the damn things impossible to resist."

Susan and Kathleen hurried after the deputy as she marched over to one side of the yacht club's parking lot. "We won't be able to see the finish line as well, but we'll get a lot more privacy here."

"Why do we need privacy?" Kathleen asked, after Janet had confiscated a shoe box brimming with fireworks from six long-haired teens.

"I thought you might be interested in my reports on the Taylors."

"We sure are," Susan assured her.

"Well, starting with the dead man then." She pulled some sheets of computer printer paper from her jacket pocket. "To begin at the beginning. Humphrey was the older son of the Taylor family. Five years older than Ted, in fact. There wasn't anything odd about his childhood that I could find. Grew up with his family in a suburb in New Jersey and attended the Colorado School of Mines after high school. Four years later he graduated and went off to work in Alaska for one of the big oil companies. First he worked in exploration for a year or two and then he spent three years helping get the pipeline finished. After that he took off for the Mideast—Saudi Arabia, Kuwait, Libya. I don't know much about it, but the list of where Humphrey Taylor had been living for the past twenty years could be described as a list of most of the oil-rich parts of the world. Then a few years ago he retired. Just traveled around for a few years, and then he got tired of being an expatriate or something and he came home. He's doing some part-time consulting in the Boston area, but he's not doing it for the money, because he's not making much.''

''But he could have made a lot of money working in oil all these years, right?'' Susan asked.

''He probably did. One of the reasons these oil companies can keep people working overseas is because of the big salaries, numerous perks, and tax advantages. Of course, a lot of that has changed in the past ten years or so, but Humphrey has been doing this for a long time. He should be fixed for life.''

''And his personal life?'' Kathleen asked. ''Was he married before or anything like that?''

''There's no record of it. In fact, there's not much record of his personal life at all. He was arrested for DWI in Alaska in 1974, but he was young at the time—twenty-four—and it was his first offense of any sort, so he was let off with a warning. And that's all. At least there's no record of anything else. The office in Ellsworth is checking with the customs department to see if there was anything significant in his life overseas, but we may not hear about that right away.''

''But most Arab nations aren't all that willing to keep around workers who don't obey their laws, are they?'' Susan asked.

''I don't know. But I was wondering about that,'' Janet answered. ''I have a friend whose son dropped out of college and got a job of some sort in the United Arab Emirates. However, when he wasn't working, he was busy with wine, women, and song. The government objected to everything but the songs, and he found himself on a plane home very quickly—and it was only because his uncle is a member of the United States Senate that he didn't find himself in an Arab prison. Tolerance isn't a byword in that part of the world."

"And that's all that we know about Humphrey Taylor?" Susan asked.

"Right now," Janet Shapiro answered.

"I know someone who might be able to get us more—if there is anything more. I'll have to call him, though. Is there a phone in the yacht clubhouse?" Kathleen asked.

"There isn't even a clubhouse," Janet Shapiro answered. "But there's a shed over near the dock with the gas pumps, and there's a phone hanging on the wall behind the door. If anyone hassles you, tell them that I asked you to make the call—official business, you know the line."

Kathleen nodded and took off.

"And Tricia and Ted?" Susan asked.

"Until their divorce, they were the most boring of couples. They're the same age. He's the second son of a family with only two children—the parents are dead, by the way; they died in an automobile crash in Colorado about five years ago. He went to Ohio State and met Tricia there. He was always interested in architecture and majored in that. She majored in English lit. They got married less than a month after graduation. Oh, I thought this was interesting. The T. T. initials belong to the girls more than their parents. He's an Edward and she's a Patricia." She looked a little embarrassed. "I know it has nothing to do with this, but I thought it was interesting. . . . Damn those kids. I hate the Fourth of July. All these damn fireworks. I'd better get over to the water and check this out. No one should be lighting fireworks in the middle of a crowd!"

But when they arrived at the dock where the loud crack had originated, they discovered that it hadn't been the explosion of an illegal firecracker. It had been a gunshot.

TWELVE

Janet Shapiro was pacing the floor of Susan's living room. "A sniper. That's just what we need now. A sniper in the middle of the one weekend of the year when everyone is making loud noises to celebrate. I'm probably going to go mad. Why does this happen when I'm on duty? Whenever Andrew is around, the most excitement we get is an auto accident or a drunk and disorderly. I'll have a nervous breakdown and that'll show him!"

Susan, who had never heard anything but feminist statements from this woman, would have been amused if the situation had been less serious. She wondered what the kayak racers must have thought as they rounded the point before the yacht club and spied people screaming and running from the long floating dock that had served as the finish line for as long as the race had been held. She got up and went to the window, trying to remember everything in order.

The floating dock was attached to a long, stationary dock, and the first shot had smashed into one of the massive pilings that held the wood in place. The second had hit one of the poles that carried the banner commemorating this year's event. The third had grazed the mayor's cheek—right through his jeans. "My newest pair, too—only one hole in the left knee," he was heard to complain in the food line at the baked-bean supper at the community church. Some of the islanders thought he was using his injury as an excuse to be first in line for May Ables's raspberry pie. There were a lot of people around who wouldn't mind getting shot slightly— if it meant a guaranteed piece of that pie.

Susan tried to focus on less frivolous subjects. The problem with being around Kathleen so much was that it was hard not to keep thinking about food. Most people had fled, and after everyone was sure the shots had ceased, and had returned, it was impossible to get any consensus on where, exactly, they had come from. Finally two of the young men whose firecrackers Janet had confiscated admitted that they had stashed another supply in the crotch of a large apple tree near the drive to the club—and that someone had crushed the box climbing in and out of the branches. Kathleen had agreed with Janet that the top of the tree was the right location, considering the various entry points of the bullets. Shells on the ground were found to match the bullets, and the gun itself was discovered a few feet away. An old thirty-odd-six, it was the weapon of choice for most of the deer hunters on the island. It might take a while to trace down the owner, but it would be done. State investigators would be checking all this out, but Susan was willing to accept the expertise of her two friends.

Who, she wondered, was the sniper shooting at? There were dozens of people around, but Susan couldn't help thinking that prominent among the fans cheering on the paddlers were Sally Harter and Judy Briane. Both women had been standing together on the dock right under the pole that had been hit. Sally had been staring out to sea through binoculars and had seen nothing. Judy had been talking with the island's mayor.

"There's no reason to assume that this is related to the murder," Janet, still pacing, reminded Susan. "No reason at all. It's just as likely that the shot was fired by an islander in a rage over property taxes or something like that."

"Did you ask the mayor if he had any ideas?"

"He thinks it's his ex-wife, and he wants me to arrest her immediately. The Taylors aren't the only couple around with divorce problems."

"Do you think . . . ?"

"Don't bank on it. She's living in Santa Fe. She hated that man when she left him, but she hated living in Maine more. I don't think she'd set foot in this state for any reason whatever. But I called the police down there to check out her whereabouts. It's just a formality. I really don't think she did it."

"Any other ideas?"

"Well, I'm hungry, and I always think it's interesting to get opinions from other people who were at an event like this afternoon's, so I was wondering about going over to the second seating at the bean supper. . . ."

"That's a wonderful idea." Susan didn't have to look up to know that Kathleen had once more been enthusiastic about food.

"The girls . . ." Susan began.

"I just spoke with Monsieur Touve on the phone, and he said they were helping him prepare appetizers for his party tonight and he would feed them dinner if we'd pick them up around eight or so. He said that they were happy there and he thought they should stay."

"Then let's get going while there's still some food left."

A lot of churches, granges, and various other clubs in Maine survived on money made at various suppers. Covered-dish suppers, bean suppers, chowder suppers, lobster and clam suppers, were popular. Members made and brought the food. Tickets for one, two, or three seatings were sold, and everyone was happy. Money was made and people got a chance to sample some of the best home cooking in the world. Despite the problems of the past forty-eight hours, Susan discovered that hunger was the prominent thought in her mind. "I'll drive," she offered.

But her phone rang, and Kathleen ran to get it. "I'm expecting this. Why don't you go with Janet, and I'll follow in your car?" she called out.

"Fine."

"How is she going to find the church?" Susan asked, following Janet to the police car.

"She can always follow the scent of beans—or she can ask someone."

"You know, I was wondering if you got reports on the Brianes or the Harters," Susan said.

"I did. Or, at least, I got the official reports. They're not very interesting, I'm afraid. Of course, I wasn't all that interested in them until this afternoon. The men have vanished, by the way. Nothing mysterious. They're out fishing."

"They're always out fishing," Susan complained. "Has it occurred to you that fishing alone in the middle of Penobscot Bay is a pretty good excuse to explain why no one can find you?"

"And that they could be someplace else?"

"Yes."

"Like shooting at their wives?"

"Well, it's a thought, isn't it?" Susan asked.

"I wouldn't rule it out, but I can't find much connection between the three families. . . ."

"They have a connection with each other, though. Paul Briane and Sally Harter are in love with each other."

"Excuse me?" Janet Shapiro put her foot on the brake and pulled over to the side of the road. "So why don't you just tell me how you know that?"

Susan explained the conversation she had overheard the night before.

"Wow. That's some busy household, isn't it? I'm beginning to be glad I live on an island," Janet said.

"Like the mayor?"

"Okay. Like the mayor. Maybe life is the same all over. So tell me what you know about the Brianes and the Harters."

"The only thing they have in common—except for falling in love with each other—is that they're both old friends of the Taylors'. They all go back to sometime around college.

"I know that Sally was Tricia's roommate in college and that she and Ryan were together at the Taylor wedding, but I don't know about the Brianes," Susan said.

"Well, Paul and Ted grew up together. They were both

Boy Scouts. They played on the same soccer team in high school, but they lost touch when they went off to college. They became reacquainted about five or six years ago when the firm Ted worked for was hired to design the sanitarium that Paul was building. . . ."

"Then he's rich?" Susan asked.

"Not that rich. He got a lot of his doctor friends together, and they all invested in a corporation that he headed. It was a smart move on their part. They got a good, healthy return on their money. It was hard to lose money in the eighties, of course, and the time was right in other ways as well. Paul Briane got in on the beginning of the 'cure your current addiction/self-help' boom. It's sure not like being a struggling artist. He's been minting money. In fact, he expanded that original clinic into four more all over the country, and he's opening new ones in San Diego and Boston in the next six months."

"Where does he live now?" Susan asked.

"Just outside of Pittsburgh. Someplace called Bethel Park . . ."

"And where do the Harters live?"

"In Pittsburgh—not surprising if Paul and Sally are involved. But the Harters are in the middle of a move to Massachusetts. Ryan's business hasn't been as successful as Paul's. His small cable company was swallowed up by a media giant last year, and he was out of work. Recently he found a job with one of the biggest cable groups in the Northeast. They needed him immediately. He's been staying in a hotel in Lowell for the past four months, in fact. And Sally's been back in Pittsburgh trying to sell the house."

"And falling in love with a married man," Susan added.

"That, too."

"I gather neither couple has any children?"

"True."

"And do the wives work?"

"Sally does some free-lance editing for a few publishing companies. She has ever since her marriage apparently. And Judy's a professional fund-raiser. She got her M.B.A. while

Paul was in medical school, and she's had her own business for the past fifteen years—apparently very successful. She works as far away as Cleveland.''

"Any hints that either marriage is in trouble, other than what I mentioned?''

"I've just got facts, nothing personal as yet."

"Is there any sign that either couple had a connection to Humphrey rather than Ted and Tricia?''

"Unfortunately not. Of course, I tried to check into that. Certainly Sally and Paul would have known him when they were young, but even then, he was Ted's older brother. And five years older. He would have been away in college by the time Paul and Ted hit high school. And Sally probably met Humphrey at the Taylor wedding, but that's about it as far as we know. I don't see any reason that we shouldn't ask Mr. and Mrs. Taylor about that."

"Ask Ted and Tricia?''

"Damn right. They'll probably be thrilled to think that we're considering someone else as a suspect, don't you think?''

"I suppose so."

"Then shall we head to the supper? I'm starving."

"Good idea," Susan agreed as Janet started the car.

The second seating of the supper was well under way when Susan and Janet walked in the door. The church hall was filled and a long line wound its way around the wall as people waited patiently to get to the tables containing food. Beans, baked in a hole dug on the opposite side of the church from the cemetery, were featured, of course. But dozens of casseroles offered a larger choice. Homemade bread, biscuits, and rolls were piled high on plastic trays, and glasses of iced tea and fruit punch were being poured by aproned women into paper cups from frosty metal pitchers. Susan was wondering if there was a chance that someone would see the deputy and offer to let them cut into the line when she heard her name. Kathleen was calling to her from a position near the tables.

"Come on!" She waved her over. "I saved you a place."

"Good girl." Janet approved. "But I think I see some people who might help us. Save a seat for me at your table, and I'll join you there."

"Everything looks wonderful." Kathleen was peering ahead at the food when Susan joined her. "I have some interesting information that means probably absolutely nothing."

"The phone call?" Susan asked, smiling at the man who was looking over Kathleen's shoulder.

"Yes. It was from a friend of mine at Customs. I worked on a few narcotics cases with him back in the city, and I knew he would help me out."

"Even on Saturday?"

"The man's good—and he's compulsive. If you called him in the middle of the night, he'd get up and find out what you needed to know. He'll die of a heart attack one of these days. Until then, he's invaluable."

"Customs?" Susan was confused.

"Remember Humphrey Taylor was abroad all those years. The U.S. Customs Office would know of anything significant that went on in that time."

Susan had become very aware of the attention they were getting. The people in line were quieter than normal, and she was sure that everyone had identified them as the summer people who found the body. "Maybe you should tell me after we sit down. Janet's going to join us then."

"Fine. Grab a plate. I think we're finally going to eat." Kathleen looked over the table. "Everything looks wonderful."

They spent the next few minutes progressing from greed to guilt, filling their plates to overflowing before allowing their minds to consider the chosen calories.

"Hi. Want to sit here?"

Susan looked down and found her favorite bookstore owner's nephew waving to the four seats surrounding him. "I'd enjoy your company," he added, glancing at the three girls who were giggling away a few spaces behind Susan and Kathleen.

"Great. Thanks. This is Kathleen Gordon. She's staying with me this summer. And, to be honest, I don't remember your name."

"Nathan Foster." He stood up politely, offering his hand.

"Nathan is helping out his aunt at TIME HAS CRITICIZED—the bookstore I told you about."

" 'Told' is not the word," Kathleen said to the young man. "She comes back from Maine with piles of wonderful books and raves about your aunt's store all winter long. I'm planning on getting over there as soon as possible. I'm looking for books on rock gardening and herbs, and old mystery novels—and, of course, women's novels. And my husband is interested in graphics, and maybe you have something about that. . . ."

"He has everything," Susan assured her. "And we'll go over there as soon as we have a free minute."

"Has the little girl been found?" Nathan asked. "My aunt says that half of the people who came into the store today were talking about the search party. Sounds like they've been pretty thorough."

"That's good to hear, but they haven't found her yet," Susan answered.

"Everyone on the island is talking about the gunshots this afternoon," Nathan continued, showing an ability to talk and eat at the same time that Susan had often observed in the young.

"Were you there?" Kathleen asked.

"In one of the kayaks. I'm new at the sport and I didn't do very well. . . . To be honest, I was one of the last three paddlers to come in. So I didn't see what happened. And I don't think I heard anything worth reporting. I heard about the gunshots, of course, but by that time, it was a little like playing telephone. As every kayaker came in, the ones who had arrived previously told him or her about the shots. By the time I arrived, you would have thought that the mayor was lying on the dock in a pool of blood—at least. Imagine my surprise when I found him here gorging on the last two servings of crab casserole!''

"It's not a situation that would encourage accuracy," Kathleen agreed. ''You didn't happen to hear anything that might help us find the person who was shooting, did you?''

"Well, a lot of people don't think the mayor was the target.''

"Why not?'' Susan was barely willing to pause in her eating for just two words. The food was wonderful.

"I don't quite understand it, but apparently he's one of the most popular people on the island. He's honest, not having an affair with anyone's wife, kind to children, does a lot for the year-round community, et cetera, et cetera. Maybe not a saint, but certainly not someone to inspire a murder, is the general point of view.''

"Any idea who was being shot at?'' Kathleen asked.

"No, but . . . Maybe I shouldn't say anything.''

"Speak,'' Susan ordered, stuffing a fried oyster in her mouth.

"Its just an impression,'' Nathan said quietly. "I don't want you to jump to any conclusions based on something like this. . . .''

"Please tell us,'' Janet Shapiro asked, sitting down beside the young man. "We won't hold you to it if you're wrong. And if you're right, you'll be helping a lot of people. It's important to know the truth here. We're a small island, and something very dramatic has happened. We need to find out who's responsible before we all start suspecting each other— and destroy our community.''

"Well . . . there was a man who kayaked with me most of the way. I guess we were the worst of the group except for Gillian. . . .''

"Who?''

"Gillian's my girlfriend. We kept each other company during the race. She's teaching me to paddle, in fact. She could have gone faster, but . . .'' He looked at the faces of the three women and changed his topic. "You want me to get to the point, don't you?''

"Sounds like a good idea to me," Janet said with a kind smile on her face.

"There was a man in a kayak who started the race in the beginning of the pack, but somewhere along the way, he slowed down. I stayed in the back the entire way. I knew I'd never win. I was just doing it for the experience. . . . Okay, I am getting to the point. The man I'm talking about joined me at the rear for about the last quarter of the race. I noticed him right around Eagle's Nest Island. And he stayed near us from there until the finish line."

"Do you know who the man is?" Janet asked.

"I didn't then, but someone in the crowd, after we finished, said that he was staying out with the man who was murdered. Anyway, when he got back to the dock, he got confused or he heard the story wrong or something. . . ."

"And?" Kathleen prompted.

"And he thought that it was his wife who had been shot. . . . I thought that might be significant."

"It may be," Janet agreed. "Tell us exactly what happened."

"Well, I'm not completely sure. Gillian and I arrived at the dock at almost the same time he did. There were a lot of people wandering around, but I didn't think about it at the time. I didn't expect a lot of cheering fans. For heaven's sake, we came in last. But people were there, and a large number of them were kneeling on the dock. I know now they were looking at the bullet holes. At the time I had a vague idea that I'd stumbled into a group of Muslims praying—which should tell you something. I'm not used to being in a kayak. I was beat. Know what I mean?"

"We'll take everything you say with a grain of salt," Janet assured him.

"We understand that you don't want to be blamed if your impressions are wrong. We'll take your fatigue into account," Kathleen said.

"Go on." Susan still hadn't cleaned her plate.

"Okay. Well, as we arrived at the dock, a few of the people around noticed us and clapped rather weakly and ran to hold our kayaks while we climbed out. You know how the dock gets thinner at the end? Well, Gillian and I were on one side, and this man was on the other. I don't know if he got there before or after we did.

"But Gillian asked what was going on, and my aunt, who had closed the store just so she could see our finish, said that there had been gunshots—or something like that. I really don't remember exactly. Anyway, Gillian was in front of me and she said something, and then I realized that the man across the way was saying that his wife had been shot."

"Not 'killed'?" Janet asked.

"No, definitely 'shot,' because that's when I figured out that everyone was looking for holes in the dock."

"And what happened then?"

"My aunt explained that only the mayor had been shot and that the injury was minor. That no one had been seriously hurt. And that's all. . . . It's probably stupid, but his reaction struck me as strange. It was almost as though he was expecting his wife to be shot. Unless I misunderstood . . ."

"How did he find out that she wasn't shot?" Janet asked.

"He saw her. She was standing on the other dock. The part that's closer to land. The part that's stationary."

"What did this man look like? Was he blond or brunet?" Kathleen asked.

"I don't know."

"What?" Susan had finished her dinner, but that was the only question she needed to ask.

"He was wearing a wet suit. One of those things that completely covers his hair. Only his face was exposed."

"Then what did his wife look like?" Kathleen asked.

"I have no idea. There were a half dozen women standing around. He pointed to them and said something like 'No, I'm wrong. There she is,' or something like that. I haven't been very helpful, have I?" he asked, obviously disappointed.

"You've been very, very helpful," Susan assured him.

He looked doubtful, but he stood up and said, "Then I'd

better get back to the shop. My aunt is going to need help tonight.''

''You're certainly making her summer easier,'' Susan said, watching at least a half dozen young girls sigh as Nathan flipped his ponytail over his shoulder and left the room. ''And what did you learn?'' she quietly asked Kathleen. ''You promised to tell me about it at dinner, remember.''

''I don't think it's significant.''

''You sound like Nathan,'' Susan hissed in her ear.

Janet and Kathleen exchanged looks. ''Listen,'' Susan said, ''I know I'm upset, but it's my house, my vacation, my traditions—''

''What I learned is that Humphrey Taylor stopped working about four years before returning to the United States,'' Kathleen said, eager to forestall any more family stories— interesting though they were, she added to herself. ''It's probably not significant at all,'' she said aloud.

Janet Shapiro leaned across the table. ''Everything about him could be important. What did your source say?'' Most of the people were leaving the hall, and the three women could speak without being overheard.

''Humphrey Taylor was very successful in the Mideast. He started his own company after the first five years there and he made a lot of money. My source was a little fuzzy about exactly what part of the oil business Humphrey worked in, but whatever it was, he was very successful. No problems that would appear in anything official, and nothing in his file that indicated there was any reason for officials to be suspicious of him . . .''

''Like transporting weapons?'' Susan asked, thinking of the spy novels that her husband loved.

''Or drugs. Or anything. He looks like a man who worked hard and got rich in the oil industry, and there's no indication that he was anything but. He didn't get involved in politics. He didn't run off with the daughters of tribal chiefs.''

''And then he just quit?'' Janet asked.

''Cashed it all in and came home, is how my friend put it,'' Kathleen said, looking at the note in her hand. ''There's nothing suspicious about it, by the way. The time was right to sell—he made a whole lot of money. And he was probably tired of living abroad. Maybe he missed his family.''

"So he came home, wrecked his brother's marriage, and adopted that family?'' Susan asked sarcastically.

"I don't know why. I only know what happened. And that's what I know.''

"What we don't know is what type of person Humphrey Taylor was,'' Janet mused.

"Too bad he died before we met him,'' Kathleen said, popping the last piece of roll in her mouth.

"But Janet's right. That's what we have to find out,'' Susan agreed. "Why don't we go pick up the girls? Maybe they can tell us something. And we should stop at home for warm clothing and bug spray.''

"Where are we going?'' Kathleen asked.

"Square dancing on a mountain.''

THIRTEEN

Susan and Kathleen had picked up Theresa and Tierney in the middle of Monsieur Touve's party, and now they were driving back to Susan's house.

"I don't see why we shouldn't go to the pie-eating contest. They might have blueberry, and that's my favorite. Theresa, I'm sure Daddy would let us if we asked him," Tierney was explaining.

"How can we be in the parade and enter the pie-eating contest, too, Tierney? That woman with the long red braids said that the contest starts as soon as the parade is over. What are we going to do with Karma? We can't bring her to a place with so much food. She'd pull our arms off," Theresa asked.

"I wish Titania were here to take care of Karma. She should be. She's her dog!"

Susan looked over her shoulder at the pouting child in the backseat and tried to cheer her up by changing the subject. "How was Monsieur Touve's party? I understand he's a wonderful host."

Tierney perked up and chattered about the event they had just left. "It was fun. There were a lot of neat people there. We met a lobster fisherman and his wife, who is a modern dancer, and there was a woman with green hair. And everyone was talking about the shooting this afternoon. Know what I think? I think it's a mad sniper and he's going to kill everyone on the island one by one." Tierney seemed to be enjoying the gruesome thought.

"That's what some of Monsieur Touve's guests were saying," Theresa agreed somewhat reluctantly.

"Then Monsieur Touve invited some very silly people to his party. There is no mad sniper on the island. It was probably someone who had been drinking and who just wasn't thinking," Susan insisted, not believing a word she was saying.

"That's what Theresa said," Tierney agreed, looking to her older sister for confirmation. "She said it couldn't possibly have anything to do with us or with Uncle Humphrey's death."

Theresa smiled at Tierney, and Susan thought how quickly they were being forced to grow up because of the mistakes adults around them were making, and how sad it was. They were just arriving at the turnoff to Susan's home, and the girls had been chattering throughout the drive.

"Are you two sure that you want to go all the way to Acadia? The dancing doesn't start until midnight, and we probably won't get back here until seven or eight in the morning. And with the parade and everything else tomorrow, you'll be pretty tired. . . ."

"Excuse me? How long does this thing last?" Kathleen asked.

"All night!" Tierney bounced in her seat, excited at the thought.

"She's kidding." Kathleen stared at Susan.

"No, she's right. It starts with square dancing at one of the schools in Bar Harbor."

"When?"

"At exactly one minute past midnight on July Fourth. They dance for a few hours and then there's a big pancake breakfast. And when that's over, at about four or four-thirty, everyone gets in their cars and drives up to the top of Cadillac Mountain."

"In Acadia National Park," Tierney sang out from the backseat.

"And then there's more dancing in the parking lot at the top of the mountain. . . ."

"And how long does that last?"

"Until the sun comes up—or until it's well past the time it should have come up. The weather in Maine can be unpredictable."

"And if the weather is bad, they don't dance?" Kathleen asked, searching the clear blue sky for a cloud or two.

"No, if the weather is bad, they don't dance until the sun comes up—that could be days—but they do dance. No one ever let a little rain spoil their fun. But you girls might want to come back early; you know you'll all want to be awake for the fireworks tomorrow night," Susan called over her shoulder into the backseat. Actually, she knew that they wouldn't be tired. If they were, they could nap in the car. She and Kathleen were sure to be exhausted, though.

"You, of all people, wouldn't want to break a family tradition, would you?" Kathleen teased her friend, trying to keep the mood light. They had talked privately on the way to pick up the girls, and they had agreed that they were worried about Titania. Very worried. After all, someone was running around shooting people, and it very well might have something to do with the Taylor household. But they didn't want the younger sisters to know that.

"I wonder how Karma is," Susan said, discovering that she really did care—a little.

"She's fine." Tierney spoke with assurance.

"She just goes to sleep when she's alone," Theresa added quickly. "But she'll be happy to see us."

"And have dinner," Susan said, pulling the car up to the house.

"You're right. We'd better get her right away—she must be starving. Come on, Tierney." Theresa was out of the car almost before it stopped.

"They can take care of her. Let's go collect the stuff we need for tonight."

"I want to call home," Kathleen said. "If my mother or Jerry call late, they're going to wonder why we're not here. They probably think we're getting a lot of extra sleep." They were in the house now, and Kathleen headed upstairs while

Susan went to the kitchen. She'd better pack some munchies. Knowing Kathleen, she'd be hungry before they got to bed, and the girls were always ready for a snack; pancakes wouldn't be served until the middle of the night. She grabbed a saucepan and went to the refrigerator. A thermos of hot chocolate might be just the thing. A few minutes later, Kathleen found her still staring into its brightly lit interior.

"What are you . . . ?" she began her question.

"When did we buy milk?" Susan interrupted urgently.

"Last night when we went shopping. There was a whole half gallon. Why?"

"Look." Susan pointed at the empty carton on the top shelf of the refrigerator. "Wait a second," she added, shutting the door and looking through the cabinets. "We're also missing crackers and cheese, and some cookies." She peered into the Pepperidge Farm box.

The two women stared at each other. Kathleen spoke first. "She's as safe here as she could be anyplace else."

"That's probably true. And I have a way of making her safer." Susan reached for the phone. "And I'll get to work on that as soon as I call Janet Shapiro and tell her to call off the search."

"I wish you had told those people they couldn't follow us," Tierney complained, grimacing out the back window of the Jeep at the BMW behind. "I don't like them. I don't know why they came to stay with us. No one likes them."

"Mommy and Daddy have been friends with them for a long time; they must like them," her sister protested.

"They don't act like they like them. Everyone is so nervous! No one is having any fun! I thought we'd all be happy if Uncle Humphrey died, but it's just making everything worse!"

Susan looked at Kathleen. "I think you should be careful not to say anything like that in public," Susan suggested carefully.

"But it's true!" the child protested.

"You don't want everyone to think you murdered him, do

you, stupid! You should learn to keep your mouth shut!'' Theresa spit out the words angrily.

Susan looked in her rearview mirror at the older girl's face. Theresa was pale, lips clenched between her teeth. It was hard to gather information with them around, but she was glad that she was able to protect these two—and now Titania—from . . . from what? she asked herself. Could anyone honestly believe that one of them was a murderer? She moved her mirror and saw the fury in Tierney's face and decided that maybe she had made the right decision. "Do you think your mother or your father will come see the dancing?" she asked, keeping her tone casual.

"They didn't say anything about it, but maybe." Tierney cheered up at the thought. "Are we going to be able to dance?"

"Probably not. This is really just for people who know how to square-dance. But it's lots of fun to watch, believe me. It's a fairly long drive. You could take a nap, you know."

"I'm not tired," Tierney insisted. She proved her lie by falling asleep in less than five minutes.

"Had you ever met your uncle Humphrey?" Kathleen quietly asked Theresa when her sister was breathing deeply. "Before he came home from the Mideast?"

"No. We'd heard about him, of course. My father used to tell us great stories about how when he and my uncle were boys they used to get in trouble dressing the dog in their best clothing and then walk it down the street—and how they built a raft and took it out in the middle of a river without anyone knowing, and it fell apart and they had to be rescued by the Coast Guard. Of course, Uncle Humphrey was a lot older than that when we met him."

"But you knew that he was in Alaska and the Mideast, didn't you?" Susan asked.

"I think Alaska was before we were born, but we knew about Saudi Arabia and Kuwait and all. He used to send us really neat presents for Christmas. Like belly dancer dolls that even have tiny finger cymbals on their fingers. And these wonderful little carved boxes. And funny beads—worry beads, they're called—that are antique amber. They have real bugs embedded in them. It sounds gross, but it isn't,'' she assured the adults.

"Did you or your parents ever visit him when he was abroad?"

"My father did. Just once, that I can remember. It was a few years ago. Maybe four or five. It was when my grandparents died. I think Uncle Humphrey was in Egypt then. My father brought us back those funny scarves that men over there wear on their heads. And a beautiful necklace of some blue stones for my mother.''

"Lapis lazuli," Susan suggested.

"That's right!" Theresa sounded pleased. "I think it's a really pretty name, don't you? Exotic."

"This may sound like a stupid question, and I'm not trying to pry, but it might be important. . . ." Susan began.

"I know. Janet Shapiro said that we should tell you anything you want to know, so it's okay."

"Did you like your uncle before you found out that he was going to marry your mother? Before you were told about the divorce?"

There was a silence while the girl thought over her answer. "I don't think so," she began slowly. "So much has happened that it's a little hard to remember. I know that sounds stupid. . . ."

"It doesn't at all. And it's not your age. Most adults would find the changes you've been through to be more than a little confusing. I'd like to hear about it, though, even if you can't remember exactly."

"You see, we were so excited about meeting him!" the child burst out. "We'd heard about him for so many years, and then, when we found out that he was actually going to live near us after all this time, we could hardly believe it. Titania was studying the Mideast in school, and she thought she could get him to come in and talk to her class, and we thought he would tell us stories about camel rides and the pyramids—no one else that we know has an uncle who's lived in places like that. So," she continued, her voice changing, "I guess we were expecting too much."

"So you didn't like him right away," Susan guessed.

"We didn't even get to see him right away. We wanted to go to the airport to meet him, and my parents wouldn't let us. Some dumb excuse about us having to go to a choir rehearsal at church."

Susan took that with a grain of salt, knowing how far children will go to get out of something that they didn't want to do. "But he did come and stay at your house, didn't he?" she guessed.

"Yes, but he walked in the door and hardly had a chance to say hello—to meet us really—when my mother said that he had terrible jet lag after being on a plane for eleven hours and that he had to go to bed right away. Then he was up in the middle of the night. I heard him talking to my father."

Susan had always wondered why jet lag was a problem for adults and not children, but there wasn't time to speculate on that. "But when you did get a chance to talk to him? What did you think then?"

"He was dull! Boring! Not at all like someone who traveled all over the world, more like a businessman, just like anybody else!"

"That must have been a disappointment," Kathleen said, glad her smile didn't show.

"And he wasn't friendly. He kept saying that getting used to his new job was keeping him busy, but he just stayed in his apartment and hardly even spent any time with us."

"Did he speak at Titania's school?"

"He said he would, but he kept putting it off and so it just didn't happen."

"Did you notice that he was falling in love with your mother?" Susan asked, hating to have to inquire into something so hurtful to the girls.

"Not at all. I didn't even think that she liked him, but my father says that may have been something called a ploy. That means that she was trying to get everyone to think that she didn't like him when she was falling in love. There's a girl in my class who's allowed to watch anything she wants on

TV, and she says that happens all the time. But I didn't think someone like my mother would do that,'' she added quietly.

"Maybe she didn't have any choice. Sometimes adults fall in and out of love. . . .'' Susan began, not really meaning what she was going to end up saying.

"She had a choice. She could have stayed with my father.''

There was no answer to that, and Susan wasn't going to insult the girl by pretending otherwise. "Theresa, did your parents' divorce come as a shock to you? I know Titania says that it did to her.''

"We had no idea. They had arguments, but everybody fights. Of course, they had been fighting more and more recently, I guess. But I didn't ever hear them talk about divorce. My mother used to have this joke about it. She'd say that she would never divorce him, but she'd kill him! Oh, I didn't mean that! She would never kill anybody. Never!''

"It's an old saying, Theresa. I don't think she meant it any more than the millions of other women who say things like that.'' Susan was afraid the child would shut up and they wouldn't learn anything else.

"That's right. A lot of people say that type of thing. That's what I told Titania, but she wouldn't believe me.''

"Titania?'' Susan repeated quietly.

"Yeah. Titania overheard my parents talking about how Uncle Humphrey had destroyed their life. But there's this girl in my class whose parents got a divorce, and she told me that it was her father's secretary's fault. I was talking to my mother about that—this was last year before she and my father split up—and she said that outsiders don't cause divorces. That divorce is the result of the actions of the people inside the marriage.''

"Uh-huh.'' Susan didn't know whether she agreed or disagreed, but she certainly hoped Theresa would keep talking.

"Titania says that Uncle Humphrey hated my father, that he wanted to destroy him, to take everything that he had—his wife, and his house, and his family. She said that we couldn't let that happen. We weren't going to let him have us. We were going to drive him away.''

"And that's what you were trying to do when you put pudding in his pockets and removed one of the cellar stairs?"

"Yes."

"Do you know why Titania is hiding?"

"She said she had to. She said everything would be all right as long as she stayed away. And I'm not going to say any more."

"Good. Shut up," her sister mumbled, turning over and pulling her sweater up around her ears.

"What did you think of Humphrey when you got here? Was he like you remembered him being?"

"Are any of us the way we were when we were young?"

Leave it to a psychiatrist to think he was answering a question by asking a question, Susan thought. "But you judge people professionally. That's what you're trained to do. I just wondered what you thought about Humphrey. You knew him when you were young, didn't you?"

"I grew up with Ted and Humphrey, in fact. We lived about two blocks away from each other in an old-fashioned town—the type of place that just doesn't exist anymore. Humphrey was older, of course. But he must have been very tolerant, because we spent a lot of time with him. I remember we all went camping together—the summer before I was in eighth grade. Just the three of us and that damn dog of Ted's. It poured rain. We spent two days in a dirty, leaky four-man tent with a smelly golden retriever—and we had a wonderful time. I've thought of that trip a lot over the years. Children are not small adults, and don't let anyone tell you differently. Any sane adult would have hated the experience.

"Of course, we saw Humphrey less and less every year after he went to college. That's usually true. The people who leave home tend to disconnect, and by the time they have their degree, they really don't return to the fold unless there's a real occasion—a ceremony usually. Humphrey went off to Alaska right after college. He did graduate work at the University of Alaska, as well as working, I believe. I know he was at Ted and Tricia's wedding, but if he came home after that, it was during a time when I was away. I don't remember seeing him again until last week.''

''But you stayed good friends with Ted over the years?'' Susan asked.

''I hired his firm to design my first clinic. We were both surprised when we rediscovered each other. But you know how it is with old friends; we introduced our wives and started getting together when we were in the same town. Which wasn't often back then.''

Susan and Paul turned their attention back to the dancers who were whirling around, skirts flying, heels stomping. The annual square dance was quite a sight. Except she noticed that Paul wasn't really watching. He was keeping an eye on his wife, who was at the other side of the large gymnasium.

Susan glanced around the room. Kathleen had agreed to take care of the girls while Susan collected more information. She spied her yawning in a corner. Theresa was standing nearby, talking earnestly with a girl who looked the same age. Tierney was being given a private dancing lesson by a cheerful man who looked old enough to be her great-grandfather. Apparently square dancing was marvelous exercise; Susan hoped she would have as much energy when she was his age.

''When did you meet the Harters?'' She continued asking Paul questions.

Well, that got his attention. ''Why do you assume that we knew each other before arriving on the island?''

''Your wives seem to be good friends,'' she answered, pleased to think that she had gotten some reaction from him.

''How long have you been coming to these things?''

He seemed to be much more comfortable asking than answering questions, Susan thought. ''Twenty-five years. Maybe more. They've been going on almost thirty, I think.''

''Unusual event,'' he commented noncommittally.

Susan, ready to defend her traditions, opened her mouth,

but shut it before leaping into an unnecessary battle. "How did you like the race today?" she asked, changing topics.

"You didn't hear about my disaster?" he asked, attempting to laugh.

"No . . ." Susan still didn't know if he had been the paddler who trailed with Nathan and Gillian or if that had been Ryan. Now, she thought, it looked like . . .

"I capsized before the race was half-over. Stupid beginner's mistake, which makes it more embarrassing, of course. I was helping another paddler who had gotten tangled in one of those floating boxes that the lobstermen use to store their catch, and I didn't pay enough attention to what I was doing. Naturally, the next thing I knew, there I was in the water. I really thought I had a chance of coming in with the winners, too. I had been taking it easy, waiting to pick up speed at the end of the race." He shook his head. "Dumb, dumb mistake. By the time I had gotten back in and pumped out my kayak—or, in this case, your kayak—I knew I wasn't going to finish in the top half. So I just turned around and went back the other way. There were some large birds on one of the small islands we'd passed that I wanted to check out. And besides—" he laughed at his own weakness in an intentionally good-natured way "—I hate to lose. Could have ruined my whole day.

"Would you excuse me? I think my wife wants . . ." He hurried off, it not being necessary to finish that sentence to civilized people.

Susan turned away. Paul Briane might hate losing, but what Susan hated was being taken for a fool. Where was that man's wife?

But Judy Briane found her before Susan had even begun to search.

"We need to talk," the woman insisted before Susan could even offer a polite greeting. "Why don't we go sit on those chairs over there?" She pointed. "There seems to be some privacy."

Susan followed the other woman across the room to where

a half dozen folding chairs had been set up and then abandoned, out of the path of the dancers.

"Does this thing last all night?" Judy Braine asked, being careful not to muss her washed-silk skirt as she sat down.

"Yes."

"What? Oh, you're kidding, aren't you?"

"No, I'm not. It lasts till sunrise. There will be food served soon, though."

"Not to me. I'm going to head back to the Taylors' house. I don't care if I find both Ted and Tricia dead in the middle of the living room floor. I'm too old to stay up this late."

"I hate to admit it, but you may be right," Susan said, sitting down and yawning. "Do you like the Taylors?" she asked, deciding that it was too late to bother with tact.

"Not really. And I certainly didn't like Humphrey. What a bore," she said, picking a piece of lint from her suede sandals. "He kept telling stories about things he and Ted did when they were young. The man had spent the past twenty-five years in fascinating parts of the world, and he talks about some small town in New Jersey. A complete bore."

Susan remembered how Titania had thought that Humphrey wanted her family. Maybe the poor man had been lonely all these years, she thought, realizing that no one was upset that Humphrey was dead. No one seemed to care. Even Tricia hadn't expressed a whole lot of grief. Susan stared at the dancers. The late hours hadn't dampened their enthusiasm!

But Judy was continuing her story. "I'm here because of my husband, to be honest. Ted asked us here in a way that made Paul think it was important that we come—an obligation of an old friend or something. Paul is very big on relationships. He thinks they're the backbone of the individual—sort of an extreme concept of 'you shall be known by the friends you keep,' or something. So when Ted called a few months ago, we put aside our plans for a few weeks in Montauk, and here we are. Wherever the hell this is. There's some good shopping up here, though. A lot of artists seem to live in Maine. Heaven knows why."

Because it's beautiful, inexpensive, tolerant of individual differences, and a whole lot of other things that you're too dumb to see, Susan lectured silently. "I couldn't believe the shooting this afternoon," was what she said, hoping to get Judy's thoughts on another topic. "I wasn't anywhere nearby, of course. But I heard that you were actually talking with the mayor when he was wounded."

Judy Briane glanced across the room, where her husband was talking with Sally and Ryan (so much for his excuse to leave Susan), before answering. "I thought the popping sounds were just some more of the fireworks that children in this place seem to love so much."

"But when the mayor was shot," Susan prompted.

"To be honest, I didn't even know then that something serious was going on. He leapt up a little and yelled ouch. I thought he'd been attacked by a blackfly or mosquito. He didn't really get shot, you know. Just grazed actually. But, of course, when someone said there was shooting, I was scared to death. I could have been killed, for heaven's sake. We were terrified. . . ."

"We?"

"Sally and I. We were there together. Waiting for our husbands to arrive. Sally and I are always together waiting for our husbands to arrive."

Not always, was what Susan thought. Not always.

"But that's what I want to talk to you about," Judy continued. "I want police protection. Sally and I both do. We could have been the targets. We could have been killed. You must talk with that deputy. She just laughed when I did, but maybe she'd listen to you."

"I don't think it will help you, but I'll speak with her when I see her," Susan said, knowing it would do absolutely no good. "But why would someone want to kill you or Sally . . . ?"

"There's Sally now," Judy interrupted. "I hope she talked the men into leaving."

Sally was walking around the dancers, waving at them. "We're going to leave. Ryan and Paul are exhausted after the race today, and Tricia will probably insist that we attend some of the town's celebration tomorrow. . . ."

"Oh, yes, that's what we're here for. To see one of the last old-fashioned Fourth of July celebrations in America or some such garbage. How Norman Rockwell!" Judy yawned. "Let's go."

Susan said good night and stayed in her chair, her eyes moving from the two couples to Theresa and Tierney. The girls were having a wonderful night. One of the nicest things about Maine is that people always have time for what's important, like paying attention to children. She saw a group of women carrying plates out of the kitchen to tables that had been set up on the stage at one end of the room, and got up to offer her help. Tomorrow she would have to figure out a way to protect Titania while allowing her to participate in some of the day's activities.

All three girls should have a chance to participate in "the last old-fashioned Fourth of July celebration in America"— before they really did become just an artist's rendering of the past.

FOURTEEN

"I ADMIT IT, YOU WERE RIGHT. IT WAS WORTH IT. THERE was something about the sunrise over the water and the dancers swirling around. . . ."

"And the happy faces of those two in the backseat," Susan added.

"Definitely that," Kathleen agreed. "They're charming little girls. I just wish Titania wasn't missing all this."

"I've been thinking about that, and I have a plan," Susan said, steering her car carefully over the winding roads.

"Well, just let me know what I need to do."

"I will."

They drove along in silence for a while, with Susan remembering other Fourth of July celebrations, and Kathleen dozing lightly.

"I feel," Susan started quietly, "that we're missing something major and that, if we find it, everything will fall together and we'll have our murderer."

Kathleen peeked over her shoulder into the backseat.

"Don't worry. They're dead to the world. You know how children sleep."

"Well, then," Kathleen whispered, "I've been thinking about it, too. Maybe we should look for motive. Everyone at the Taylor house had the opportunity and the means to kill Humphrey, but who had the motive?"

"Ted, certainly," Susan said even more quietly. "Revenge for taking his wife and family—and his dream house, for that

175

matter. Maybe he killed his brother hoping to get it all back. It's certainly possible.''

''I hate to say it, but it's probable. That's got to be where Janet is looking.''

''But there must be others,'' Susan insisted. ''What if Humphrey found out about Sally and Paul? One of them might have killed him to make sure their relationship remained a secret.''

''Why is it a secret? There are no children involved. Why don't they just get two divorces and remarry?''

''Good question. I suppose one of them doesn't want that to happen—or maybe they're both happy being married and having an affair on the side. Would someone commit a murder just to maintain the status quo? Have you been thinking about the shooting, too?''

''Yes, but wait,'' Kathleen suggested. ''We should consider Tricia's motive first. She might have discovered that she didn't love Humphrey after all—that she'd made a mistake.''

''So she kills him? Why not just get another divorce?'' Susan asked. ''Why did she suddenly fall in love with Humphrey in the first place? No one seems terribly impressed with him. What made her suddenly give up her first marriage and leap into a second anyway?''

''Just because outsiders don't understand the attraction doesn't mean that it isn't real.'' Kathleen, a beautiful young woman very happily married to an older widower, reminded her. ''Besides, she didn't lose all that much. She has primary responsibility for her children, both houses. . . . All she did was exchange one brother for the other.''

''That's an interesting way of looking at it.'' Susan drove along, wondering who had gained from Humphrey's death, until Kathleen asked a question.

''Do you think the murder was planned or that it happened on impulse?''

''Probably planned.'' The answer came slowly. ''Humphrey was probably lured over to my house on some pretext or other and then killed. The house wasn't occupied at the time, and no one except Burt knew when we would show up.

It was possible that the body might not be discovered for some time.''

"Maybe." Kathleen sounded doubtful. "It's really too bad that we haven't been able to get hold of Burt Jamison.''

"You think this had to do with the house being just half-opened? I was wondering about that myself. Do you think someone killed Humphrey in the living room and then put the shutters back up—but why? What sense would that make?''

"None. If we had some sense, we'd have some answers—and we might know who killed Humphrey.''

"How about the shooting yesterday?'' Susan asked, thinking that they had fit a week's worth of activities into the last twenty-four hours. "I've been wondering if we have any idea where either Ted or Tricia were during that time.''

"Supposedly Ryan and Paul were both in their kayaks racing around the island. If it had to do with our group of suspects, it must have been Ted or Tricia. We should find out. Surely . . .'' Kathleen started, and then stopped.

"You're right." Susan agreed with what Kathleen hadn't said. "It couldn't be Titania. She's only thirteen, for heaven's sake.''

"I just hope her age protects her from the sniper," Kathleen said.

"We have to hurry and figure this out.''

"And watch after these two and try to get their older sister to some of the activities so that she has something good to remember about this time, et cetera, et cetera. How do you expect to get all this done?'' Kathleen muttered.

"We're mothers. We're good at doing a lot of things at the same time," Susan reminded her friend, a determined look on her face.

"Did you see that sign? We just passed it," Kathleen asked as they arrived on the island.

"The one announcing the 'Red, White, and Blueberry Breakfast' at the Grange hall? It's a waffle breakfast. They serve huge Belgian waffles with blueberries, strawberries, and whipped cream. You're not hungry, are you?'' she asked, disbelief in her eyes.

"We are.'' Theresa spoke from the backseat, surprising the women.

"We're starving,'' her sister confirmed.

"Well, we can't have starvation on the Fourth of July,'' Susan said. "Let's stop—if you're sure you don't need to get home and finish your float. The parade starts at noon, you know.''

"Oh, it's been finished . . .'' Tierney began, and then stopped, giving her sister a guilty look.

"I think they already know,'' Theresa said to her sister, and then turned to the adults. "You had Mrs. Shapiro call off the search, didn't you? I heard someone talking about it at the dance. How did you figure out where Titania was hiding?''

"I should have realized earlier than I did,'' Susan answered. "Karma would never have happily gone into the boathouse unless Titania was already in there. That dog is a social beast. And, then, there was food missing from my kitchen.''

"We really should go back to her,'' Theresa said.

"Don't worry. Halsey's been looking after your sister— and she's a great cook. They're probably sitting in my kitchen eating blueberry pancakes this minute.''

"We are still not going to talk to you about Titania,'' Theresa assured them.

"That's right. We promised her,'' Tierney agreed.

"Then why don't I drop you three off at the breakfast and then head on home to make sure everything's okay there. I can come back and pick you up in an hour. To be honest, if I eat one more meal, my jeans are going to burst.''

"Great!'' Kathleen picked up the cue as the car pulled into the parking lot of the pretty white hall. Red, white, and blue crepe billowed from the rafters, pots of geraniums were perched on every windowsill, and trios of American flags hung on either side of the deep blue front door.

"Wow. I think I smell whipped cream," Tierney yelled, spilling out of the car. She was followed closely by her sister.

"They do serve coffee, don't they?" Kathleen asked, slamming the car door behind her.

Susan was surprised to find Ted Taylor sitting in the light blue rocker on her front porch.

"I had to get away," he said. The early morning sun caused his red beard to sparkle, and Susan remembered how she had first spied Titania's shining cap of hair across the cove.

"I thought you were staying at the inn," Susan said, confused.

"I spent the night in my . . . in my house," he explained, looking a little embarrassed. "After all, she was my wife for years, and I did design and build that house. . . ."

"You don't have to explain to me."

"Everything would have been fine if our houseguests hadn't returned in the middle of the night," he ended rather belligerently, and then calmed down. "I'm sorry. I'm a little high-strung today."

"That's certainly understandable," Susan said, thinking that this problem was his own damn fault. "Did you just want to get away or did you want to see me for something special?" She was anxious to get inside, to see if there was any sign of Titania—or Halsey—or even Karma.

"I just wanted to get away," he repeated, staring across the cove.

Susan dropped down in another rocker, resting her head and closing her eyes. What made members of this family mistake her home for a retreat? she wondered. She couldn't go inside in case Ted wanted to join her and they discovered his daughter. She decided to ask some questions. If nothing else, maybe he would take offense and leave. "Were you at the race yesterday afternoon? The kayak race around the island?" she asked.

"No. I was wandering around one of the large cemeteries in the middle of the island. It always amazes me how many cemeteries there are here. This island must have been a busy place at one time."

"Very. But the main industries, shipping, fishing, quarrying granite, became smaller and smaller, or, in the case of shipping, nonexistent. Everyone left. But what did you expect to find in the cemetery?"

"Peace. Quiet. The same thing I was looking for this morning, I guess." He looked over at her. "What else do you want to ask me?"

"Do you know where Tricia was during that time?"

"You are investigating systematically, aren't you?"

He sounded a little sarcastic, and Susan resented it. "You asked me for help," she reminded him angrily.

"You're right and I apologize. Trish was probably at the end of the race—the yacht club. At least that's where she told me she was going to be."

"No one saw her there."

"I can't help that," he answered.

"Then maybe you can tell me something else. Why are the Brianes here? And the Harters?"

"The Brianes are here because Paul and I were good friends. You've been asking a lot of questions, so I'm sure you've heard about that. Paul is always talking about a certain camping trip we once took with Humphrey and Chesapeake. . . ."

"Who?"

"Our dog. Well, Paul has turned that trip into part of his own personal mythology; he probably recites that story for all of his patients at one time or another. I just thought it would be nice for Humphrey if Paul was along. Of course, I'd forgotten what a bitch Judy can be. And Paul said something about the Harters moving to Boston, and I guess everyone felt the more the merrier, and that's how Sally and Ryan happened to get invited. Why?"

Susan ignored his question. "Did you know that Paul and Sally are having an affair?"

"Really? You're sure? Why, that old scoundrel. So that's

why he wanted the Harters here. I'll be damned.'' He smiled broadly.

Susan wondered why she got the impression that this new information caused him some relief. ''You didn't know about it then?''

''No, but I sure wish I had. Not that having the Harters here hasn't made everything easier for Trish—you know that Sally was her college roommate, don't you?''

Susan nodded.

''Trish has needed friends around. Things have been very difficult for her the past few months.''

''Do you mean that she'd decided that marrying your brother was a mistake?''

''Not really a mistake as such,'' he answered slowly. ''But it's been very difficult with the girls and everything. You know about that. And it was difficult for Humphrey to adjust to being back here, I think.''

''Why did he come back?'' Susan asked.

''Why?'' Ted seemed surprised by the question. ''I guess he just wanted to come home, got tired of living abroad and all. Most people get more conservative as they grow older, and then they want to return to the things they grew up with, don't you think?''

''I suppose so,'' Susan said absently. She was listening to the sound of a car coming closer. ''I think I'd better check—'' she began, getting up.

''I guess you're finally settled in,'' Ted said, looking around the porch.

''What?''

''Everything's put away. Even the pile of stuff that was dumped here in the corner.

''I guess I'd better be getting back, too,'' he added, as Susan realized simultaneously that the float the girls had built was missing and that Janet Shapiro was joining them.

''I'd better be getting back home,'' Ted repeated, after greeting Janet. ''You'll know where to find me if you need me,'' he added to both women.

''Would you answer just one more question?'' Susan

asked, and continued when he nodded. "Did you hate your brother?"

"No." The words came out slowly. "I loved my brother. At one time, when I was a kid, I loved him more than anything in the world." He nodded and then left.

Susan and Janet watched him cross the lawn, walking toward the path that led to his dream house.

"You think you know who did it, don't you?" Janet asked when Susan didn't speak for a while.

"There are things that don't fit. Every time I think I've got an answer, I realize there are pieces hanging all over the place."

"Sounds like you may be closer than I am. I sure hope so. We don't have much time, you know. A murderer on the loose is a real threat to kill again. Where'd you lose Kathleen and the two Taylor girls, by the way?"

Susan explained their whereabouts, and then asked her own question. "Where's the float?"

"Downtown in the garage of a friend of mine, waiting for the parade to start. Aren't you going to ask about Titania and Halsey? You don't have to. Happens they're the same place the other two girls are. Don't worry. Halsey's family is running the kitchen at the breakfast this year. They'll keep Titania safe and out of sight."

"I keep wondering if she has the missing piece of the puzzle. . . . I need some coffee. Would you like some?"

"Went to the square dancing, did you?" Janet chuckled. "Why don't we join Halsey and the girls? We can go in the back way—remember you're traveling with the sheriff's deputy."

Susan put away thoughts of a shower, clean clothing, a nap. At least the coffee would be good if the Downings had anything to do with making it. "Let's go. Maybe you can fill me in on some things as we drive."

"Like what?"

"Like what you've found out about the shooting yesterday. I keep coming back to that. Could any of the Taylors have taken those shots? Or maybe Ryan?"

"Why don't you ask about Paul? Even if you believe his story about capsizing, he could have had his accident less than halfway around, paddled back, hidden his craft—an ideal boat for concealing a rifle, by the way—taken those shots, and then vanished. Everyone who saw him paddle said he was exceptionally proficient and very strong. And traveling by land and traveling by water are two entirely different things; what's a short distance by land is a real trip by boat—and vice versa. He just might have done it.''

"Ryan?''

"He didn't appear to be a good paddler, but he could have faked his incompetence. I talked to Nathan like you suggested. He was working too hard to keep track of who was around most of the time. And his girlfriend was concentrating on him. She said she was worried that Nathan was way over his skill level.

"It does, by the way, look like Judy was the target—or possibly Sally, although she wasn't quite as close to where the bullets hit. Ted or Tricia could have done it. Tricia admits to being there, and Ted's story of wandering in a deserted cemetery is difficult to believe. But possibly true. And I sure don't know why either of them would want to kill Judy.''

"Or maybe just scare her,'' Susan suggested. "Remember she didn't get hit.''

"Our mayor's a nice man, but he's had a slight ego problem since his wife of thirty years announced that she was sorry, but she'd discovered she was a lesbian, and took off to the Southwest with a very young female lover. I sure wouldn't want to be the one to tell him that his gunshot wound was a warning to someone else!''

Both women were giggling as they pulled the sheriff's car around to the back of the town hall.

They entered through the kitchen door and were immediately wrapped in the fragrance of fresh berries, sugar, and warm dough. Four people stood around a large table in the center of the room. Four round waffle presses lay before each person, and as Susan watched, dozens of waffles were produced and, still steaming, passed through an open hatch to the main meeting room, where they would be doused with fruit and cream and eaten by islanders who came every year for this unusual treat.

Susan spied Halsey making waffles, and hurried over to her. "Where . . . ?" she began her question.

"In the storage room," Halsey answered, pointing to a pine door.

Susan opened the door and peeked in. Three red heads and a fourth with long, golden ears looked up at her from their seats on the floor. Between the girls and the dog were the remains of at least a dozen plates of waffles. "It's good to see you all together again," Susan said, surprised that dogs burped. She had always thought indigestion was a human problem. "I'd like to speak with Titania alone, if you two would go outside for a bit. . . . I'm not going to yell at her," she added, seeing the dismay on Tierney's face. "I just want a few minutes, and then we can all head down to the parade route. Okay?"

"It's okay. Go on out," Titania urged her sisters. "Mrs. Henshaw's trying to help us, remember.

"You don't mind that I was hiding in your boathouse, do you?" she asked as the door closed behind her sisters. "I couldn't think of anyplace else that was safe where I could keep track of Karma." The dog was licking unseen scraps from a plastic plate and didn't bother to acknowledge her name.

"I don't understand why you've been hiding," Susan said. "Did you think someone was going to hurt you?"

"I'm still hiding," Titania insisted stubbornly. "And I'm still not going to tell anyone why."

Susan opened her mouth to speak.

"And I'm not going to tell you why I'm not going to tell you."

Susan tried not to smile. "Okay. But can you tell me why you think there's a message hidden in the pictures carved into the mantel?"

Titania frowned and then thought for more than a few minutes before answering.

Susan was willing to wait.

"I don't want to tell you who I heard it from. . . ."

"That's fine. Just tell me what you feel comfortable telling me."

"All I can say is that there's a picture of someone in the mantel that gives something away—something important!"

" 'Gives something away.' " Susan repeated the phrase, hoping the girl would elaborate.

She didn't.

"And this has to do with someone in your family?"

Under different circumstances, Susan might have been impressed with Titania's caution.

"It has to do with Uncle Humphrey's murder," was all the girl would say.

"Are you in danger?" Susan asked.

"I have to hide," was the only answer.

"Do you want to see the parade? And hide at the same time?"

The girl's eyes sparkled. "Yes. Can I do that?"

"I think so. I have an idea. I just hope it's safe." Susan stood up and pulled a half dozen large gold tablecloths off a shelf behind the girl. "I'm going to borrow these and ask the deputy to take me home. I have some things to do, and then I'll meet you all wherever the float is stashed. We'll put everything together and we'll all get a chance to be part of the parade."

Susan thought the parade was going splendidly. A record number of groups had entered. The island's high school band, an adult community band, a kazoo band from the Baptist retirement home, and two young college students playing bagpipes performed, spaced far enough apart for each to be appreciated. There were marchers as young as three months (in her father's backpack), as well as the island's oldest living veteran. Nathan, seeing that the Taylor girls had chosen a circus theme, had pulled juggling balls from his pocket, made a newspaper hat for his head, and juggled along after them. They were certainly the tallest float. Susan, Janet, and Kathleen had pulled off the wheels and attached the lion cage with Karma inside to the roof rack of her Jeep. Tierney and Theresa, kneeling on a small wooden chest propped across the passenger seat, stuck their heads through the sunroof and waved. Titania, hidden by the improvised curtains, could peek at the action. Everyone was having a wonderful time. Except for Karma, who threw up three times and then fell asleep.

Susan drove slowly along the parade route. She saw Kathleen. She saw Janet. Norman's aunt waved a small whole earth flag as they passed; his girlfriend just smiled proudly. Beth Eaton, wearing one of her own handwoven creations, called out to the girls. Monsieur Touve applauded loudly and yelled, *"Magnifique"* a couple of times. Even Susan's favorite potter allowed a slight smile to bend the corners of his lips as the dog lifted her head and threw up. But there was no sign of Ted or Tricia Taylor. And she didn't see either of the Brianes or the Harters. But Susan wasn't terribly upset. She didn't know exactly who the murderer was, but she had a pretty good idea of why Humphrey was killed, and she thought she might even have the evidence that would prove it. She smiled as one of the parade organizers waved her into a parking spot provided for participants.

Tierney slid down and shimmied into the rear of the Jeep. "That was fun," she exclaimed to her sister. "Did you see everything? Did you see the gigantic sea monster? I think that was my favorite. Do you want me to save you a piece of pie? Or maybe a whole pie? I could enter the contest and just refuse to eat, couldn't I?"

"I'll take care of your sister," Susan insisted, remembering to speak quietly. "She'll get all the blueberry pie she wants. I promise. You and Theresa just have fun. Either Kathleen or I will be waiting for you on the dock by the booth where the fishermen's wives are selling lunch. So be sure to come there right after the contest is over, okay?"

"Okay!" Both girls leapt from the Jeep and ran toward the tables set up with dozens of pies.

"You stay here for a minute. I'm going to get Karma down

from the top of the car and bring her inside to you," Susan said, getting out of the car.

Nathan was still by their side, and with his help, Karma was taken from her improvised cage and, after a short walk to the nearest tree, allowed into the back of the car. One thing about this dog, she certainly appreciated people who cared about her. She put her head in Titania's lap with a loud sigh and closed her eyes.

"Wait here. It may get hot, but I'll be as fast as I can. I just need to find Janet or Kathleen. Then we can figure out what to do with you. Will you be all right?"

Titania nodded, and Susan hurried off.

There were dozens of people to greet, old friends, islanders, people she hadn't seen in almost a year, people she should catch up with, people she wanted to catch up with, but Susan smiled, waved, promised to call, to stop in . . . and continued to look for Kathleen and Janet.

She found them standing by a massive coffee urn that was just beginning to perk. Kathleen was looking a little tired. Janet was sternly lecturing three small children on the dangers of fireworks. She sent them away as Susan appeared. "What can I do?" she asked. "Their grandfather drove all the way to New Hampshire to buy fireworks for the kids. Why doesn't he just cut off their fingers and be done with it?" She ran her hand through her hair. "Don't mind me. I always get like this on the Fourth. And usually we don't have a murderer loose somewhere."

"I told Theresa and Tierney that one of you would meet them here after the pie-eating contest was over."

"I'll do it," Kathleen offered.

"Great. I'm going to spend more time with Titania. I have to convince her to trust me. I'm sure that she must hold the key to all this."

"Have you noticed Ted and Tricia around?" Kathleen asked. "Janet told me about last night, by the way. But if they're getting back together, you'd at least think they might start paying some attention to their children."

"No one's going to argue with you about that. They're

more concerned about their houseguests than their own children. . . .'' Susan started, and then stopped suddenly and grabbed Kathleen's arm. ''That's it. They worry more about their houseguests than their own children. I can't believe that we didn't see it before. You stay here. I'm going back to Titania. Maybe we can exchange information. And if her information is what I think it is, we'll have our murderer before the fireworks begin!''

But when Susan returned to her Jeep, the rear door was open, and long, golden hairs were the only sign of its recent occupation.

FIFTEEN

"I'M TELLING YOU FOR THE LAST TIME. NO ONE HAS SEEN
either Ted or Tricia since lunch on the pier today. I haven't
seen them. My wife hasn't seen them. Sally and Ryan haven't
seen them. And it's been days since the girls were around."
Paul Briane brushed his hair off his forehead and glared angrily at Susan. "You don't seem to understand our position
here. We're houseguests. We came to Maine to relax for a
week or two. It's not our fault that there's been a murder. We
want, naturally, to do what we can. We want to be supportive. But we're not directly involved. This has nothing to do
with us. Now I must get back to my wife. She's insisting that
we all go to view the fireworks this evening—together."

He practically spat out the last word, and Susan watched
as he stomped off through the woods. When he was out of
sight, she ran down to the boathouse and yanked open the
door.

"Titania! Karma! Are you there?" She peered into the
dim interior, but the only life was arachnoid, and brushing
a tiny brown spider from her eyebrow, she slammed the door
shut and ran up to her house.

Janet Shapiro was patrolling the island in her car, and
Kathleen had commandeered Nathan's disintegrating vehicle
for the same purpose. Susan was going to check out her
house, make two phone calls, and then join the search for
Titania.

If only, she thought, bounding up the stairs, they knew
whether the child had been kidnapped or had once again

disappeared for some reason of her own. She would have felt better if the girls' parents hadn't vanished, too.

A quick search revealed that there was no one in her house, but she really hadn't expected there to be. She knew there was no reason for anyone to come here anymore.

Susan made a mug of instant coffee (double strength, the kind Jed called sludge, she remembered wistfully, missing him) while she dialed the phone. The first call, the most important one, was to the person in charge of the morgue where Humphrey's body was still stored. Janet had assured her that even on a holiday, she would find a person willing to answer her questions, and Janet had been right.

The man on the other end of the line was happy to help. It had been a slow week and he remembered Ted and Tricia well. They were distinct. You never knew how people would react to the death of their loved ones, but Ted and Tricia were the first couple he'd met who had found it an occasion for a full-scale marital battle. Pressed for details, he admitted to listening pretty closely to what had been said. Like many divorced couples, they reviewed how much they hated each other, how unhappy they were that the wrong people seemed to be the ones to die, how happy each would be to watch the body of the other lowered into the cold, damp ground. His problem was, the man ended his report, that neither of them wanted to accept responsibility for this body.

Tricia said she wasn't even a blood relative. Ted pointed out that she had loved him enough to marry him, so why wouldn't she take care of him now that he was dead? She said that there was, after all, a spot in the family plot waiting for this particular body. He said he'd be damned if he'd spend all eternity lying next to the man who had robbed him of everything he loved. She said, well, what do you expect me to do with him—throw him in the ocean? He said that was the best idea he'd heard yet and he should have done that to begin with. . . . Yes, ma'am, he was sure that's what had been said. He'd even given some thought to it at the time— about whether the body would come in with the tide or sink to the bottom to be eaten by lobsters and crabs. Seemed almost like a kind of justice there, didn't it? Considering how many crabs and lobsters were eaten by humans every year . . . Why, yes, she sure was welcome. Anything he could do, any time at all . . .

The second call was lucky. Susan hated to call her husband when he was so busy at work, but this was truly an emergency. Only Jed would be able to answer this question. He was the family member in charge of the boathouse. And his answer confirmed something she had suspected all along. Susan sat quietly, mulling over what she had learned.

There was a large clump of dog fur hanging from the edge of her tablecloth. That animal always left fur there as she walked by. She had cleaned an identical piece off this morning. . . .

They'd been here! And they probably wouldn't have come here if Titania hadn't realized the significance of what she'd known for a while. Did that mean she was alone? Surely no one else would allow the dog to tag along. Unless it was someone whom Titania didn't suspect.

Susan walked slowly back to her car. They (Titania and the dog? Titania, Karma, and someone else?) had not found what they were looking for, she was sure of that. Where else would they look? She got into the driver's seat, but just sat and thought for a few minutes. She put the key in the ignition. There was no place else to look. If Titania wasn't alone, the people she was with had probably left the island. Susan cursed and drove off down the road, into the long line of cars headed toward the center of town.

There was only one place to be tonight: watching the fireworks that were shot from a small offshore island, bursting into the sky before they merged with their own sparkling reflection in the ocean. The show would begin as soon as darkness fell, so Susan wasn't surprised that all the traffic seemed to be heading in the same direction, and it wasn't until she had parked her car in the playing field next to the elementary school, which had been turned into a parking lot for the occasion, that Susan overheard people discussing the accident.

She was having trouble believing her ears when Kathleen joined her, coming up from behind and grabbing her arm. "Did you find them?" she asked urgently.

"No, what's everyone saying about the bridge?"

"A truck full of fish oil sideswiped a van carrying haddock fillets. They hit in such a way that the sides of both trucks were peeled back, mixing fish with hundreds of gallons of oil. The accident happened at the top of the bridge—the highest point—and the mess spilled in both directions. Some people are predicting that the cleanup is going to take all night. At the very least, the bridge is closed for the next four or five hours."

"When did it happen?"

"During the parade. I know what you're thinking. There's no way anyone could have taken Titania off the island by car. . . . Does that mean you've reason to think that she's been kidnapped? There are always boats. . . ."

"No." Susan refused to think about that possibility. "Where are the girls?"

"They've staked out a spot near the water to watch the fireworks. They're okay—they're with Nathan and Gillian." Kathleen picked long hairs off the black slacks she wore. "What a mess," she muttered.

"Wha . . . Where did you get covered in that?"

Kathleen looked surprised at the urgency with which Susan asked the question. "Nathan's car. It was a pigsty. Full of dog hair—and what a smell! I think someone was sick recently in the backseat. Where are you going?"

Susan was running down the road and called her answer back over her shoulder. "To find them. To find Nathan. Come on. You know where he is."

Nathan and Gillian had gotten the girls into the perfect position to see the show. The youngsters were perched on a large granite boulder leaning against the public dock that jutted out into the water. Happily the tide was going out, so Theresa and Tierney had their own safe promontory. Gillian was looking back into the crowd and, noticing Susan and Kathleen, waved at them.

"Nathan!" Susan flung both arms in the air and yelled. "I need to talk to Nathan!"

Gillian poked her boyfriend in the ribs, said something in his ear, and he turned, saw the women, and returned their waves.

"Come here!" Susan and Kathleen yelled simultaneously. "We want to talk to you!"

Since they had attracted the attention of everyone within hearing, Nathan had no trouble making his way through the crowd; people moved aside for him.

"Did you give Titania and Karma a ride in your car recently?"

"Karma? The dog is named Karma? That's neat!"

"Nathan, listen to me! Did you?" Susan insisted that he answer her question.

"Yes. Did I do something wrong? She kept peeking at me through those curtains in the back of your Jeep during the parade. Then, after it was over, I was looking for Gillian when Titania found me and asked if I would drive her and her dog to your house."

"And you did."

"Of course. Did I do something wrong? I assumed she was going to meet you. When we got to the house, you weren't there, but Titania said she had to look for something inside the house and asked if I would wait for her.

"And you did." Susan repeated herself.

"Yes. She ran to the front of the house, and I stayed in the car with the dog. But then I wondered if Karma—that's really a neat name. . . ."

"Go on!"

"Well, I gave the dog a chance to find her favorite tree, and she ran off. So I ran after her. And by the time I got back to the car, Titania was opening the back door to your house. Well, the dog ran in." (Susan remembered the fur in her kitchen.) "And Titania and I dragged her out."

"Was she carrying anything?" Kathleen wanted to know.

"Nothing that I saw; I mean, she might have had something in one of her pockets, but she didn't have anything in her hands. Is she okay?'' he asked worriedly. "I didn't know that I was doing anything wrong."

"You didn't," Susan assured him. "But what happened next? Did you bring her back here?"

"Well, she wanted to go to the historical society museum over on the other side of the island." (Clever girl, Susan thought; she hadn't even thought of that.) "So I took her there, but it was closed, so I asked where she wanted to go, and we were heading downtown when we spied those two women who are staying at the Taylor house. . . ."

"We know who you mean," Susan assured him.

"They were coming out of that little gift shop that's in the front parlor of The Island Inn, and Titania yelled at them and asked me to stop."

"And she went off with them?"

"Yes. She ran over and talked with them first, and then she came back to the car and told me that she was going to go with them. I don't think they were too thrilled when she got the dog from the back of the car, though. The poor animal was covered with her own vomit."

"And have you seen her since then?"

"No, I—"

"Did her sisters mention seeing her?"

"No, but I was telling Gillian about it, and she said that she saw those women in their car—they have that hot BMW, don't they?"

Susan nodded.

"Well, she saw them going down the road, and Titania wasn't with them. Or the dog either."

"And they are pretty likely to be found together," Kathleen said quietly.

"I guess I shouldn't have let her go off with them," Nathan said sadly. "If she's hurt or something—" he seemed to have a difficult time saying the last word "—it will all be my fault."

"There's no reason to think about that. We need you to keep Theresa and Tierney together."

"Right," Kathleen said as the young man headed back to

the rock. "Don't let either of them out of your sight. And don't let them take off with anyone other than their parents."

"Fine," Susan whispered when they were alone. "Except that one of those parents could be a murderer."

"I thought you knew who it was."

"I think I know why Humphrey was killed, but not who did it," Susan corrected her. "Let's head down to the water and see who appears to watch the fireworks. I'll tell you all about it on the way."

"They're wonderful. They get better every year," Susan said, despite the fact that she was not one of the crowd whose eyes were turned toward the sky as hundreds of green and white stars danced through their patterns and then fell into their own reflections in the sea. Susan was watching the Brianes, the Harters, and the Taylors, the latter couple having appeared nearby after the fireworks had already begun.

"There's Janet." Kathleen pointed. "We should tell her what Jed said. . . . Oh, look. Those are my favorite—the ones that go off all at once like that."

Susan glanced in the direction Kathleen had indicated. "I don't want to stop watching. . . . Damn!" She jumped as someone behind her threw a loud cherry bomb into the air.

A dog barked, and Susan whirled around, hoping to see Karma's enthusiastic face—with Titania beside her. But it was a poodle, clasped in the arms of an elderly lady who was enjoying the fireworks as much as any child. Susan returned to her former occupation. She was determined that if anyone was shot at tonight, she would know of six people who didn't have a gun in their hands at the time.

But she was having a difficult time keeping track of everything. The island's fireworks were generously augmented by private contributions. All around her on the shore, children waved sparklers in the air. Roman candles were shot over her head into the sky. Dozens of boats bobbed around the harbor, from big schooners to private sailing yachts, to lobster boats, rowboats, and even a kayak or two. And on each, people were celebrating in their own way. Bottle rockets were especially popular, shot from wine and beer bottles that had been recently emptied. Everyone was having a very good time. She looked over her shoulder and noticed that even Janet Shapiro had surrendered to the mood and was enjoying the sights.

She returned to her self-appointed task. Tierney and Theresa were on the rock in the water with Gillian and Nathan (no one was taking any chances there), the Brianes and the Harters (Judy and Sally giggling together in front of their husbands, probably laughing at someone, Susan thought) leaned against their BMW illegally parked in the middle of the road—but tonight no one would care—and the Taylors were sitting as far apart as possible on the narrow wooden steps leading up to one of the town's antique stores.

Susan returned to the girls, whose two little red heads were illuminated by the fireworks, and wondered where Titania was—and if she was safe. She looked at the adults involved in this again. Surely none of them would hurt that child . . . that child whose mother was suddenly missing! Damn!

Ted Taylor was sitting alone on the steps. Tricia was nowhere in sight. Susan checked the Brianes and the Harters; neither couple had moved. Tierney and Theresa were fine. "Stay here, I'm going to find Janet," Susan said to Kathleen, taking off.

Janet Shapiro was leaning into the open trunk of her police car. Susan ran toward it.

"This will be fine. But be sure to wash it off well when you get home, and if there's any swelling or pus, you go right to the medical center first thing in the morning. . . ." Janet patted the young boy's head before he ran off. She snapped her first aid kit shut and was reaching up to close her trunk when Susan joined her.

"Something's happened." Janet didn't say the words as a question.

"Tricia's vanished."

"She was sitting on the step with Ted the last time I saw her. . . ."

"But now she's gone. I was looking somewhere else. I didn't see her leave. I don't know—"

"Anyone else moved?" Janet interrupted, scanning the scene. A large clump of explosives flew into the air as a girandole spun around on the ground, and it was light enough to see everything easily.

"No . . . Look, Kathleen is waving!"

As they watched, Kathleen leapt from the rock to the pier, climbed over and around all the spectators there, and across the road to where Susan and Janet waited.

"She went around the back of those houses. I saw her go. That's where her car is parked." Kathleen panted.

"You stay with those girls, make sure they're protected. . . ." Janet called out, following Susan in the direction Kathleen had indicated.

"I—" Susan began, jogging slowly.

"Go! You're twice as fast as I am," Janet ordered, puffing up the sidewalk.

Susan ran. She ran past her own car, the sunroof still open from this afternoon. She ran past dozens of teenagers, making a token effort at hiding their beer cans as an adult chugged past. She almost tripped over two small boys lighting tiny tablets that grew into smoking snakes as she passed. She ran as fast as she could around the corner to the parking lot of the grocery store where the Taylors had parked. The car was there. Locked, she discovered when she tried the doors. But Tricia Taylor had disappeared.

Or maybe she had not been coming here at all? Maybe she had been going to take advantage of the chemical toilets set up in front of the post office tonight? Maybe there was nothing suspicious about this at all. . . .

So why was Judy Briane sneaking around that corner? Susan stopped herself from walking right up to the woman. Maybe, just maybe, she could follow her to Tricia—or to Titania.

The celebration was really under way now, and the sky was lit up more often than it was dark. And that made it easier to follow Judy Briane as she headed back down to the water, moving through the crowd, her eyes looking toward the sea.

"What's going on?" Janet had caught up. "Where's Tricia? I certainly don't see her."

"I lost her," Susan answered, not turning around to reply. She wasn't going to take a chance at losing sight of her prey. "I got up to her car, and it was locked, and she wasn't around. . . ."

"Did you look in the trunk? Was there a rifle in the trunk?"

"I . . . what?"

"Ted Taylor caught up with me after you left. He said his wife had put a rifle in the trunk of the car before they left the house tonight. She didn't know that he knew."

"What sort of stupid . . ." Susan was too appalled to go on. "He didn't leave it there?"

"He took the shells out of it. He thought that, since she couldn't do any harm with it . . . That man is obviously not thinking right. The woman is the mother of his kids, for heaven's sake!"

"She couldn't be wandering around the crowd with a rifle in her hands," Susan muttered, her eyes still on Judy Briane. "Someone would notice. Someone would stop her."

"But she could be up on one of those buildings," Janet muttered, looking over her shoulder.

Susan glanced around at the happy crowd. A sniper. It was too horrible to think about. "Let's just hope she didn't bring ammunition."

"What's happening?" Susan asked, seeing that Judy had turned around and was heading straight toward them.

"My husband," Judy called out, running to them. "My husband is gone. You have to help me. He's trying to kill me!"

Janet and Susan exchanged alarmed looks.

"Did he have a gun?" Susan asked.

"Do you know where he might have gone to?" Janet asked, still thinking of the rooftops.

"I think he brought a kayak down to the harbor earlier. I think he was going to try to leave the island. The clinics are in my name, too; he had to kill me! He was going to kill me and then leave the island!''

Janet realized that they had a hysterical woman on their hands. "Get in there," Janet ordered, pointing at a dark green plastic shed standing on the corner of the street. Large white block letters proclaimed it to be an official STATE O' MAINE PORT O' P.

"What?"

"Get in. I'll tie a sign around it saying it's out of order. You'll be safe enough. No one would think to look in there.''

"That's disgusting. I can't. . . ." Judy protested in a horrified voice.

"You could, of course, just stand here and risk getting your head blown off.'' Janet peered into the dark shadows around them.

"Okay. But find him and come get me out as soon as possible.''

Susan was trying not to laugh over the look on Judy Briane's face. After all, this was serious. But still . . .

"Let's get going," the deputy insisted, slapping the OUT OF ORDER sign across the door. "Be sure to keep that thing locked, and don't open it unless you know one of us is standing outside," she called into the inadequate air vent, getting only a muffled reply. "Come on. We've got work to do.''

The fireworks finale was beginning. The members of the audience, knowing from experience that a long pause in the action was necessary to get the last large barrage of explosives ready, were busily burning up their small personal stockpiles.

"Maybe if we split up," Susan suggested.

"Good thought. I want to get to where I can check the rooftops. . . .''

"I'll head down by the water then," Susan agreed. "But if I find anyone, what do I do?''

"You just ask the closest and biggest fisherman you see to jump on the suspect. Look frantic. They'll come through for you.''

Susan was left alone on the sidewalk with this doubtful bit

of advice for comfort. She stood still for a minute and then decided that the best thing she could do was check on the girls. She trotted down the street, arriving back at the water's edge as the finale began.

White chrysanthemums filled the sky, followed by the loudest explosions yet. Susan looked around. How could she protect anyone in this crowd? How could anyone distinguish gunfire from fireworks? Red, white, and blue sparks followed the first display, fanning out in every direction. Susan, glancing down at the reflection, saw two kayakers, their cigar-shaped cylinders in what seemed to be rather close proximity to the sparks. Some people had no common sense!

She found the Taylor girls with Nathan and Gillian. They had been joined by their father. And, as she watched, he pointed up in the sky, and their eyes followed his hand. Susan was distracted, thinking about what sort of a father he was, when Kathleen joined her.

"Look! Look!" Kathleen insisted, waving at the kayakers.

"I know. They're probably just some stupid kids. . . ." As she watched, one of them grabbed at the other, and whether it was an act of affection or anger was impossible to determine from shore.

"It's Tricia and Paul!" Susan gasped.

Susan and Kathleen ran down to the water's edge, getting as close to the sea as they could. But the light was intermittent, and the paddlers moved in and out of the shadows.

In the last loud explosion of the night, Susan and Kathleen watched, appalled and helpless, as both boats flipped over, spilling the two paddlers into the icy water.

Most of the spectators hadn't even seen the boaters, and people were drifting back home to their own private celebrations of the day. Cars stuck in the island's annual (and only) traffic jam were full of cheerful people calling out greetings to one another, comparing this year's fireworks with those of the past.

Janet had quietly gotten a small Coast Guard craft to patrol the area where the accident had occurred, and both kayaks had been recovered, but, as yet, no one else had been found. A search was being organized, and fishermen as well as law enforcement people would be giving up their night to help out.

Susan and Kathleen were standing on the now-deserted fishing pier with Ted and his two daughters.

"Sally and Ryan are taking over my room at the inn tonight," Ted said quietly. "They've already left. They'll be coming back to the house in the morning. But I thought that I should spend the night in the house with . . . with the girls." There were tears in his eyes, and he didn't seem able to go on.

Theresa was white in the light from the streetlamp, and she didn't say anything. Tierney tightly held her father's hand and scraped the ground with her sneaker.

"I think that's a good idea," Kathleen agreed. "I don't think there's any reason to try to sort this out until morning. Everything that's happened . . . has happened," she ended weakly.

Susan bent down, hoping for something comforting to say, when she was almost thrown into the water by a burst of uncontrolled affection that caused Karma to fling herself on the woman and lick her face.

"Titania? Titania, honeybunch?" Ted Taylor called into the darkness, and the animal sped away, only to return seconds later with her mistress running by her side.

"Daddy! Daddy!" Titania flung herself in her father's arms, hugging him and her two sisters at the same time.

And over the shoulder of her father, the child, tears in her eyes, smiled at Susan.

SIXTEEN

Susan's house, filled with a comfortable combination of old and new furniture, seemed the best place for
everyone to meet the next morning for breakfast, for news of
Paul Briane and Tricia Taylor, and for an explanation. Susan
had been exhausted when she arrived home last night, but
despite the excitement of the last twenty-four hours, she had
slept well, awakening refreshed at dawn.

She hurried through her shower, wondering what she could
serve her guests. She had inherited from her mother the belief that no matter what the crisis, people had to eat. Halsey
Downing had promised to show up early. Maybe . . . Reaching for a fluffy towel, Susan had a thought.

She was dressed in clean jeans, a faded chambray shirt,
and thongs, and was busy making coffee when Halsey arrived
at the kitchen door, boxes of homemade doughnuts piled
high in her arms.

"Danny's going to kill me when he finds out that I've taken
these," she said, handing the boxes to Susan. "But I had to
come. Has anyone heard from the searchers? Have there been
any arrests? How are the girls? What's going to happen to
them?"

"We should wait until everyone is here, I think," Susan
suggested. "If you have some time, would you help Kathleen
set up the large table in the living room? We can put the
doughnuts and coffee out there—and orange juice for the
girls. Napkins are right over here."

Under Susan's direction, everything was ready by the time her guests began to arrive.

The Harters appeared first: Ryan, with dark circles under his eyes, and Sally, so upset that her blouse was buttoned crooked and her hair unwashed. Between them they supported a much-tranquilized Judy Briane. Distressed less by her husband's disappearance than by the six hours she had spent in the STATE O' MAINE PORT O' P before Janet Shapiro remembered to release her, Judy Briane had remained the rest of the night under sedation at the island's medical center, muttering in her sleep about men and their less than sanitary bathroom habits.

Karma arrived next, bounding into the living room, swiping a chocolate doughnut, and vanishing behind the couch in one continuous movement. Titania, Theresa, and Tierney followed, while Ted Taylor remained outside to speak with Janet Shapiro, who drove up at that moment.

None of the girls were interested in food, although Susan handed each one a glass of freshly squeezed orange juice. She smiled at Janet Shapiro and Ted Taylor as they walked through the door, and then let the deputy take over.

Janet spoke first. Waiting for Ted to settle his girls around him, she announced that the bodies of Paul Briane and Tricia Taylor had been recovered by a fisherman a little after 5:00 A.M. this morning.

Tierney put her head in her father's lap and wept quietly, but Theresa and Titania sat silently, grim looks on their faces. "We thought that might happen," the middle child explained solemnly.

"I think," Titania started slowly in an almost adult voice. "I think that we all need to know what's been going on—and who killed Uncle Humphrey."

Janet Shapiro looked at Ted Taylor; she didn't have to ask aloud.

"I think . . ." he started, and then stopped, frowning down at his children. "In fact, I've thought about nothing else all night. If they want to know, I guess we should tell them."

"Then maybe Susan should begin," Janet suggested.

"The first part of the story is yours," Susan said, nodding to Ted Taylor.

"For God's sake, someone—" Judy Briane began.

"Shut up!" The order burst simultaneously from Kathleen, Susan, and Janet Shapiro. They should have said it three days ago. And they probably would have if they had known how well it was going to work.

"You know about Humphrey . . ." Ted began in the ensuing silence.

Susan nodded. "That he's dead. And that he died five years ago. Right?"

Ted Taylor looked down into the surprised faces of his daughters and began his tale. "It's a long story, but I guess everyone here has the right to hear it from the beginning." He took a deep breath and started. "Humphrey was my older brother—my only brother. There were just the two of us. When my parents died in an automobile accident, all the money in their estate went to Humphrey. It was assumed that he would help me out when I needed it—or divide up the money in some way that was agreeable to both of us. We were very close as children, and Humphrey had always taken care of me. Under the circumstances, it was the logical way for my parents to deal with their estate.

"At the time of my parents' deaths, Humphrey was involved in an important project in the Mideast and couldn't get home. I saw to all the details of the funeral service. Then I flew out to Egypt, with a briefcase full of papers from my parents' attorney for him to sign.

"We hadn't seen each other in years. Humphrey wasn't particularly close to my parents. Even as a child, he'd been extremely independent. But I'd always loved him and looked up to him. And after the papers were signed, we settled down for a nice visit. Only—" he looked at his daughters and continued more slowly "—something dreadful happened. We were coming home from a restaurant one night, returning to my brother's apartment, when . . . when there was a terrible accident. A car jumped the curb, hit two pedestrians on the walkway, then sped off. One of the injured was a young man, a native, who got up, dusted himself off, and vanished into the night. My brother was the other—and he was killed instantly.

"I was frantic. I was in a foreign country, a country not on especially friendly terms with the United States. There was no one to help me. So when a man who claimed to be a friend of my brother suggested that we bury Humphrey quietly, privately, that we should allow his death to go unrecorded and that I should leave the country as soon as possible, I agreed. You have to remember that I was very aware that we were in a part of the world where my own country's influence was limited. In a state where I could be locked in a prison under false pretenses and never be seen again. Humphrey and I had been talking about that the night before he died. I thought . . . I thought I had no choice. I did what was suggested."

"You did the right thing." Titania spoke up in a firm little voice.

"I did the wrong thing, honeybunch," he answered. "And I've paid for it."

"But the money. It was yours," Susan said.

"Yes. I didn't have to wait or tell anyone that Humphrey was dead to get hold of my parents' estate. Humphrey had signed papers before he died that very generously offered me as much of the estate as I wanted, whenever I wanted it. Humphrey had no family, and his business was doing very well. The money was mine—whether he was dead or alive."

"Lucky you." Judy Briane slurred her words.

"But you didn't spend it right away," Susan suggested, ignoring the woman.

"No. I was terribly upset, as you can imagine, and I just didn't want to think about it. And I didn't—not for years. I put the money in the bank and tried to pretend it wasn't there. Sometimes I'd dream about what had happened and wake up wondering if the whole thing was real or not. And sometimes Trish would mention the money . . . but most of the time I was able to forget that it existed," he added quickly. "And then I found this land and decided to build my house. Building that house had always been a dream of mine.'' He looked down at his daughters, patting Tierney on the head. ''And I guess I used the fact that you girls were growing up and I wanted to give you summer vacations that you would always remember to get what I wanted for myself. . . .'' He stopped speaking and looked away from his family.

''So you decided to use that money to buy the land and build your house,'' Susan prompted.

''Yes. There was nothing illegal about it. The money was mine absolutely. Morally . . . Well, that's another story. I felt guilty about my brother—the way I had buried him anonymously, the way I had ended up with my parent's estate. I think my guilt was the reason that it was so easy for me to be blackmailed. . . .''

''By the man that we've all been accepting as Humphrey Taylor . . .''

''Yes. He appeared right after the work was begun on the house's roof—right before the bad weather came last fall. I still don't know how he found out about Humphrey. We got a letter in the mail—from Egypt—and it spelled out a list of conditions—mainly that he wanted to be accepted as Humphrey Taylor and to share in the inheritance, otherwise he would reveal the truth about my brother's death. And, of course, he claimed that I had killed Humphrey.

''I didn't know what to do. I thought about calling the police. I knew we shouldn't accept his demands, but—'' he stopped and looked down at his daughters, seeming to get the courage to go on from their presence ''—I couldn't prove what had happened to Humphrey. And I have no idea what happened to the man who helped me bury Humphrey. I was stumped.

''Tricia thought we should go along with the charade. Just until we met this man, was what she said at the time. She said it was for the good of the girls, and she reminded me that I was building the house for them. I . . . I think she was wrong, but she was trying to do the right thing. And I'm not blaming her; it was my decision,'' he added more forcefully.

"I agreed to let this impostor into our lives because I didn't want to give up the house I was building, and that's all there was to it."

"And then your wife fell in love with this man?" Janet Shapiro asked.

"I don't know that Trish was in love with him. Trish was so selfish, so self-centered, that she may not have been capable of love. I think she saw marriage to the impostor as a way to get her hands on my parents' estate—to spend it any way she wanted. Our marriage had been in trouble for some time—and it was mainly my fault. I had been so depressed after my parents and Humphrey died that I was almost impossible to live with. And, in truth, Trish and I had always had problems. We wanted to live different life-styles. Trish wanted to be part of society, to travel and see the world. And I, of course, wanted to be at home in the houses that I built. The fact that Tricia and I didn't agree about this crisis was sort of the last straw. She was fed up with me and our marriage, and she was ready to do something else with her life."

"Did you know that she was planning to marry the fake Humphrey when you two decided to get a divorce?" Ryan Harter asked him.

"His name was Arthur Deed," Ted explained. "I don't know much about him, but he did tell us that much. And no, I was as surprised as anyone at her marriage. In fact, I might not have agreed to the divorce if I had known that was coming. I would have wanted to spare my girls that man for a stepfather. But I couldn't. So there I was, with that man living in my house, with my wife and, worst of all, with my daughters."

"So you killed him." Judy Briane spoke matter-of-factly.

"No. I didn't kill him. I wanted to, but I didn't."

"But you need to tell us something else," Susan insisted. "You have to explain why you invited the Brianes and the Harters to the island. Both Paul and Ryan said the invitation came from you, not Trish. That is right, isn't it?"

"Yes. Tricia was worried that someone would realize that Humphrey wasn't exactly like he had been. Not that there was much risk that anyone would recognize him as an impostor. Being five years apart in age, we didn't have many friends in common when I was growing up. My parents' friends are all dead or living someplace where they weren't likely to meet Arthur Deed impersonating my brother. But, of course, Paul had known Humphrey well, and Sally had met him a few times. And, more significantly, they were both going to be seeing the new Humphrey a lot. Sally because, due to her husband's job change, she was moving to Boston, and Paul because he was opening a clinic nearby. This holiday week was to be a test to see if the new Humphrey would pass. And he did—except for you," he added, looking at Susan. "You were suspicious, but I sure don't know why."

"Because of Karma," Susan explained, as the dog peeked around the corner of the couch at the sound of her name. "Paul kept telling this story of camping with a wet dog, and even your mantel has a carving of you, your brother, and your dog. But Titania said that Humphrey was terribly allergic to Karma. She even thought that you had given her the dog to irritate Humphrey's allergies. It struck me as unusual that he would have changed so much from child to adult. Most adults with terrible allergies have some sign of them as children. And, in fact, Tricia said that Humphrey (or Arthur Deed pretending to be your brother) had said that he had suffered from terrible asthma since birth. The two stories didn't fit, and the only explanation was that there were two different men. Judy complained that Humphrey had lived in exciting, glamorous parts of the world, but all he would talk about was growing up with Ted, probably because he had never lived in the Mideast. But he made a mistake when he told Tricia too much about his own childhood," Susan explained. "The other reason is that I knew a little more about Arthur Deed than you do. I knew that he had spent time on the island before. You see, there's a picture of him on the wall of my house. He had stayed in the house as a renter. And he knew about the picture."

"I tried to find that," Titania said. "I looked and I

looked—I even thought there might be something in all those photos at the island historical society exhibit, but it wasn't open yesterday.''

''The photograph is in the wooden trunk on the front seat of my car—the one Theresa and Tierney knelt on during the parade. How did you know about it?''

''I heard Uncle . . .''

''Don't worry about what you call him,'' her father suggested. ''It doesn't matter now.''

''Well, a few days ago, I overheard that man talking to someone. I didn't know who,'' she added, glancing around the room. ''And he was saying that the truth was going to be discovered if anyone saw that picture of him in the house—and that would ruin him. I didn't think much about it until he was killed, and I began to think that whatever he had been talking about might be important. But I didn't connect it with this house. I just assumed it had something to do with our house—with the mantel. I looked and looked at that thing, but it didn't make any sense.''

''A lot of people were looking for that picture. I think Tricia even realized that it might be at this house—that's why she was wandering around in the middle of the night, trying to break in when Halsey tripped over her,'' Susan suggested.

Titania nodded. ''I guess that might be who that man was talking to,'' she continued reluctantly. ''Then yesterday, I remembered the photographs that Halsey had told me she was going to help Mrs. Henshaw put up on the walls, and I realized that Uncle Humphrey might not have been talking about the mantel, and that's why I asked Nathan to bring me here. I had explored most of the house before you came up, and I had seen those photographs in the attic. I'd even looked at some of them, thinking about what funny clothing people used to wear, but I didn't recognize anyone. . . .'' She looked at Susan. ''I still don't know how you knew I'd been here after the parade, though.''

''Because you brought your shadow,'' Susan said. ''And she left some of her fur behind.''

"What I don't understand is what Mr. Briane has to do with all this," Tierney said.

"I think," Titania said slowly, "that he was in love with Mommy."

"I think so, too," Susan agreed.

"So Paul Briane killed Humphrey?" Halsey asked, sounding excited at the discovery. "Of course—he did it because he was in love with Tricia Taylor, right?"

Theresa looked up at her father. "Is that what happened?"

"I think it would explain the gunshots at the kayak race," Sally Ryan said slowly. "Judy was the target, wasn't she?"

Everyone in the room looked at Judy Briane, who was napping, a tiny line of drool dripping down her chin.

"Probably," Susan said, getting up to fetch a doughnut. Karma hurried to the table, hoping for a crumb or two, which she decided to retrieve by tugging on the tablecloth. Halsey rescued one of the platters. Janet rushed to keep the orange juice from spilling, and succeeded only in soaking herself.

"Maybe you and your sisters could take Karma down to the cove now that you know who the murderer is," Ted suggested.

"Okay," Titania agreed, but Susan noticed that she had a puzzled look on her face. "Come on, Karma."

"What I don't understand," Halsey began as they heard the girls step off the porch, "is why Paul Briane would try to kill his wife—or why he would kill the man pretending to be Humphrey Taylor. Couldn't Tricia get another divorce? Or couldn't Tricia and Paul just live together without getting two divorces?"

"Yes," Ted agreed, speaking very quietly. "But it wasn't Paul who killed Humphrey or who shot at his wife. It was Tricia, wasn't it?" he asked Susan.

She had walked to the window and saw that the girls were out of hearing range before she answered. "Yes. But maybe it really isn't necessary for your daughters to know."

"You're right. Thanks," he added quietly. "She always was greedy. Always wanted everything. But how did you figure it out?"

"It was the only conclusion that made sense. The only person who had a lot to gain was Trish. And she manipulated the situation from the beginning to the end trying to gain everything.

"I think the story goes something like this. Your parents and Humphrey died around the same time—five years ago. And that's also the time that Paul Briane came back into your life. You admitted that you were devastated at the time. So it isn't surprising that you didn't notice when your wife became involved with your old friend. She was probably disappointed that you weren't going to use your parents' estate to provide her with the life that she desired, and Paul Briane's business was beginning to grow. . . . She was very, very vulnerable."

"And then, when Arthur Deed appeared—" Kathleen began.

"I've been giving this a whole lot of thought, and I don't think Arthur Deed's appearance was a surprise for Tricia," Ted Taylor interrupted her.

Susan nodded. "I'd have to agree with you," she said to him. "This whole thing must have been set up by Tricia. I don't suppose we'll ever find out how she ran into Arthur Deed or how she talked him into posing as a dead man and taking part in her blackmail scheme. She may have promised him half of her divorce settlement or she may have convinced him that she was in love with him. But it's obvious that she prompted Arthur Deed about the details of Ted's childhood and then insisted on inviting the Brianes and the Harters here to Maine to see if he could fool people who had known Humphrey as a young man. It must have shocked Arthur Deed to discover that he was now living with his new wife on a cove where he had stayed as a young man, but he had a job to do convincing the Brianes and the Harters that he was Humphrey, and he went ahead and did it.

"It must have been a lot of work for everyone," Susan continued, talking to Ted. "But to Tricia, it was worth it. She got the entire divorce settlement and both houses. And then she intended to get rid of Arthur Deed and run off with

Paul Briane, a man she had been in love with for five years. All she had to do was push you into agreeing to accept Arthur Deed as your dead brother. And that was probably easier to do because you were so guilty about the way you had covered up Humphrey's death in the first place.''

"There are no excuses," he said sadly.

Susan agreed, but she didn't say anything. "Trish married the man claiming to be Humphrey, and then after she had the house and all the money, she was going to kill the impostor and marry Paul. . . .''

"And, just in case Paul wanted to stay married to his old wife, she'd kill her, too," Kathleen added. "She shot at her, and Paul knew it."

"Yes," Susan agreed, looking at Ted Taylor. "But you suspected all this earlier, didn't you? That's why you were so relieved when I told you about Paul and Sally meeting in the middle of the night on the other side of the cove."

"Yes, but then I got to thinking. . . .''

"And you realized that Tricia had driven in late that night and had immediately picked a loud fight with you—before she even got in the house. Right?''

"Yes. It occurred to me later that she must have left Paul, driven around the cove, gotten home, and provoked that fight outside—so that you would hear it on your way back home. Right?''

"I think so. And I'm afraid that it worked for a while. But then Janet was talking about how Paul could have kayaked back to the start of the race and run across the island to the yacht club, and it occurred to me that I was being stupid. It's different traveling on land and on water. It was Tricia who was in love with Paul. It was Tricia who met him on the other side of the cove. I missed that completely."

"But a lot of things still don't make any sense," Kathleen began. "Are you saying that your house being half-open and half-closed by Burt Jamison had nothing at all to do with the murder?"

"It had a lot to do with it. But we shouldn't blame Burt. I think he did exactly what he was told to do, and the house should have been open and waiting for us when we arrived—and it would have been if Titania hadn't half closed it up again and relocked the driveway. I should have suspected her earlier, of course. After all, she admitted to being in the house—it was logical that she would be the one person who knew that the key to the driveway was kept hanging on the wall. So she was the one person who would lock up the driveway—or unlock it later when she realized that she had inconvenienced us like she did.''

''Why would she do that?'' the girl's father asked.

''Because she was protecting Theresa. She thought that her sister was the murderer.''

''What . . . How did she ever get that idea?'' Ted asked.

''We can ask Titania, of course, but there's more than one incident that led me to come to this conclusion. In the first place, Tricia's response to the news of Humphrey's death puzzled me. I think now that she came over to my house that morning to make the point that Humphrey was still alive—even though she had killed him the day before. Practically the first words out of her mouth were that she knew Humphrey was looking forward to meeting Jed and Jerry. She wanted us to think that she thought that he was still alive at that point. She had already made a mistake in asking Halsey to come to the house Thursday morning to clean. It's not surprising that Halsey thought Tricia was strangely nervous. She had, after all, just murdered her husband. And she had probably planned an elaborate cover-up, but it turned out to be unnecessary—in fact, it was impossible to carry out. Because, you see, Titania found the body and moved it.

''That explains why Tricia was so shocked when Janet told her that her husband was dead. She thought Janet was talking about Ted—she thought that Ted had been found dead in my living room.'' Susan turned to Ted Taylor. ''And I think that, despite everything she had done, Tricia still had some feelings for you, otherwise she probably wouldn't have been so upset when she thought you had been killed.''

Ted nodded, but didn't otherwise acknowledge what she was saying.

"Tricia must have been very confused to hear that Humphrey had been found here," Susan continued. "Titania had found the body and the bait bag. I think the fact that he was on your property, along with the knowledge that among Theresa's many collections was one of bait bags, convinced Titania that her sister had taken the pranks one step too far and killed the man they thought was their uncle.

"You see, everyone keeps thinking of those girls together—almost as though they were one entity. I think it's because they look so much alike and they have such similar names. But they're very distinct individuals. . . ."

"That they are," their father agreed. "Always have been."

"Titania is the mothering one; she takes care of the others," Susan began, thinking that the girl's maternal skills had probably developed early because her own mother was so deficient in them. "And Tierney is the very sweet younger child. But Theresa is more complex than that. She's jealous of her older sister at the same time that she's proud of her. She has to find her own identity—maybe that has something to do with all the collections she has. And she's the angry child.

"You see, the pranks weren't all the same. There was more than one mind at work here. I think you knew that." She looked to Ted, who sadly nodded his agreement. "Putting pudding in someone's pockets is a long way from pulling out a cellar step and hoping someone will fall to the bottom. And doctoring a Scotch bottle with a harmless substance is different from altering the brakes on a car. Someone was even walking around the island talking about death threats to Humphrey—this was serious stuff. Titania saw that what Theresa was doing was dangerous. And when she found her uncle dead, she assumed Theresa had carried out the ultimate prank. So she moved the body. . . ."

"Humph . . . Arthur Deed . . . was a pretty big man," Sally Harter said.

"Yes. That's why Titania used a wagon to get him into my living room. . . ."

"The wagon that Theresa and Tierney made into the float

for the parade yesterday!'' Kathleen said, understanding at last.

''Exactly.'' Susan nodded. ''I called Jed, and he told me that the girls had never found that wagon in our boathouse. Jed is very, very neat. I should have realized immediately that he would never leave such a thing around over the winter. Titania probably stuffed it in there and then didn't know how to get it out without someone catching her—so she suggested that her sisters turn it into a float. There may even be blood-stains on it if anyone bothers to look.

''So after she moved the body into my house, she closed it up again as well as she could—putting up the downstairs shutters and covering up the rest of the furniture, even the chairs that didn't have anyone in them. She had been spending a lot of time in the house over the past few months, and she knew how it should look. But it didn't matter terribly much. The main thing was for the body to be away from the Taylor house, away from Theresa. And the longer it was before someone came up and stayed here, the better.

''But trying to make everything look normal at my house wasn't all there was to do. Titania was worried that someone would put all this together and assume Theresa had done it. She was probably worried that Theresa would say something that would give herself away—and she didn't want any witnesses around if that happened. That's why she thought it was so important for Judy and Sally to be out of the way when Tricia told the younger girls about Humphrey's death. So she insisted that I take Judy and Sally to Acadia. She took that opportunity to throw the rest of Theresa's bait bags into the ocean. But she was in such a hurry that she dropped one under her bed. I knew it was Theresa that she was trying to protect because Tierney had already told me about the girl's collections. Anyone who wanders the beach collecting lob-ster buoys and beach glass in Maine is going to find a lot of bait bags—it just made sense.''

''Then Titania ran away so that we would think she had done it?'' Ted asked.

''Like a good mother, she was ready to trade her life for

the girls that she loved." Susan nodded. "And she hid at my house so she could keep an eye on her sisters—so she would be around if she was needed. She even managed to get a message to me about the mantel, which she thought was the missing clue."

"She's taken on a lot of responsibility for a child her age," Ted Taylor said slowly, sadly. "It's going to take us all a lot of time to get over this, but I think maybe Titania is going to have the most difficult time of all."

No one argued with him.

SEVENTEEN

SUSAN JOINED TITANIA DOWN BY THE SAME ROCK WHERE they had first met. "It's been a sad day," she commented, sliding down to sit by the girl. "How are your sisters?"

"They'll be okay. It's going to be harder on Theresa than Tierney, don't you think? I mean, Tierney will probably have forgotten all about this by the time she grows up, won't she?"

"Maybe." Susan agreed because the girl so obviously needed for her to do so.

They sat silently for a while, watching two gulls fight over a half-opened clam.

"It's pretty here, isn't it?" Susan said finally.

"Hmmm." It was an agreement. "Do you think . . ." Titania started to ask another question and then stopped.

"Go on."

"Do you think that there's anything to heredity? That people are predetermined to become just like their parents?" Titania asked, avoiding Susan's look.

"Are you thinking about your mother?" Susan asked.

"Yes. She killed those people, didn't she? Mr. Briane as well as . . . as Uncle Humphrey?"

Susan didn't see much point in lying to the girl. "No one is ever going to know what happened out in those kayaks last night, but she did kill the man pretending to be your uncle."

"You knew that I was protecting Theresa, didn't you?" Titania asked. "But I don't understand how you found out."

"The next time someone tells you to clean your room, you might consider listening to them. You left a bait bag on the floor under your bed. I picked it up and put two and two together.''

''We shouldn't have started pulling those pranks,'' the girl admitted.

''They did go a little far,'' Susan agreed.

''Yes. But . . . well, my father almost encouraged us to do them.''

''He was caught in a trap,'' Susan said, not adding that it was one of his own making and that's usually the worst kind.

''I think it's better if Theresa and Tierney don't know about Mommy,'' Titania said seriously, avoiding Susan's eyes. ''They won't be so hurt then. Or so worried,'' she muttered.

''There's nothing that's going to stop the hurt except time,'' Susan said, resisting an urge to put her arms around the child. ''What your mother did can't be excused, and I don't think we're ever going to understand why she did it now that she's dead. It just has to be accepted. But you don't have to worry about you or your sisters inheriting some sort of bad gene that would make you kill someone. It just doesn't happen like that. Remember, you had two parents.''

''And my father wouldn't hurt a fly,'' Titania said proudly.

''That's right.''

There was a longer silence before the child spoke again. ''My father's going to sell the house.''

''I thought he might. It doesn't hold pleasant memories for him now.''

''I think he should keep it. It's the house he's always wanted, and if we stay here and don't sell it, we can make other memories, happy ones, that will cover up some of the bad things,'' Titania added earnestly.

''Have you told him that?''

''No. I didn't think he would want to hear what I had to say. He's made up his mind.''

''It may not change his mind, but you should tell him how you feel anyway,'' Susan suggested. ''And maybe he'll decide to stay. I sure like the idea of having the three Taylor girls as my next-door neighbors in Maine.''

"We like being here, too." Titania smiled. "Do you hear something? Like someone yelling?"

"I do hear someone." Susan stood up. "It's Kathleen!" She shaded her eyes and looked across the cove at the group that stood on and around her porch. "It looks like she's holding Bananas . . . and maybe Jerry. . . . There's Jed and my son, Chad." She turned to Titania. "I think my family's here. Come on over and let me introduce you."

Titania followed Susan as she hurried across the cove, waving her hands and calling out to her husband and her son. "I think they've already met Karma," the girl said. The dog was racing around and around, in and out of the water, soaking the happy gathering each time she shook her fur.

"I'm so glad you came up early," Susan said, handing her husband a glass of Samuel Adams ale.

"Thanks. I just wish we'd been here before. It sounds like you've had quite a long weekend."

"Sad," Susan commented, sitting down in the porch rocker next to her husband's. "Those poor girls."

"You mean the ones in the canoe in the middle of the cove that the dog is working so hard to turn over?"

"I guess they're going to survive," Susan said, watching the pandemonium. "If they had to lose one parent, it's best that it was their mother. She never seemed to have their interests in the, uh, forefront of her life."

"Is their father going to get out of this without any legal difficulties? After all, he did ignore the formalities of his brother's death in a foreign country."

"I talked to Janet about that. It was over five years ago. She thinks it will just be overlooked. Arthur Deed will be buried here. It turns out that there are people on the island who remember when his family rented my aunt's house. He wasn't very popular. It will be a pauper's grave."

"Maybe . . ." her husband began.

"I've already taken care of it." She smiled at Jed. "After all, he lived here for a short time. I thought we should do something. And I made a donation to the fishermen's wives' fund. There was a lot of work done to retrieve the bodies by people who didn't have to pitch in. Ted Taylor is going to do something for the volunteer firemen who spent so much time looking for Titania. They all deserve to be remembered.''

"Good." Jed approved and then changed the subject. "Chad's sure happy to be back on the island, isn't he?''

They both watched while their son paddled his kayak in circles around the girls and their pet.

"Yes, but it's sad that Chrissy isn't here this year."

Jed took her hand. "They grow up, hon. In a few years, she'll probably be sitting here watching her own children out there."

Susan blinked. "Not too soon, I hope."

"The house is going to be getting lonely with Chrissy going off to college in another year, and then Chad just a few years later," he commented.

"You know, Jed, I've been thinking about that," Susan began in a serious tone of voice. "And I have a solution. . . .''

Susan looked down at the floor where her husband had fallen when he pushed the rocker too hard.

"Why don't we—" she began.

"Hon, think of the diapers, nursery school, another college tuition to save for. . . .'' he began seriously.

"Jed," she laughed. "I just wondered what you'd think about getting a dog!"